THE ADVENTURES OF MICKEY & MAJ

BY RICK LUNDEEN

WRITER/ILLUSTRATOR: RICK LUNDEEN
BRYAN SEATON: PUBLISHER/ CEO
SHAWN GABBORIN: EDITOR-IN-CHIEF
JASON MARTIN: PUBLISHER-DANGER ZONE
NICOLE D'ANDRIA: MARKETING DIRECTOR/EDITOR
JESSICA LOWRIE: SOCIAL MEDIA CZAR
DANIELLE DAVISON: EXECUTIVE ADMINISTRATOR
CHAD CICCONI: MAGIC CARPET WRANGLER
SHAWN PRYOR: PRESIDENT OF CREATOR RELATIONS

BOOK
ONE

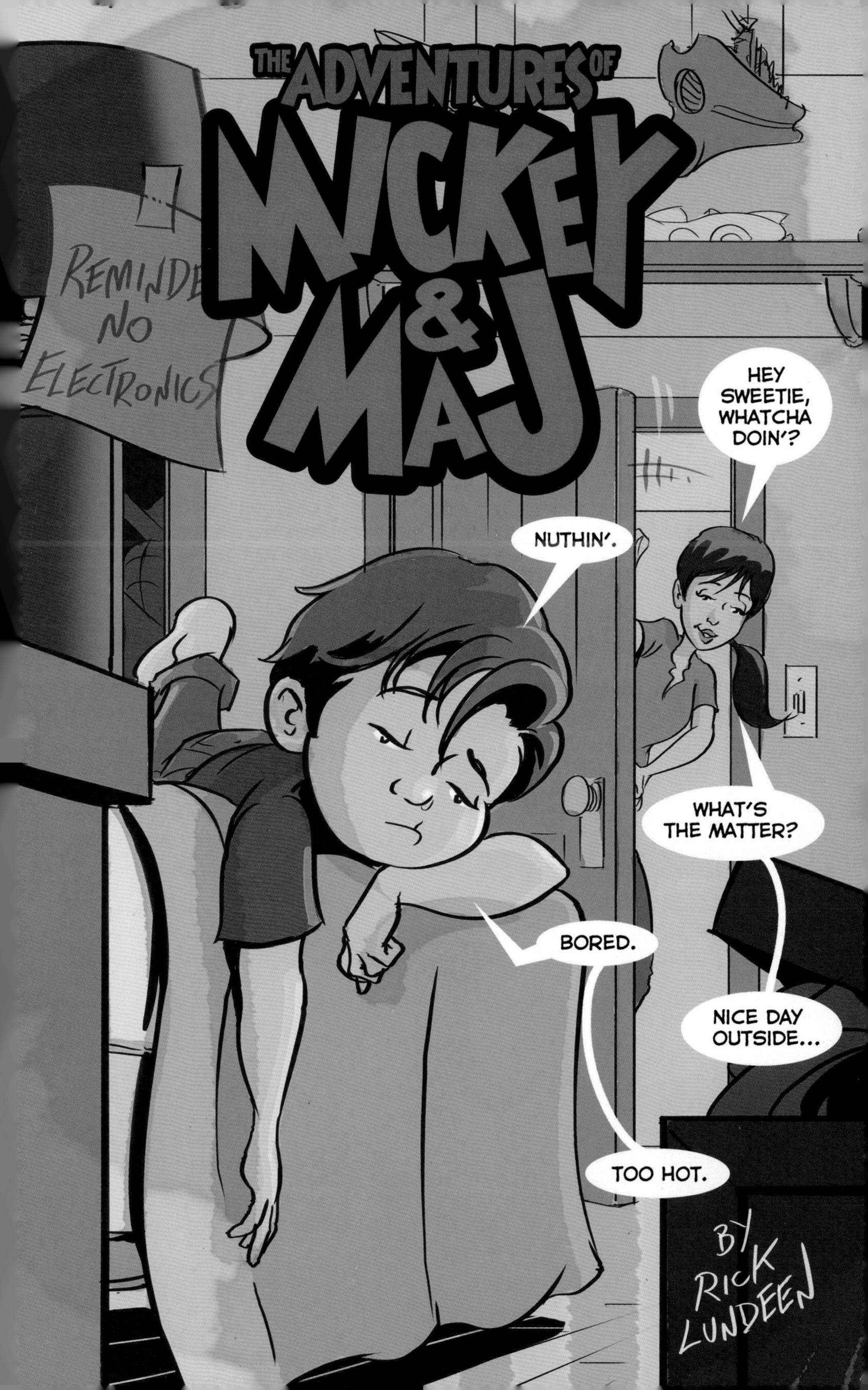
THE ADVENTURES OF
MICKEY & MAJ
REMINDE
NO
ELECTRONICS
HEY SWEETIE, WHATCHA DOIN'?
NUTHIN'.
WHAT'S THE MATTER?
BORED.
NICE DAY OUTSIDE...
TOO HOT.
BY RICK LUNDEEN

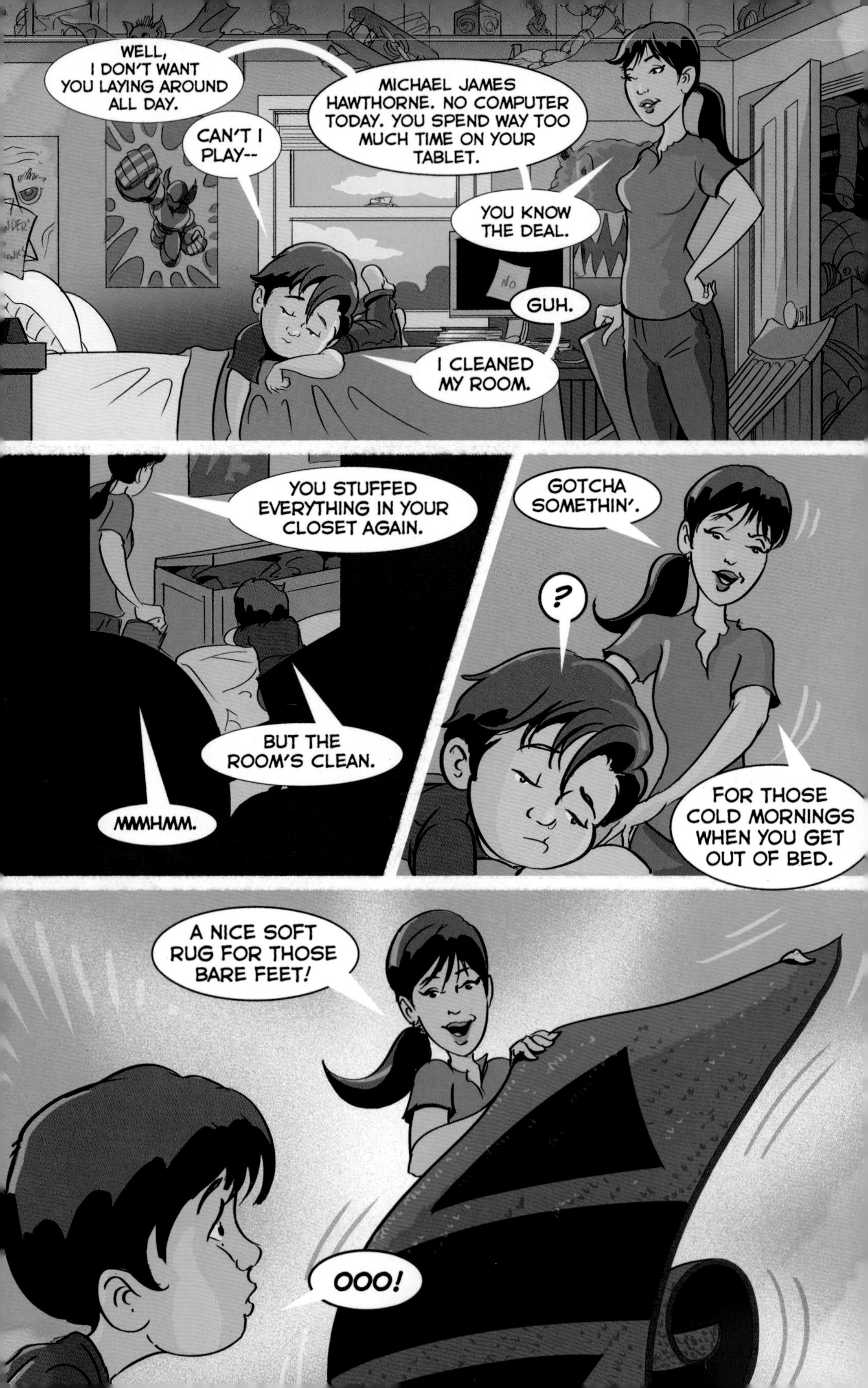

WELL, I DON'T WANT YOU LAYING AROUND ALL DAY.
CAN'T I PLAY--
MICHAEL JAMES HAWTHORNE. NO COMPUTER TODAY. YOU SPEND WAY TOO MUCH TIME ON YOUR TABLET.
YOU KNOW THE DEAL.
NO
GUH.
I CLEANED MY ROOM.
YOU STUFFED EVERYTHING IN YOUR CLOSET AGAIN.
BUT THE ROOM'S CLEAN.
MMHMM.
GOTCHA SOMETHIN'.
?
FOR THOSE COLD MORNINGS WHEN YOU GET OUT OF BED.
A NICE SOFT RUG FOR THOSE BARE FEET!
OOO!

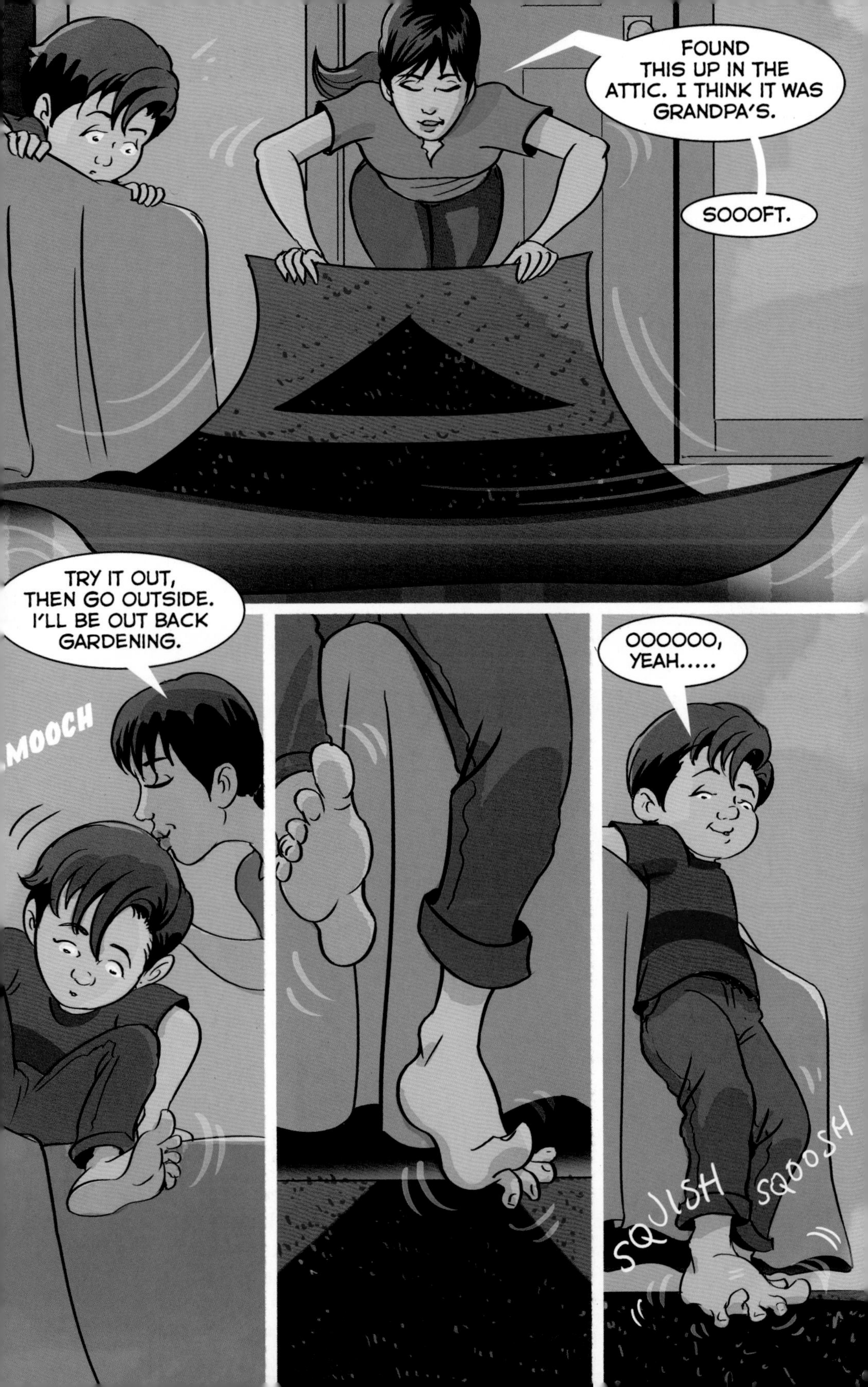
FOUND THIS UP IN THE ATTIC. I THINK IT WAS GRANDPA'S.
SOOOFT.
TRY IT OUT, THEN GO OUTSIDE. I'LL BE OUT BACK GARDENING.
MOOCH
OOOOOO, YEAH.....
SQUISH
SQOOSH

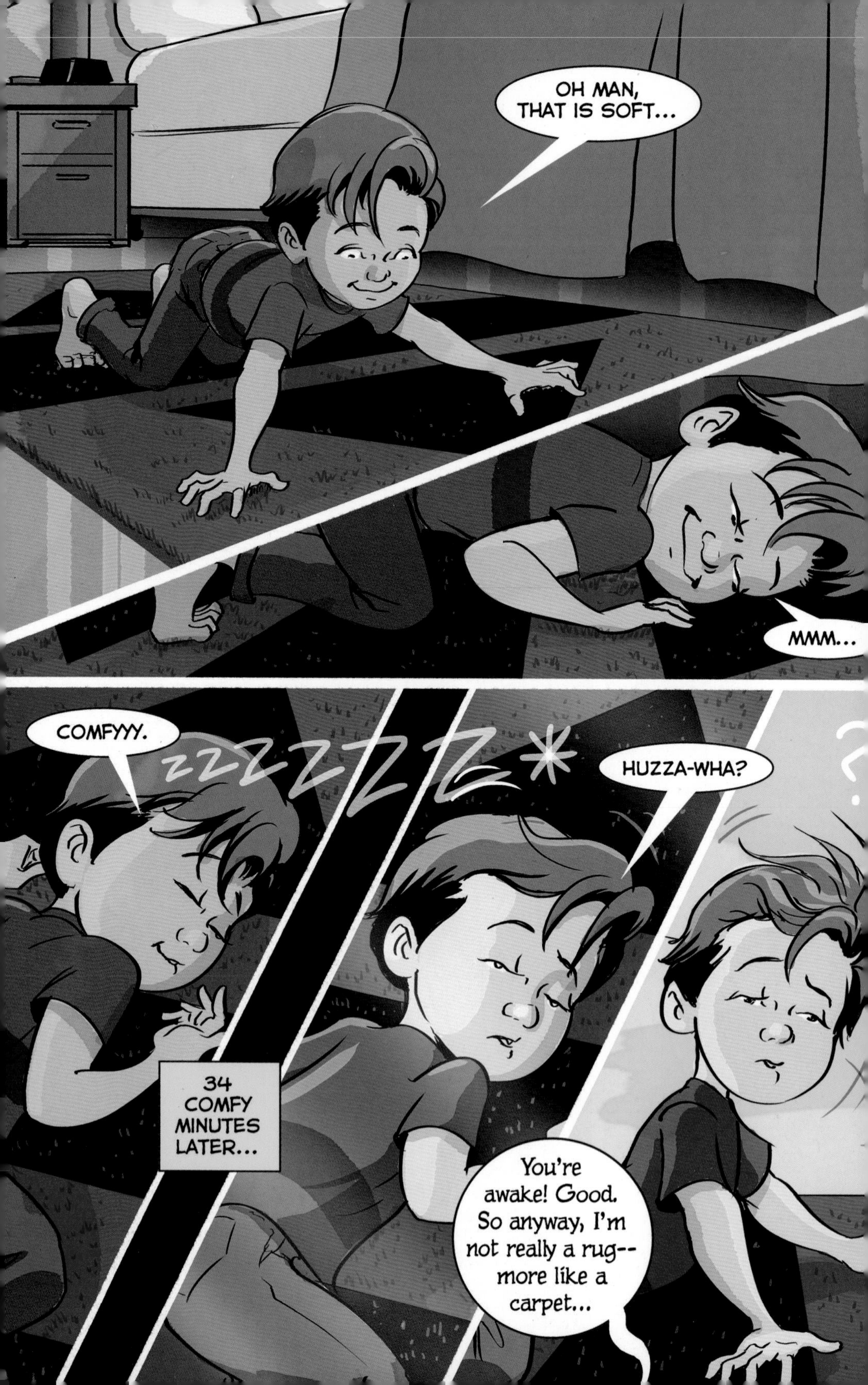
OH MAN, THAT IS SOFT...
MMM...
COMFYYY.
ZZZZZZZZ
34 COMFY MINUTES LATER...
HUZZA-WHA?
?
You're awake! Good. So anyway, I'm not really a rug--more like a carpet...

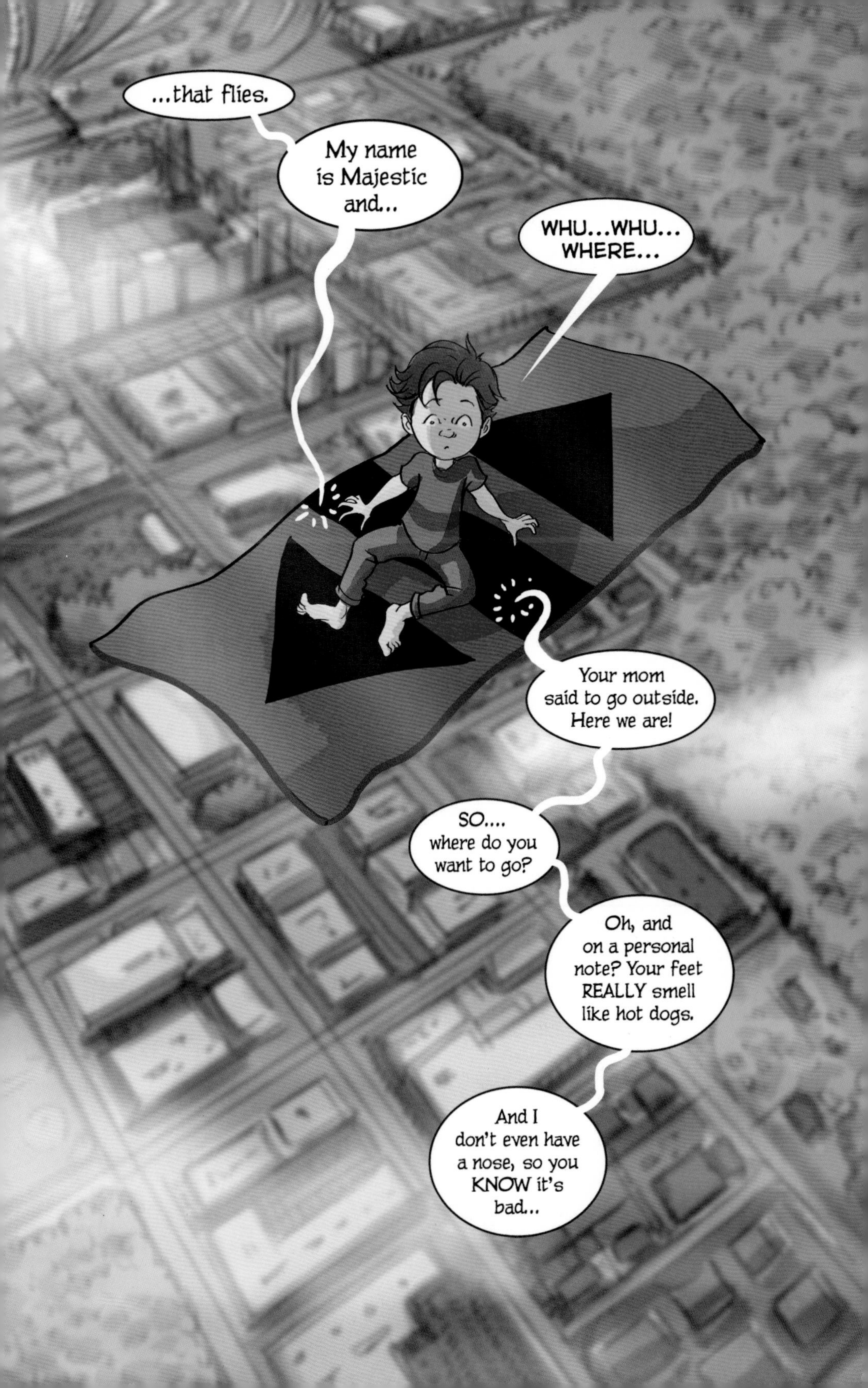
...that flies.
My name is Majestic and...
WHU...WHU... WHERE...
Your mom said to go outside. Here we are!
SO.... where do you want to go?
Oh, and on a personal note? Your feet REALLY smell like hot dogs.
And I don't even have a nose, so you KNOW it's bad...

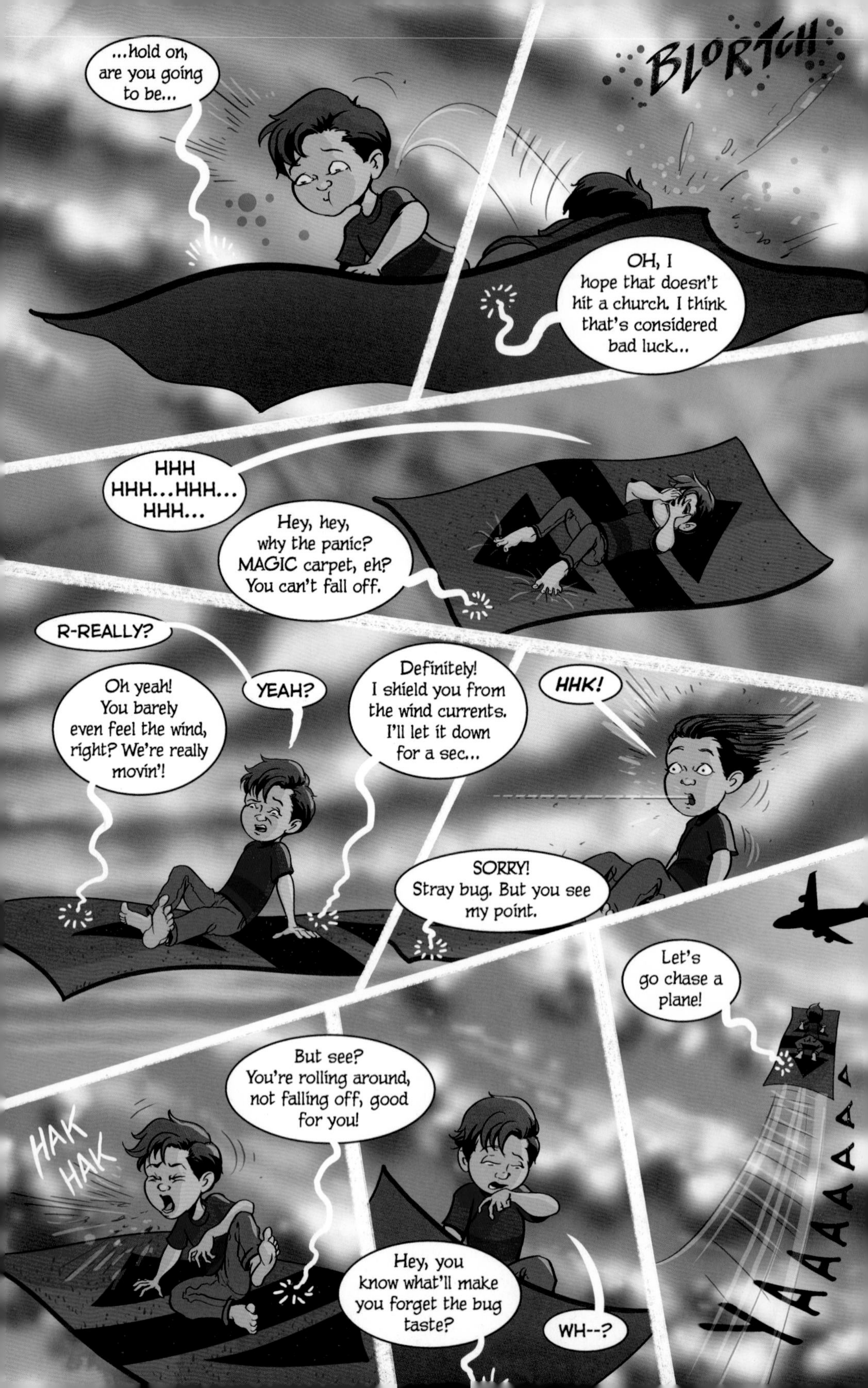
...hold on, are you going to be...
BLORTCH
OH, I hope that doesn't hit a church. I think that's considered bad luck...
HHH HHH...HHH... HHH...
Hey, hey, why the panic? MAGIC carpet, eh? You can't fall off.
R-REALLY?
YEAH?
Oh yeah! You barely even feel the wind, right? We're really movin'!
Definitely! I shield you from the wind currents. I'll let it down for a sec...
HHK!
SORRY! Stray bug. But you see my point.
HAK HAK
But see? You're rolling around, not falling off, good for you!
Hey, you know what'll make you forget the bug taste?
WH--?
Let's go chase a plane!
YAAAAAA

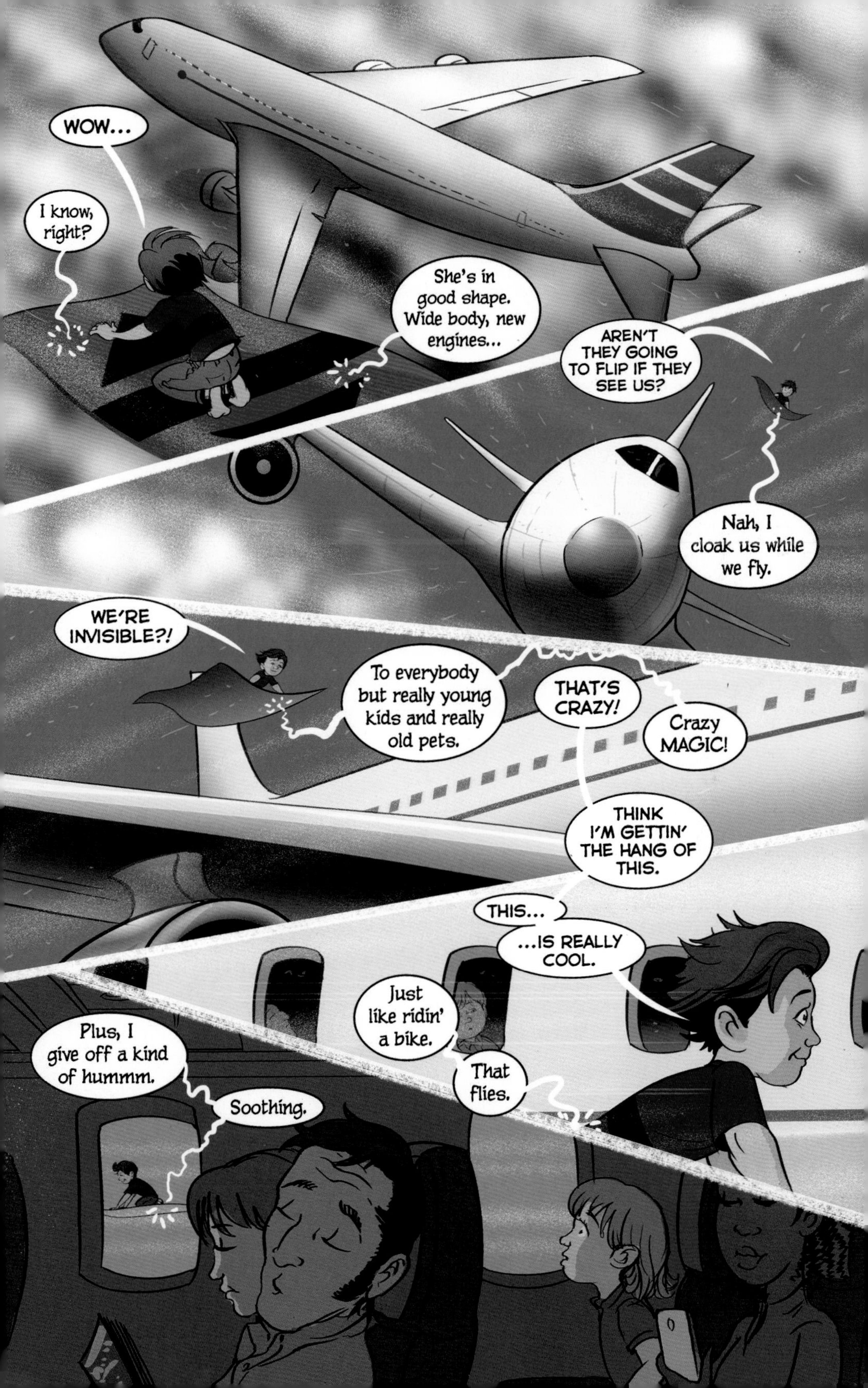
WOW...
I know, right?
She's in good shape. Wide body, new engines...
AREN'T THEY GOING TO FLIP IF THEY SEE US?
Nah, I cloak us while we fly.
WE'RE INVISIBLE?!
To everybody but really young kids and really old pets.
THAT'S CRAZY!
Crazy MAGIC!
THINK I'M GETTIN' THE HANG OF THIS.
THIS...
...IS REALLY COOL.
Just like ridin' a bike.
That flies.
Plus, I give off a kind of hummm.
Soothing.

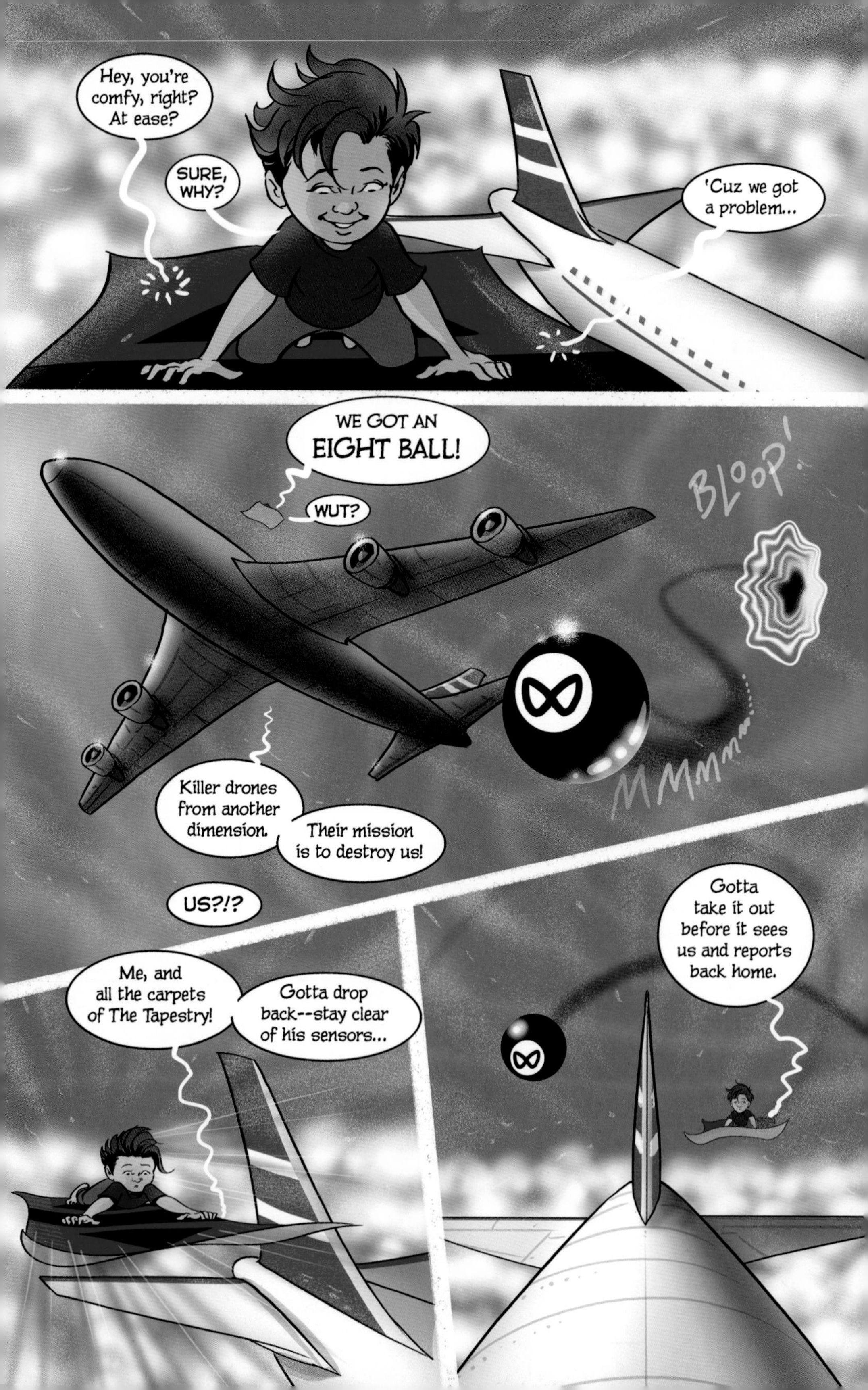
Hey, you're comfy, right? At ease?
SURE, WHY?
'Cuz we got a problem...
WE GOT AN EIGHT BALL!
WUT?
BLOOP!
MMMmm...
Killer drones from another dimension.
Their mission is to destroy us!
US?!?
Me, and all the carpets of The Tapestry!
Gotta drop back--stay clear of his sensors...
Gotta take it out before it sees us and reports back home.

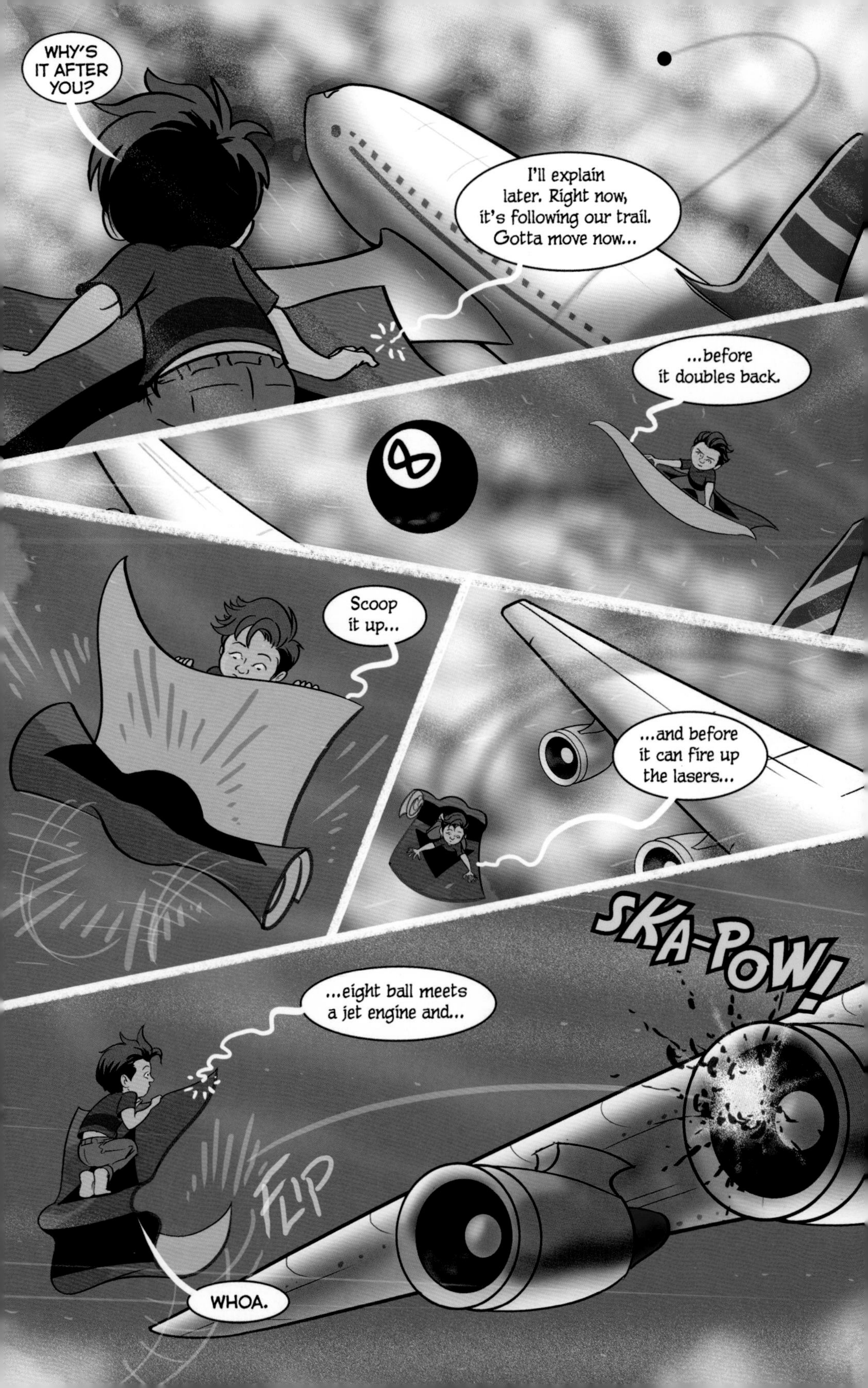
WHY'S IT AFTER YOU?
I'll explain later. Right now, it's following our trail. Gotta move now...
...before it doubles back.
Scoop it up...
...and before it can fire up the lasers...
SKA-POW!
...eight ball meets a jet engine and...
FLIP
WHOA.

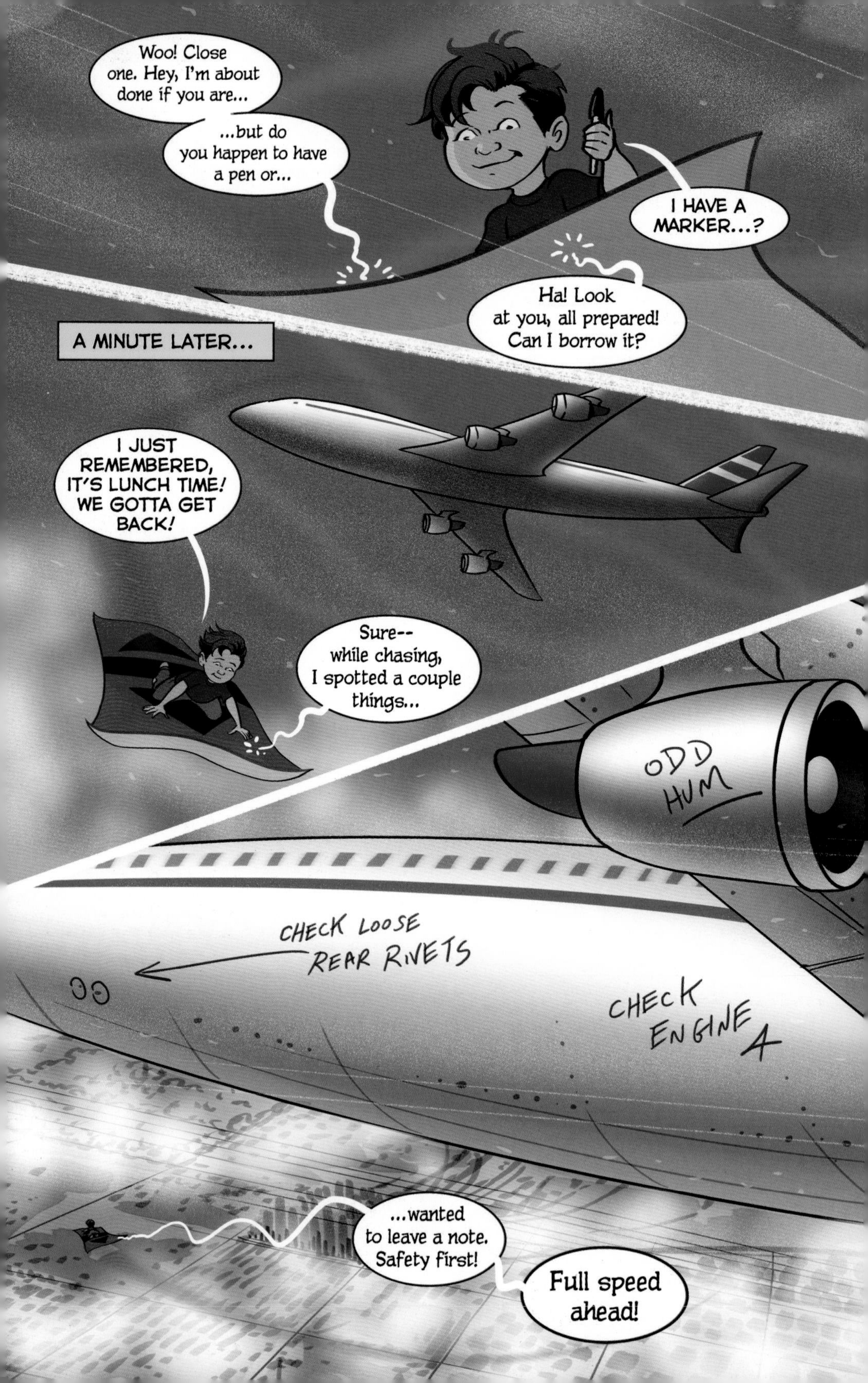
Woo! Close one. Hey, I'm about done if you are...
...but do you happen to have a pen or...
I HAVE A MARKER...?
Ha! Look at you, all prepared! Can I borrow it?
A MINUTE LATER...
I JUST REMEMBERED, IT'S LUNCH TIME! WE GOTTA GET BACK!
Sure-- while chasing, I spotted a couple things...
ODD HUM
CHECK LOOSE REAR RIVETS
CHECK ENGINE 4
...wanted to leave a note. Safety first!
Full speed ahead!

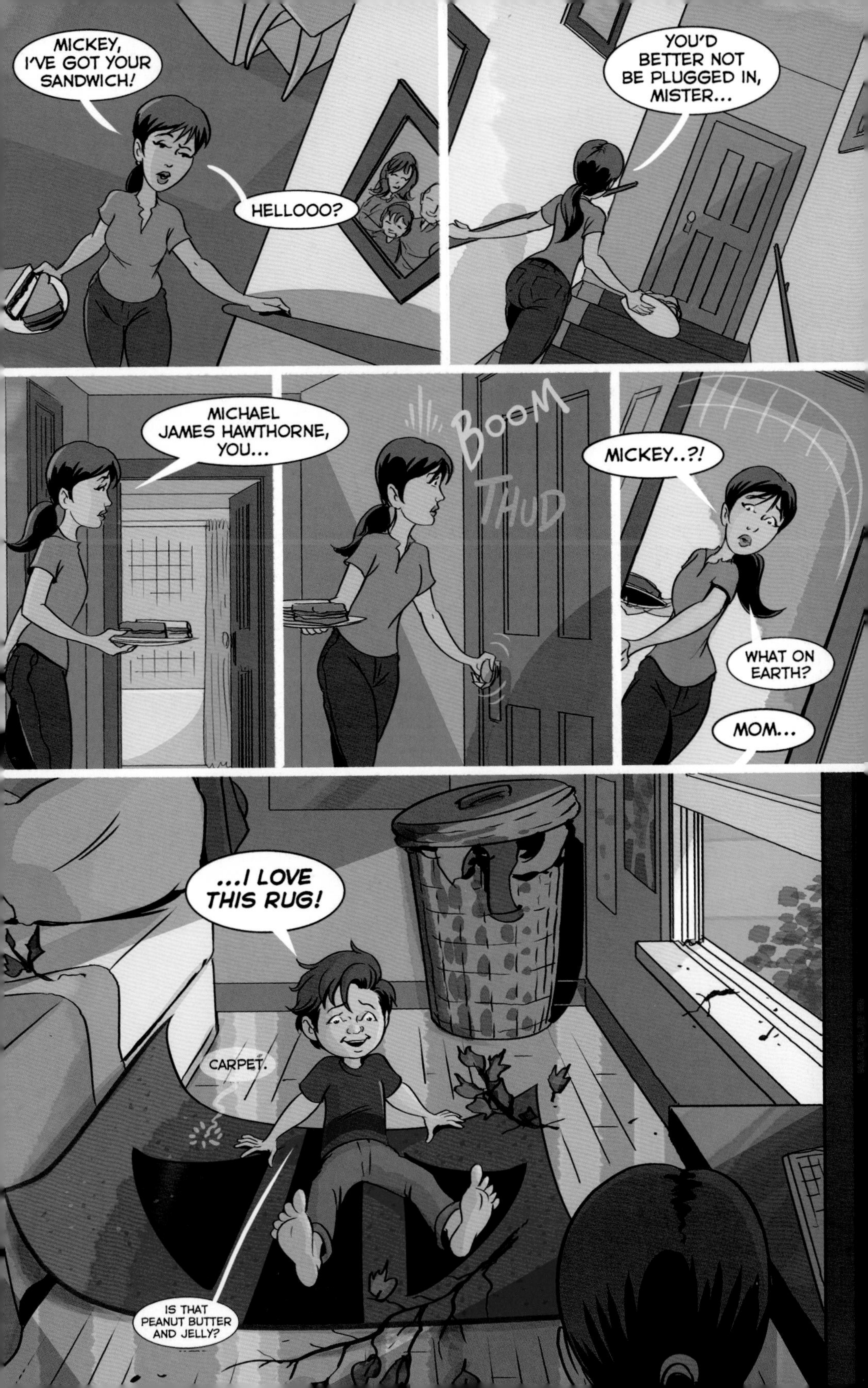
MICKEY, I'VE GOT YOUR SANDWICH!
HELLOOO?
YOU'D BETTER NOT BE PLUGGED IN, MISTER...
MICHAEL JAMES HAWTHORNE, YOU...
BOOM
THUD
MICKEY..?!
WHAT ON EARTH?
MOM...
...I LOVE THIS RUG!
CARPET.
IS THAT PEANUT BUTTER AND JELLY?

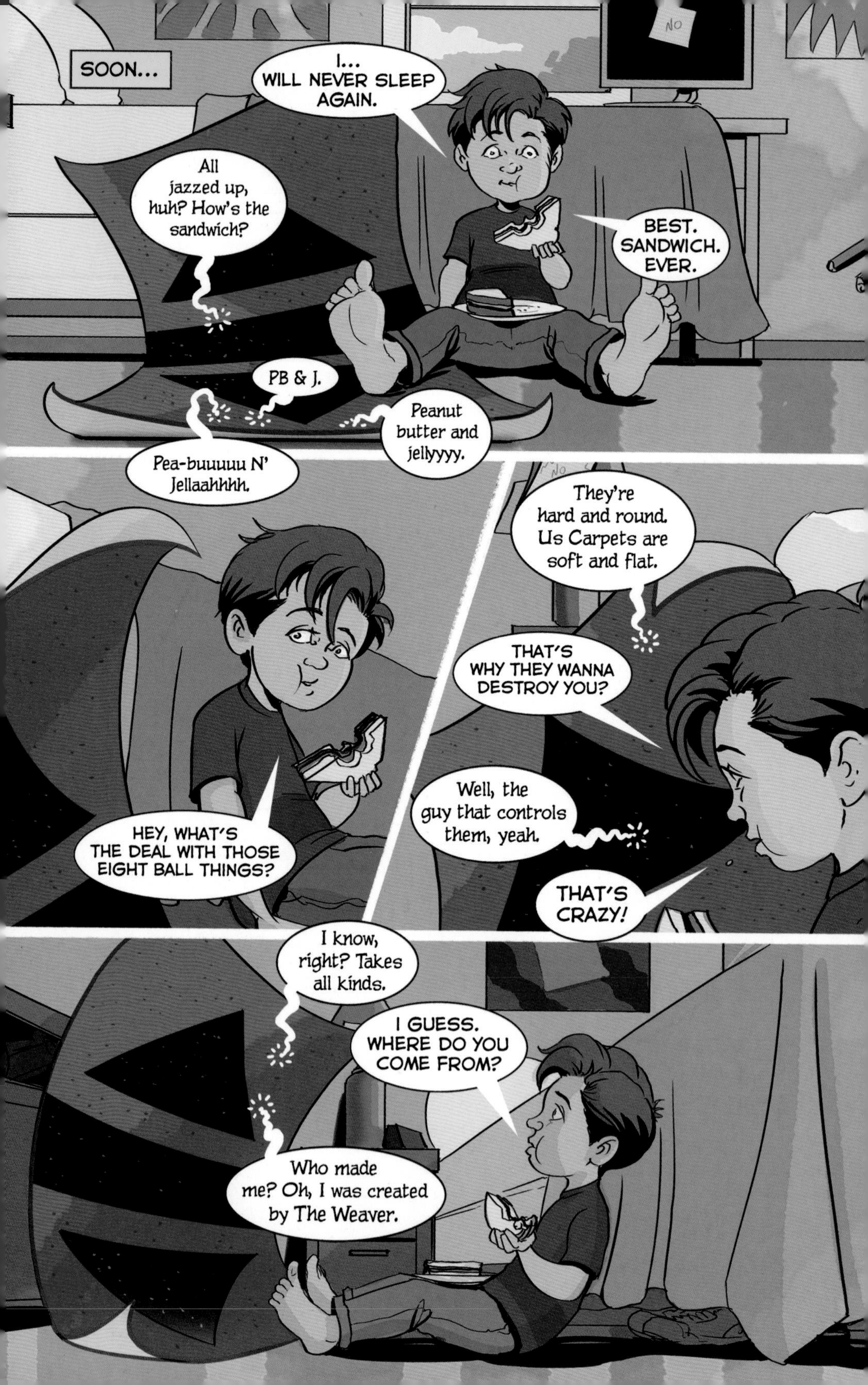
SOON...
I... WILL NEVER SLEEP AGAIN.
All jazzed up, huh? How's the sandwich?
BEST. SANDWICH. EVER.
PB & J.
Peanut butter and jellyyyy.
Pea-buuuuu N' Jellaahhhh.
HEY, WHAT'S THE DEAL WITH THOSE EIGHT BALL THINGS?
They're hard and round. Us Carpets are soft and flat.
THAT'S WHY THEY WANNA DESTROY YOU?
Well, the guy that controls them, yeah.
THAT'S CRAZY!
I know, right? Takes all kinds.
I GUESS. WHERE DO YOU COME FROM?
Who made me? Oh, I was created by The Weaver.

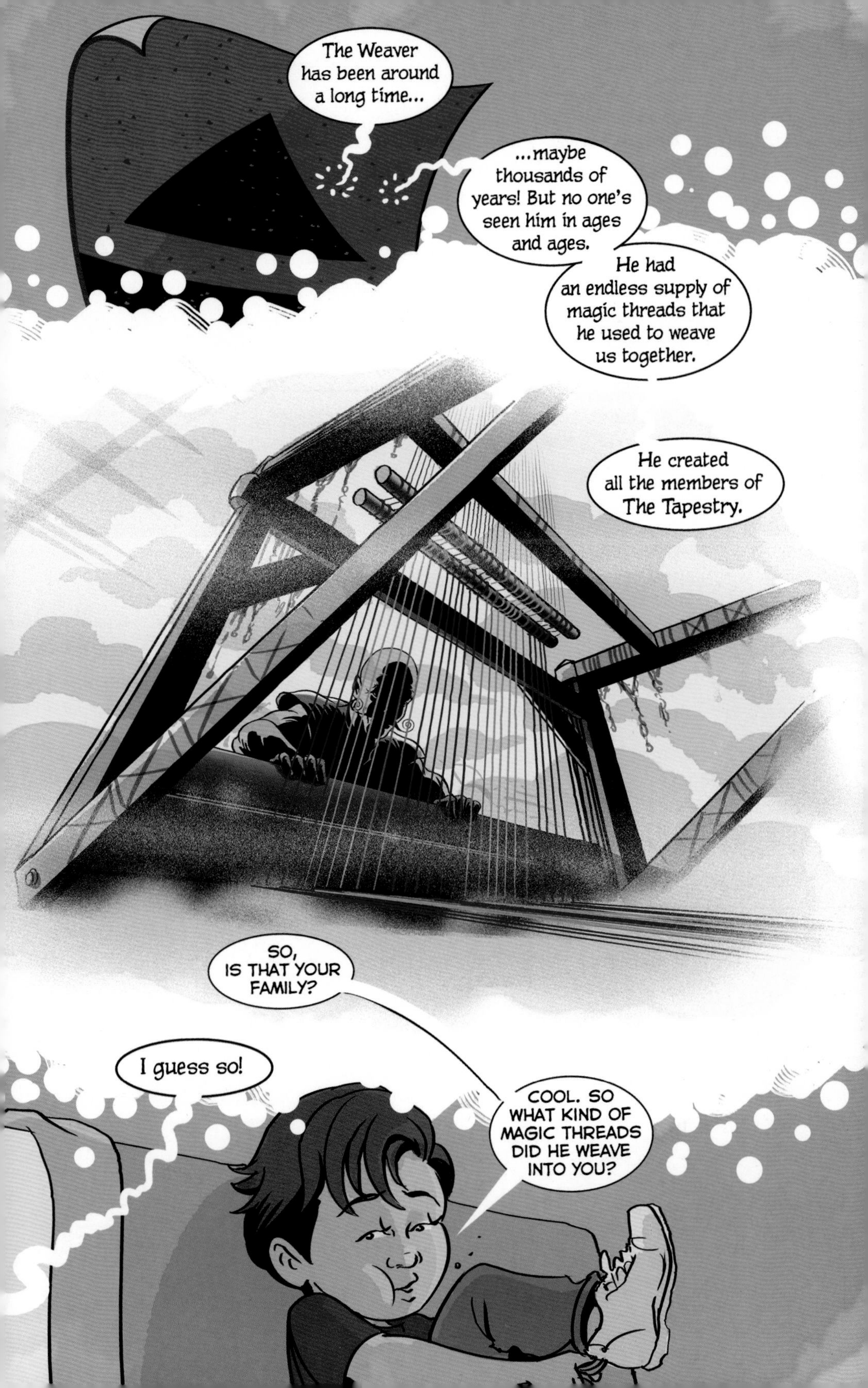
The Weaver has been around a long time...
...maybe thousands of years! But no one's seen him in ages and ages.
He had an endless supply of magic threads that he used to weave us together.
He created all the members of The Tapestry.
SO, IS THAT YOUR FAMILY?
I guess so!
COOL. SO WHAT KIND OF MAGIC THREADS DID HE WEAVE INTO YOU?

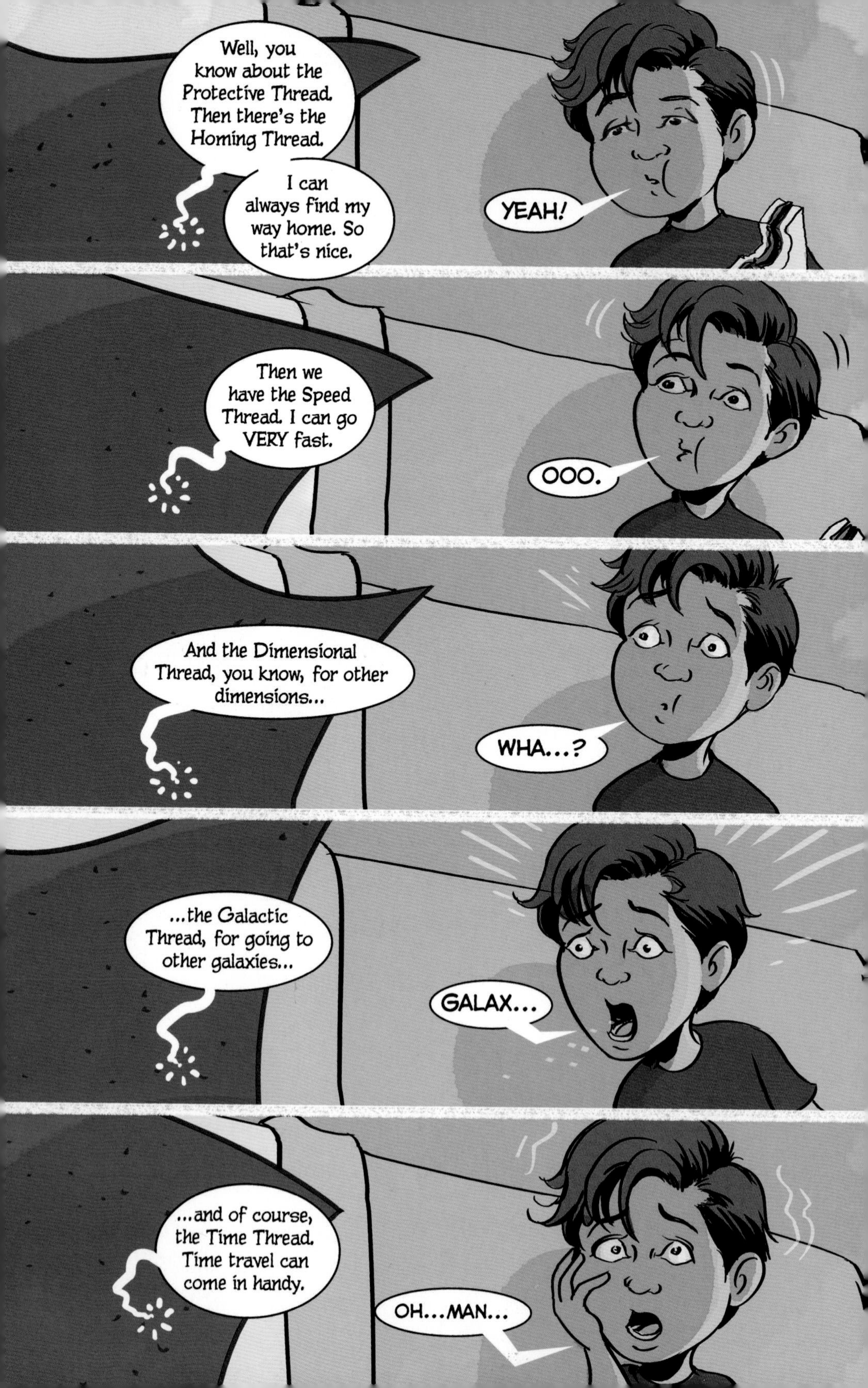
Well, you know about the Protective Thread. Then there's the Homing Thread.
I can always find my way home. So that's nice.
YEAH!
Then we have the Speed Thread. I can go VERY fast.
OOO.
And the Dimensional Thread, you know, for other dimensions...
WHA...?
...the Galactic Thread, for going to other galaxies...
GALAX...
...and of course, the Time Thread. Time travel can come in handy.
OH...MAN...

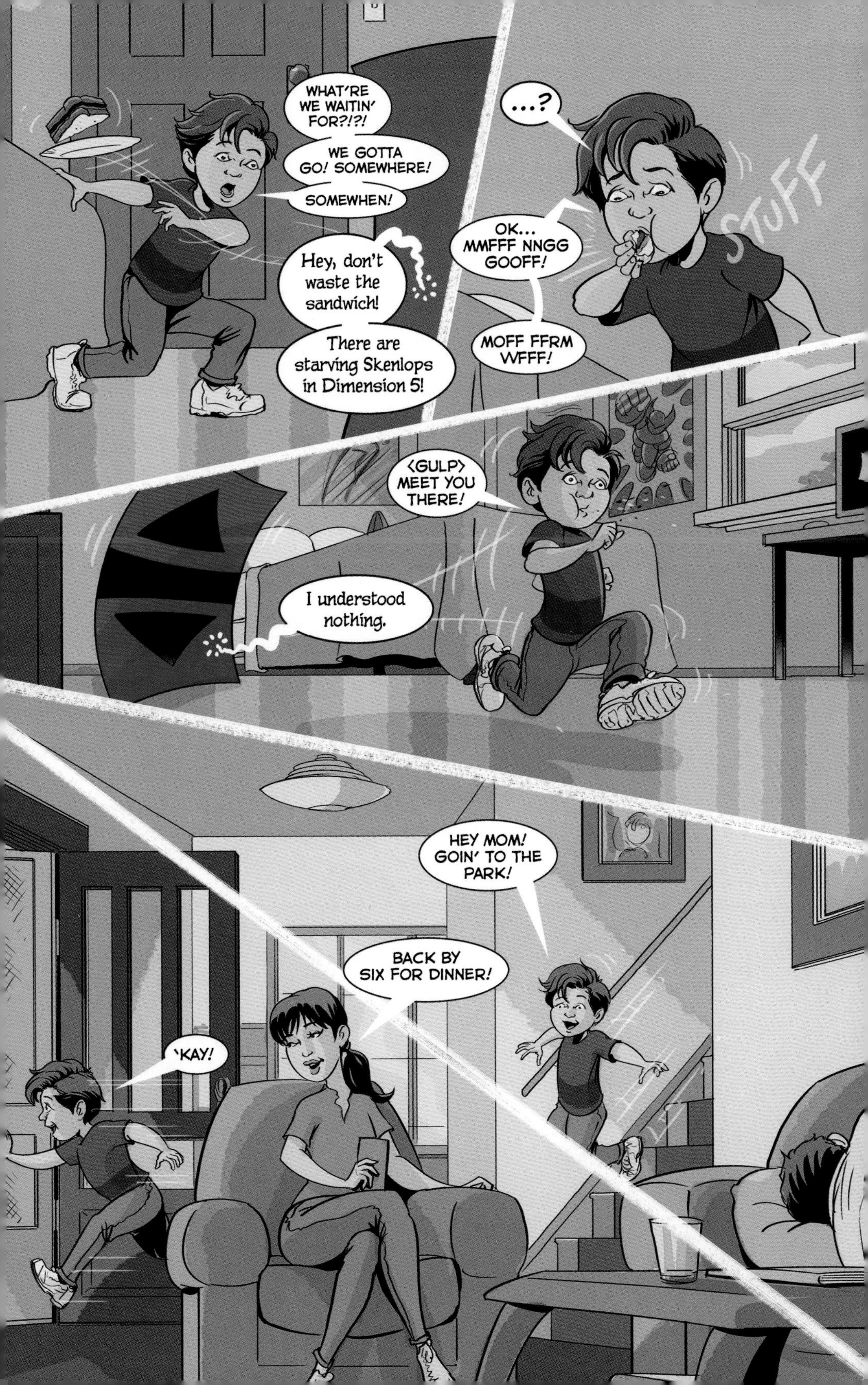
WHAT'RE WE WAITIN' FOR?!?!
WE GOTTA GO! SOMEWHERE!
SOMEWHEN!
Hey, don't waste the sandwich!
There are starving Skenlops in Dimension 5!
...?
OK... MMFFF NNGG GOOFF!
MOFF FFRM WFFF!
STUFF
<GULP> MEET YOU THERE!
I understood nothing.
HEY MOM! GOIN' TO THE PARK!
BACK BY SIX FOR DINNER!
'KAY!

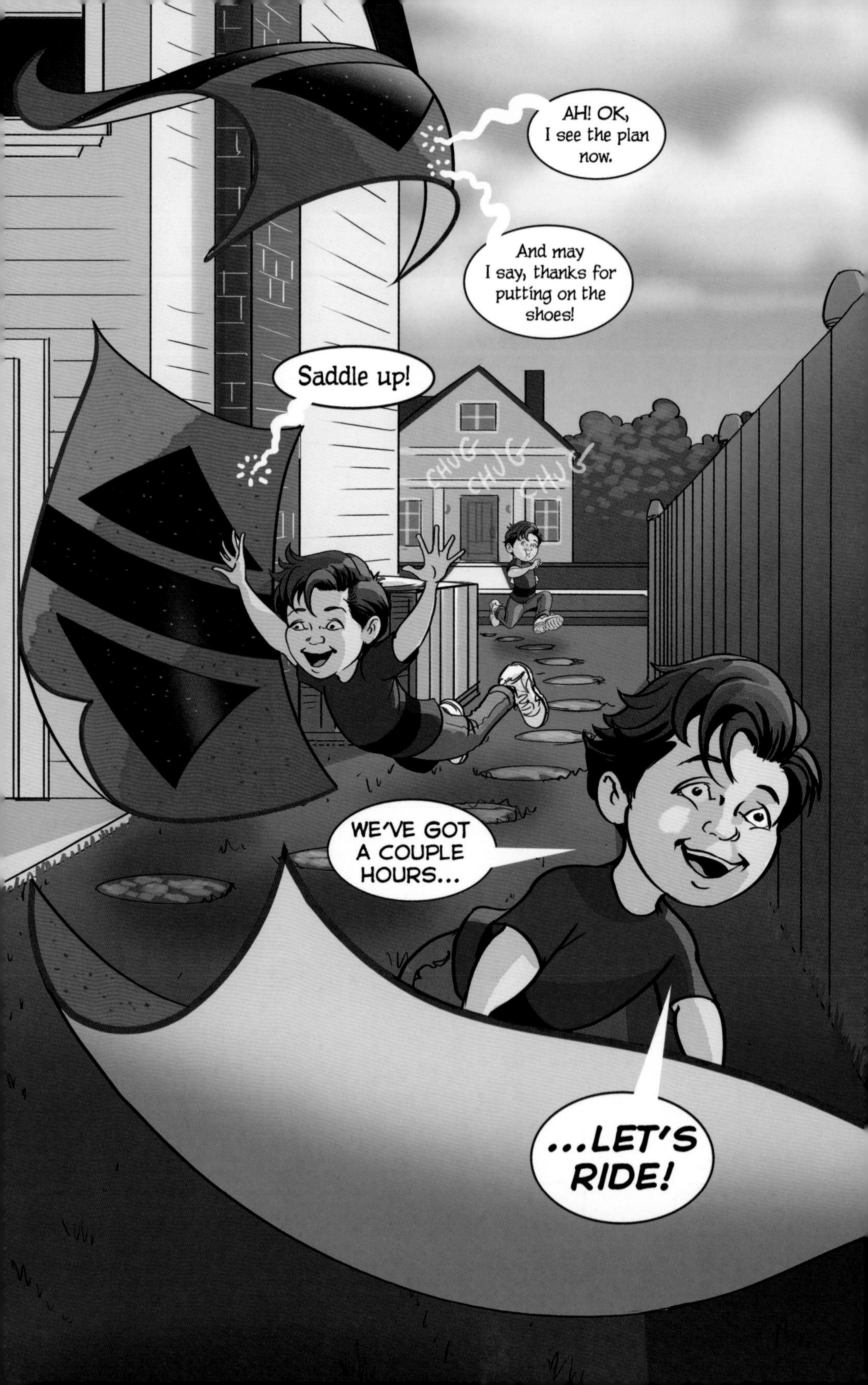
AH! OK, I see the plan now.
And may I say, thanks for putting on the shoes!
Saddle up!
CHUG CHUG CHUG
WE'VE GOT A COUPLE HOURS...
...LET'S RIDE!

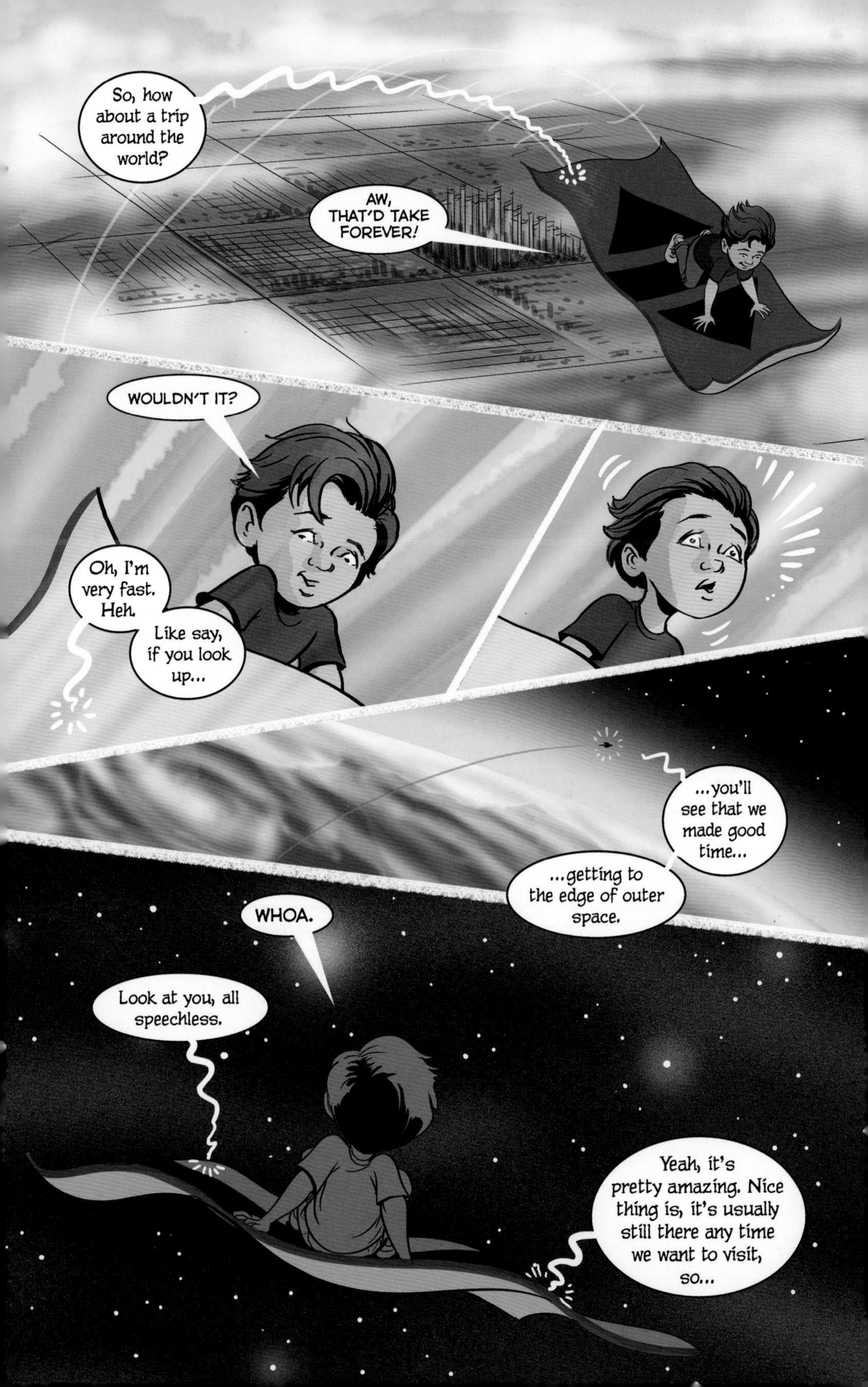
So, how about a trip around the world?
AW, THAT'D TAKE FOREVER!
WOULDN'T IT?
Oh, I'm very fast. Heh.
Like say, if you look up...
...you'll see that we made good time...
...getting to the edge of outer space.
WHOA.
Look at you, all speechless.
Yeah, it's pretty amazing. Nice thing is, it's usually still there any time we want to visit, so...

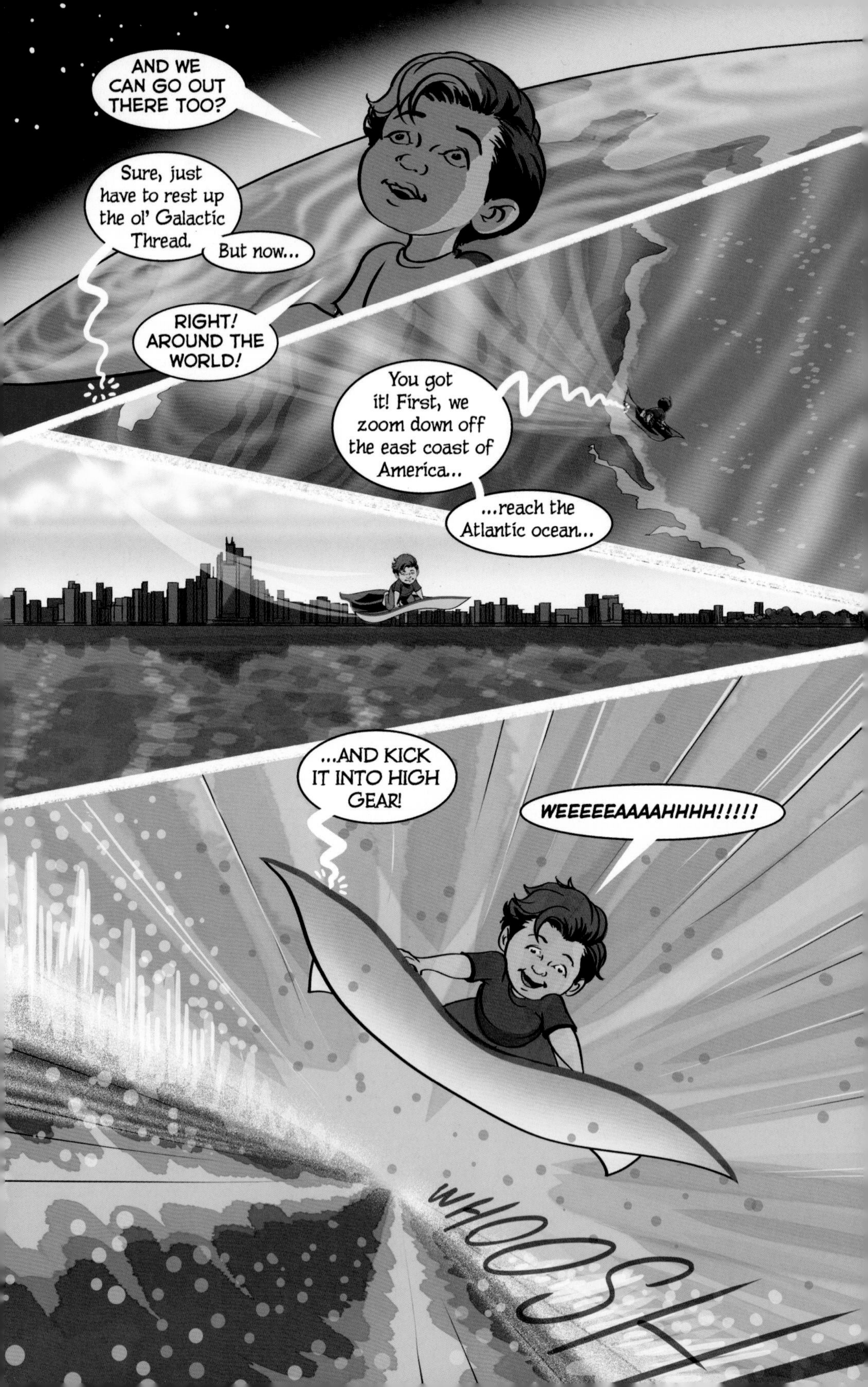
AND WE CAN GO OUT THERE TOO?
Sure, just have to rest up the ol' Galactic Thread.
But now...
RIGHT! AROUND THE WORLD!
You got it! First, we zoom down off the east coast of America...
...reach the Atlantic ocean...
...AND KICK IT INTO HIGH GEAR!
WEEEEEAAAAHHHH!!!!!
WHOOSH

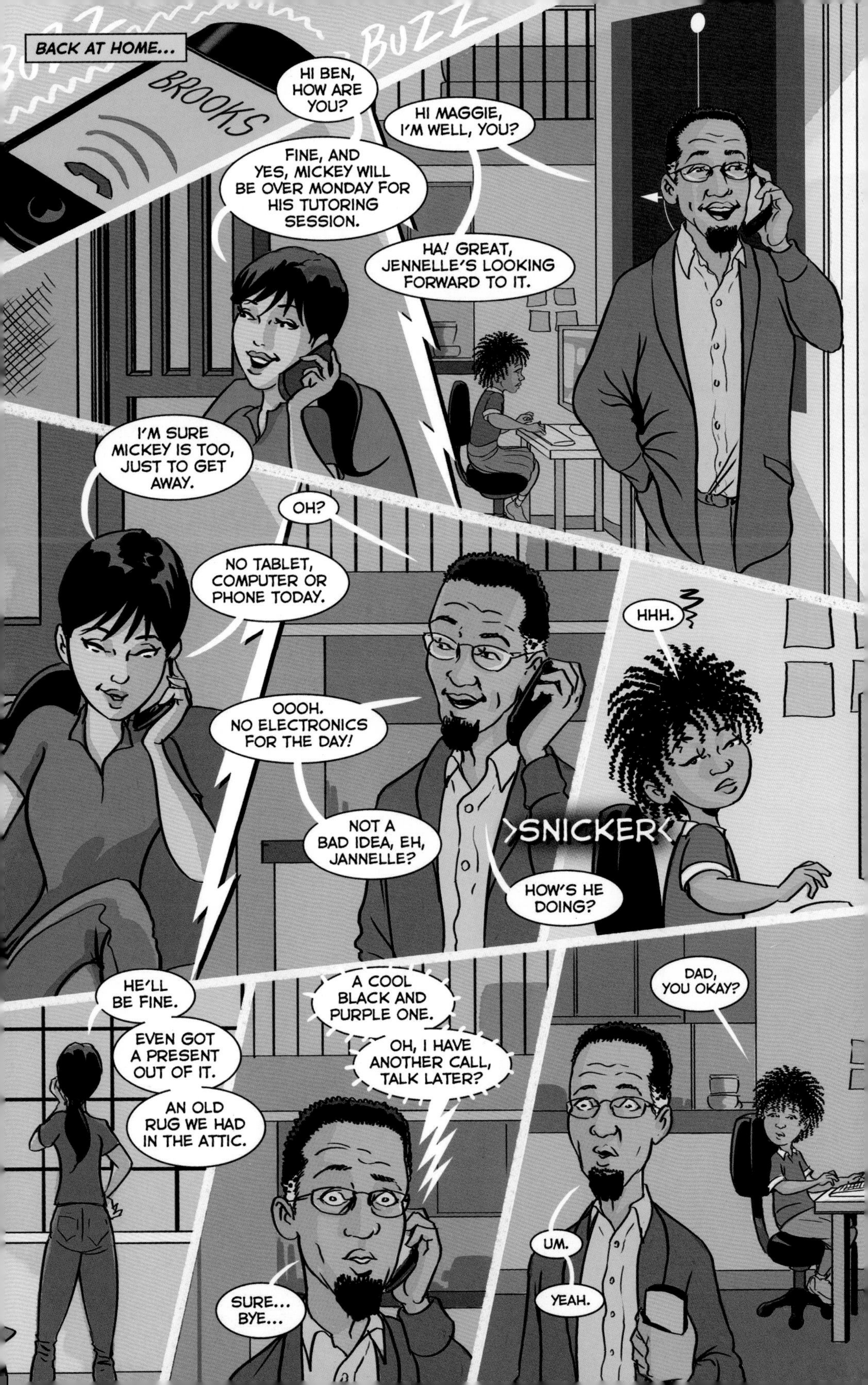
BACK AT HOME...
BUZZ
BROOKS
HI BEN, HOW ARE YOU?
HI MAGGIE, I'M WELL, YOU?
FINE, AND YES, MICKEY WILL BE OVER MONDAY FOR HIS TUTORING SESSION.
HA! GREAT, JENNELLE'S LOOKING FORWARD TO IT.
I'M SURE MICKEY IS TOO, JUST TO GET AWAY.
OH?
NO TABLET, COMPUTER OR PHONE TODAY.
OOOH. NO ELECTRONICS FOR THE DAY!
NOT A BAD IDEA, EH, JANNELLE?
HHH.
>SNICKER<
HOW'S HE DOING?
HE'LL BE FINE.
EVEN GOT A PRESENT OUT OF IT.
AN OLD RUG WE HAD IN THE ATTIC.
A COOL BLACK AND PURPLE ONE.
OH, I HAVE ANOTHER CALL, TALK LATER?
SURE... BYE...
DAD, YOU OKAY?
UM.
YEAH.

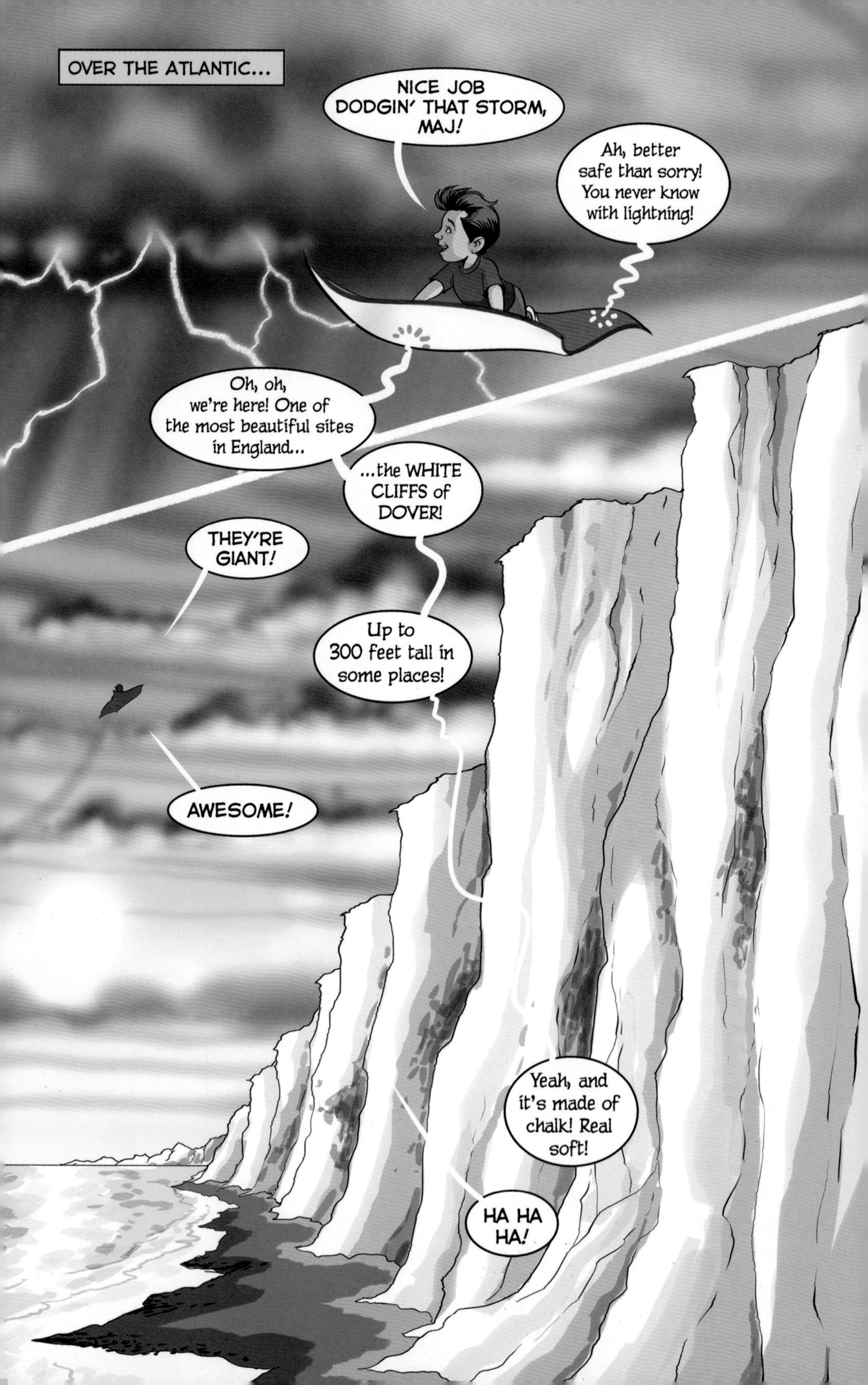

OVER THE ATLANTIC...
NICE JOB DODGIN' THAT STORM, MAJ!
Ah, better safe than sorry! You never know with lightning!
Oh, oh, we're here! One of the most beautiful sites in England...
...the WHITE CLIFFS of DOVER!
THEY'RE GIANT!
Up to 300 feet tall in some places!
AWESOME!
Yeah, and it's made of chalk! Real soft!
HA HA HA!

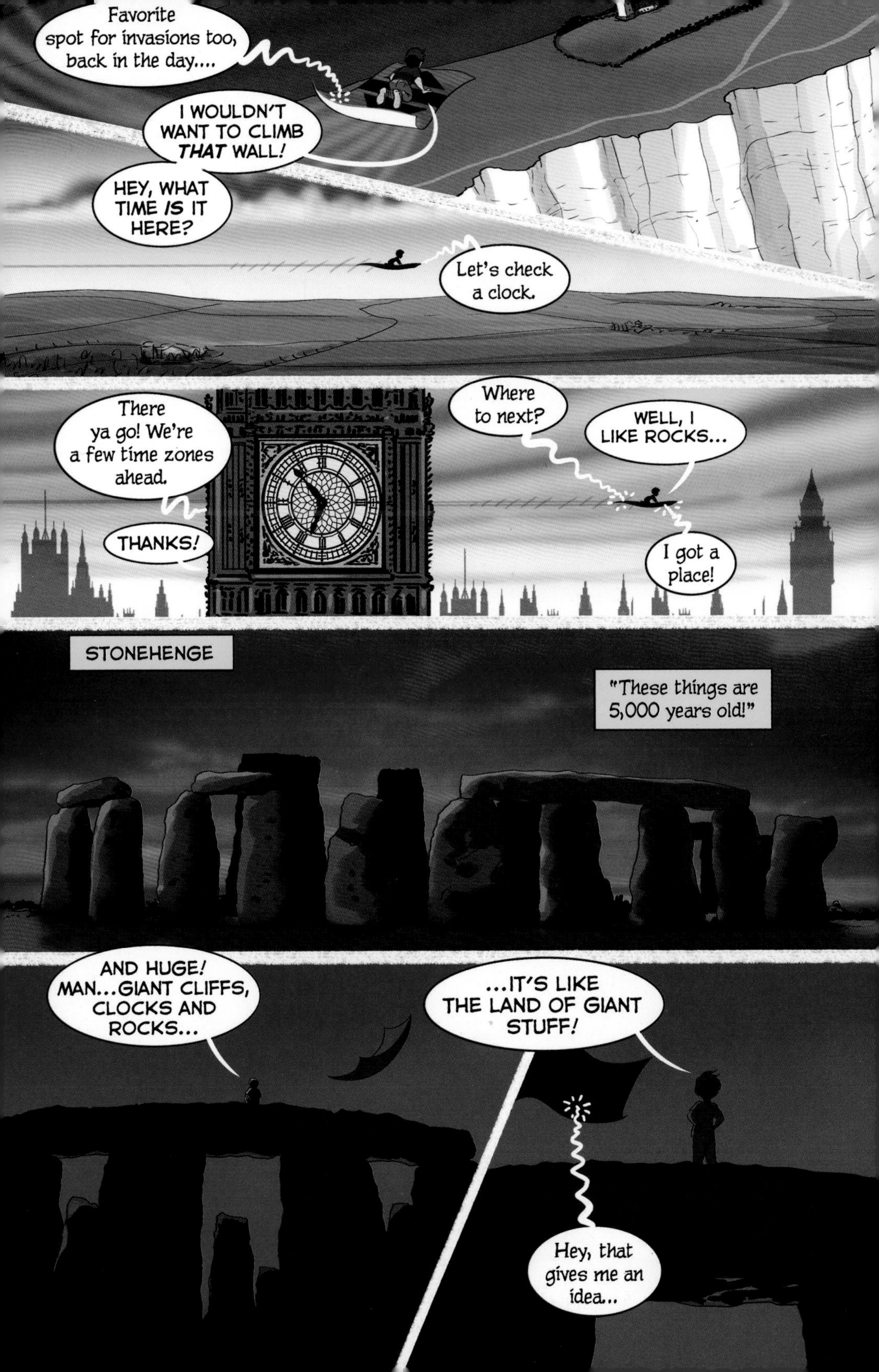

Favorite spot for invasions too, back in the day....
I WOULDN'T WANT TO CLIMB *THAT* WALL!
HEY, WHAT TIME *IS* IT HERE?
Let's check a clock.
There ya go! We're a few time zones ahead.
THANKS!
Where to next?
WELL, I LIKE ROCKS...
I got a place!
STONEHENGE
"These things are 5,000 years old!"
AND HUGE! MAN...GIANT CLIFFS, CLOCKS AND ROCKS...
...IT'S LIKE THE LAND OF GIANT STUFF!
Hey, that gives me an idea...

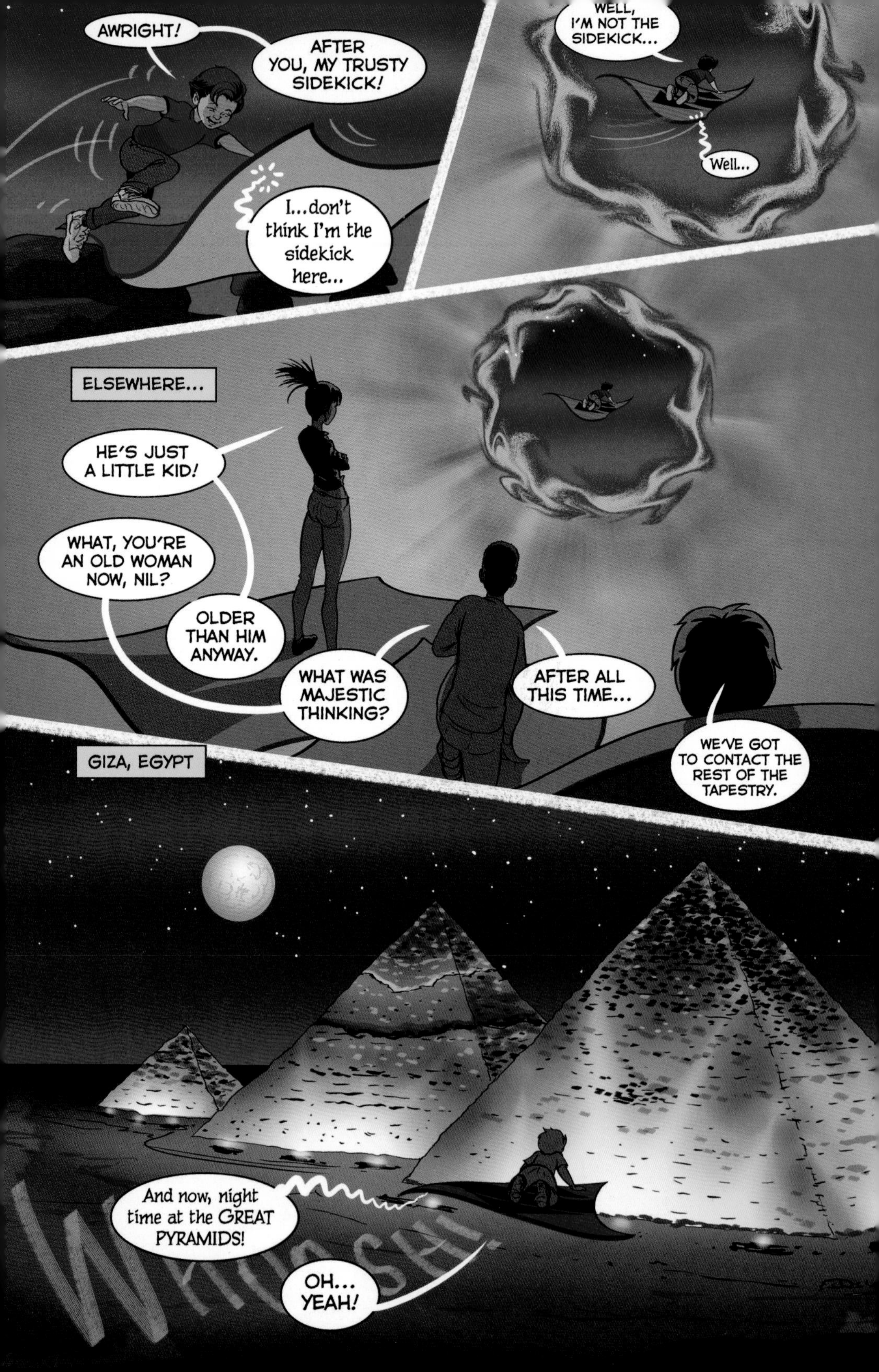
AWRIGHT!
AFTER YOU, MY TRUSTY SIDEKICK!
I...don't think I'm the sidekick here...
WELL, I'M NOT THE SIDEKICK...
Well...
ELSEWHERE...
HE'S JUST A LITTLE KID!
WHAT, YOU'RE AN OLD WOMAN NOW, NIL?
OLDER THAN HIM ANYWAY.
WHAT WAS MAJESTIC THINKING?
AFTER ALL THIS TIME...
WE'VE GOT TO CONTACT THE REST OF THE TAPESTRY.
GIZA, EGYPT
WHOOSH!
And now, night time at the GREAT PYRAMIDS!
OH... YEAH!

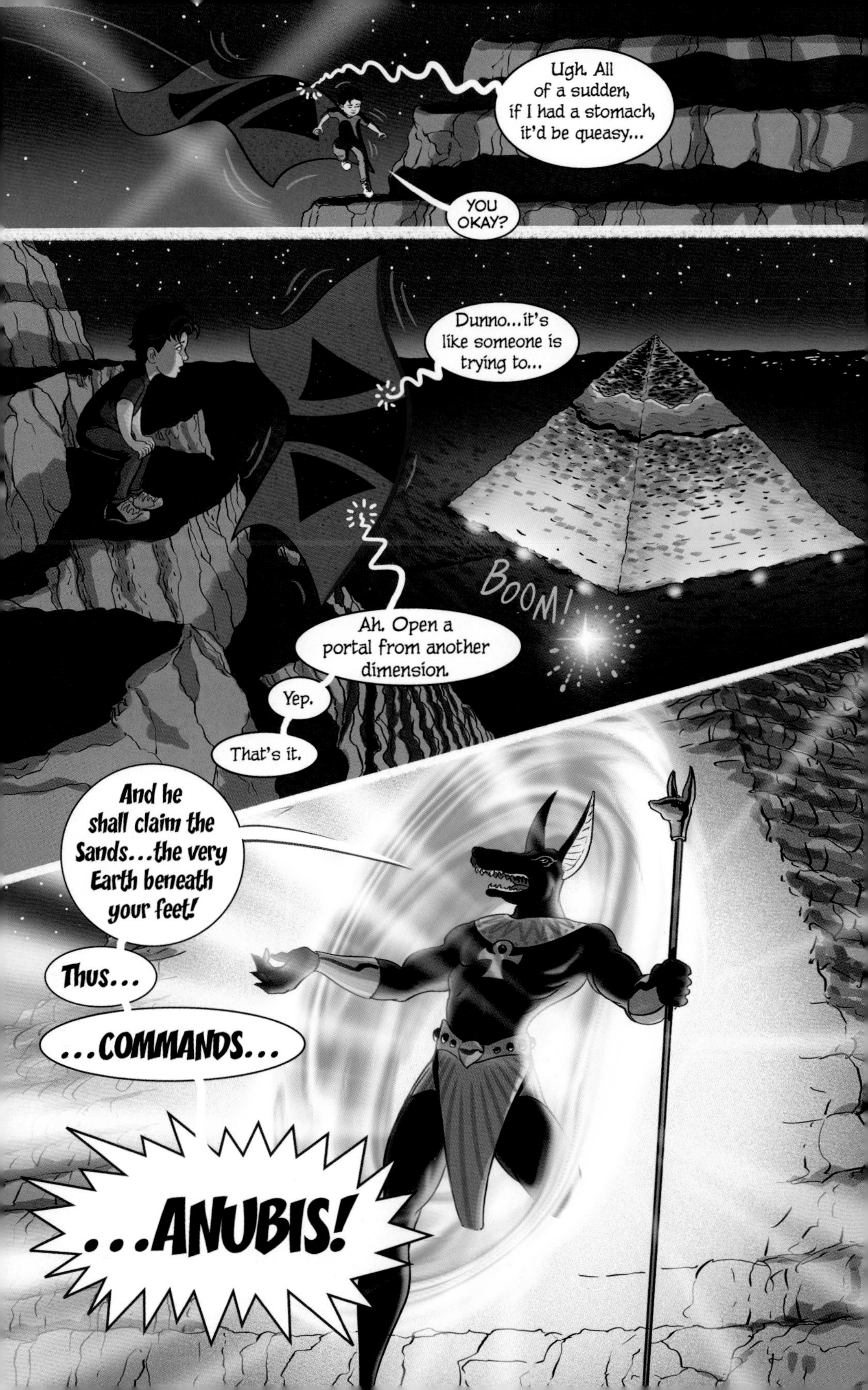
Ugh. All of a sudden, if I had a stomach, it'd be queasy...
YOU OKAY?
Dunno...it's like someone is trying to...
BOOM!
Ah. Open a portal from another dimension.
Yep.
That's it.
And he shall claim the Sands...the very Earth beneath your feet!
Thus...
...COMMANDS...
...ANUBIS!

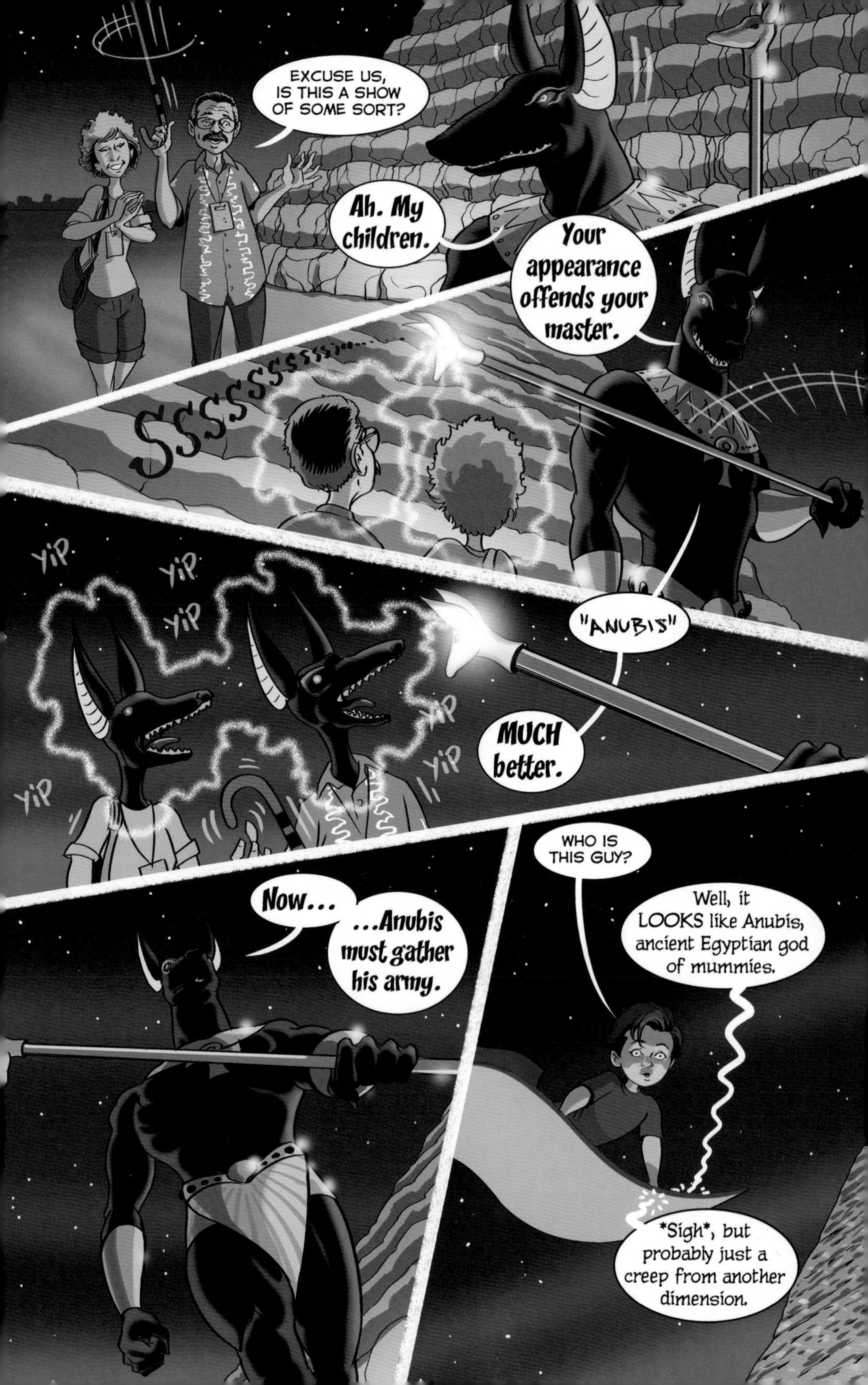
EXCUSE US, IS THIS A SHOW OF SOME SORT?
Ah. My children.
Your appearance offends your master.
SSSSSSSSSSSSS...
"ANUBIS"
MUCH better.
YIP
YIP
YIP
YIP
YIP
YIP
Now...
...Anubis must gather his army.
WHO IS THIS GUY?
Well, it LOOKS like Anubis, ancient Egyptian god of mummies.
Sigh, but probably just a creep from another dimension.

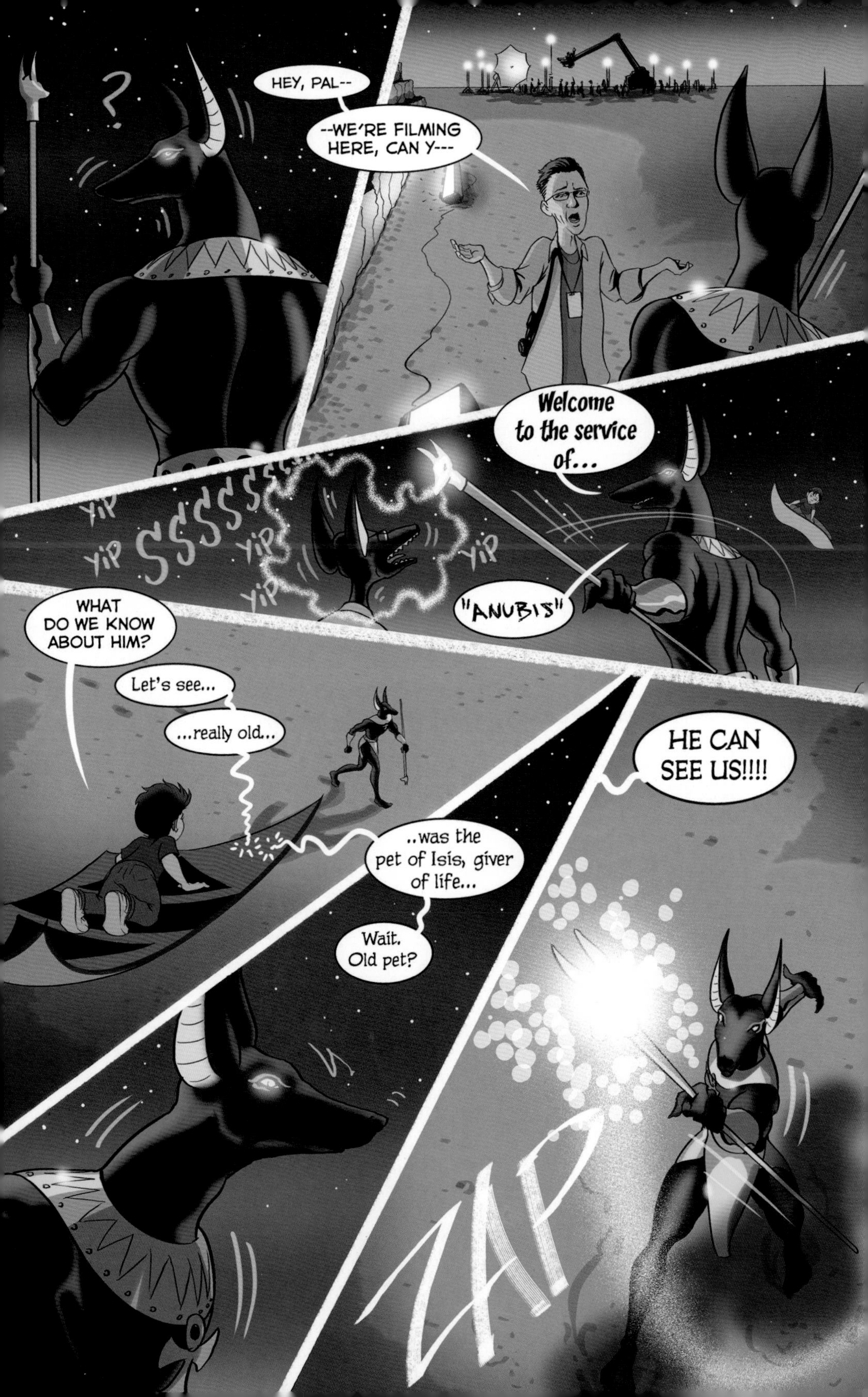
?
HEY, PAL--
--WE'RE FILMING HERE, CAN Y---
Welcome to the service of...
YIP
SSSSSSS
YIP
YIP
YIP
YIP
"ANUBIS"
WHAT DO WE KNOW ABOUT HIM?
Let's see...
...really old...
..was the pet of Isis, giver of life...
Wait. Old pet?
HE CAN SEE US!!!!
ZAP

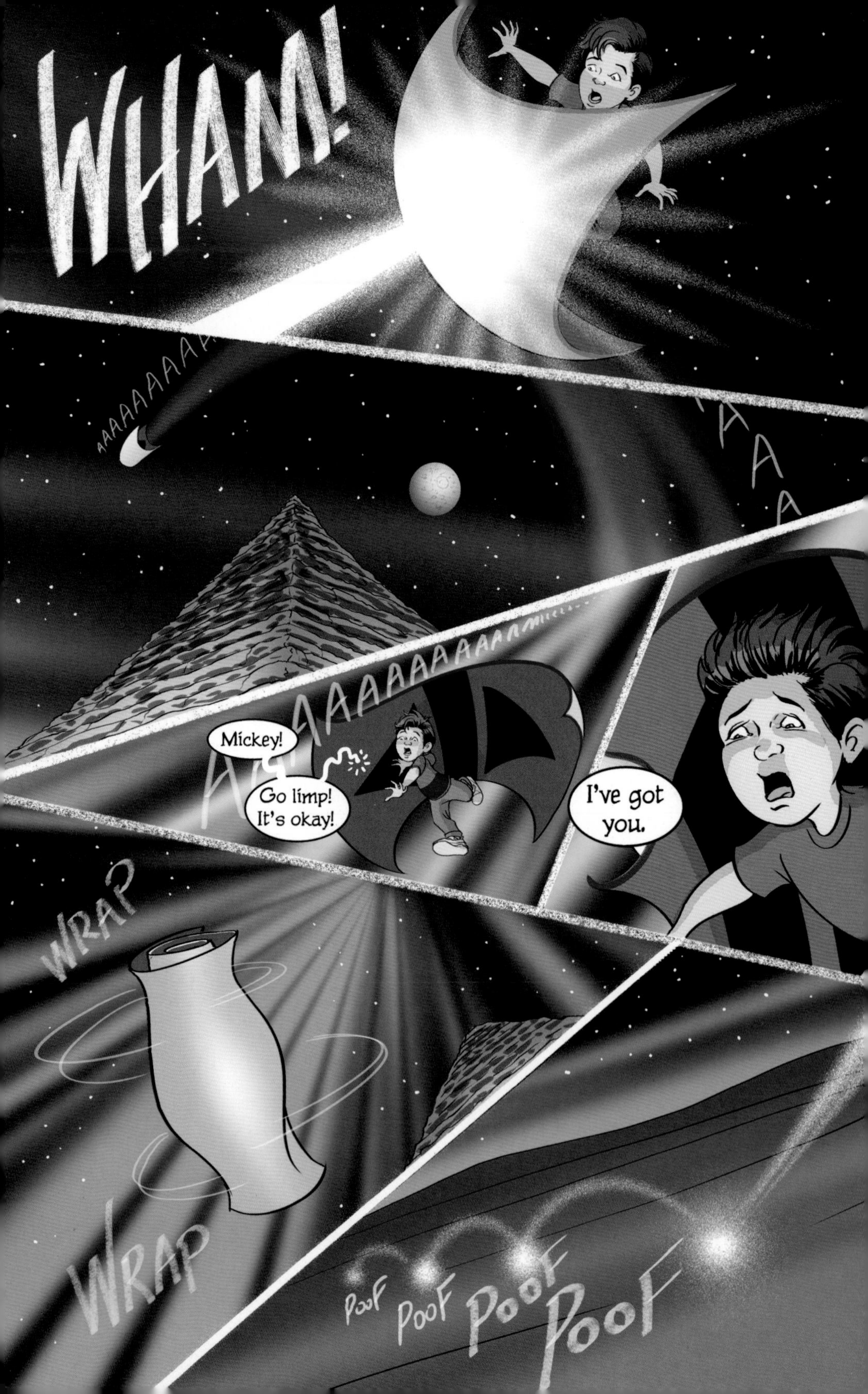
WHAM!
AAAAAAAAA
AAAA
AAAAAAAAAAAAAA
Mickey!
Go limp! It's okay!
I've got you.
WRAP
WRAP
POOF POOF POOF POOF

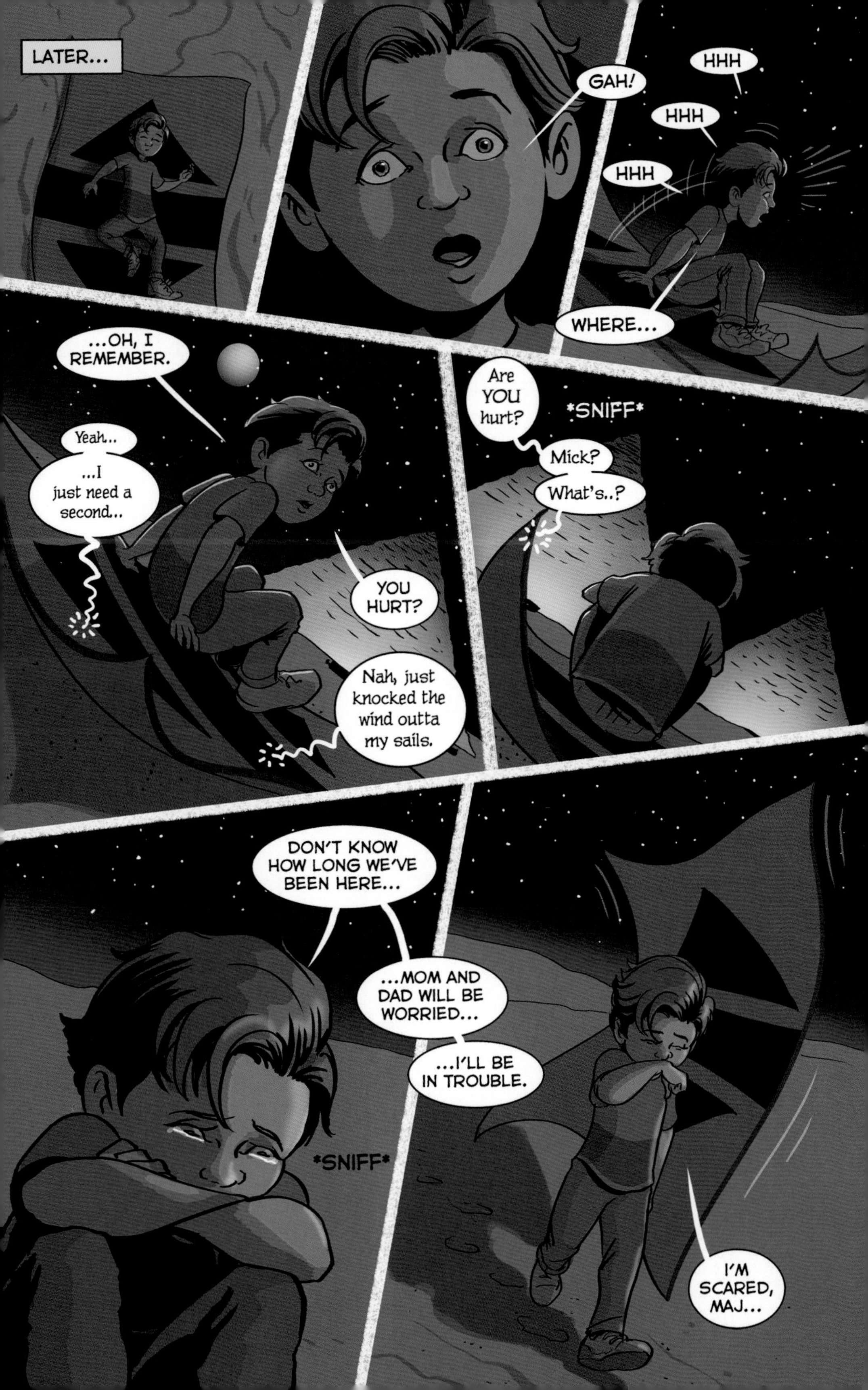
LATER...
GAH!
HHH
HHH
HHH
WHERE...
...OH, I REMEMBER.
Yeah..
...I just need a second...
YOU HURT?
Nah, just knocked the wind outta my sails.
Are YOU hurt?
SNIFF
Mick?
What's..?
DON'T KNOW HOW LONG WE'VE BEEN HERE...
...MOM AND DAD WILL BE WORRIED...
...I'LL BE IN TROUBLE.
SNIFF
I'M SCARED, MAJ...

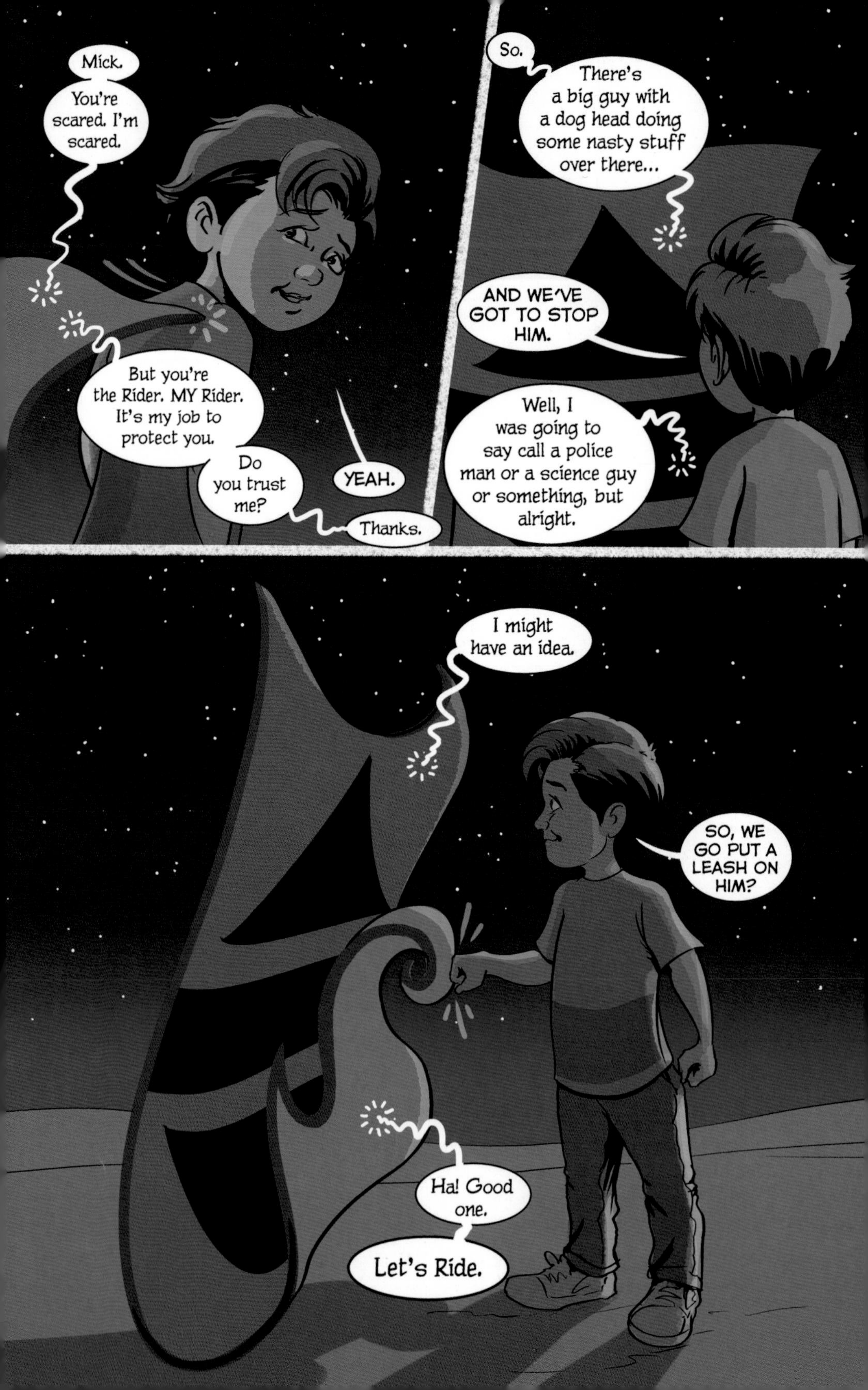
Mick.
You're scared. I'm scared.
But you're the Rider. MY Rider. It's my job to protect you.
Do you trust me?
YEAH.
Thanks.
So.
There's a big guy with a dog head doing some nasty stuff over there...
AND WE'VE GOT TO STOP HIM.
Well, I was going to say call a police man or a science guy or something, but alright.
I might have an idea.
SO, WE GO PUT A LEASH ON HIM?
Ha! Good one.
Let's Ride.

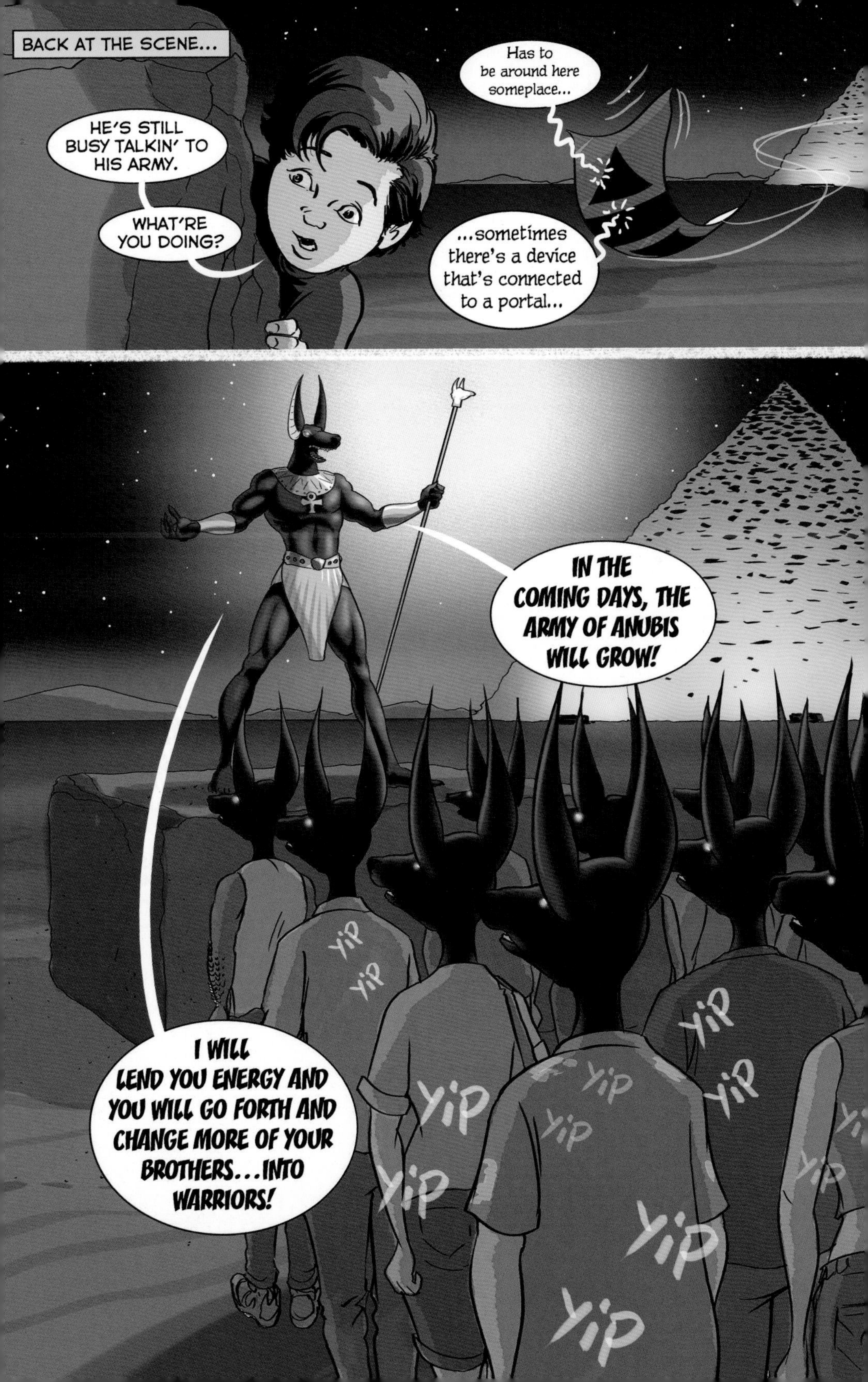
BACK AT THE SCENE...
HE'S STILL BUSY TALKIN' TO HIS ARMY.
WHAT'RE YOU DOING?
Has to be around here someplace...
...sometimes there's a device that's connected to a portal...
IN THE COMING DAYS, THE ARMY OF ANUBIS WILL GROW!
I WILL LEND YOU ENERGY AND YOU WILL GO FORTH AND CHANGE MORE OF YOUR BROTHERS...INTO WARRIORS!
YIP
YIP
YIP
YIP
YIP
YIP
YIP
YIP
YIP
YIP
YIP

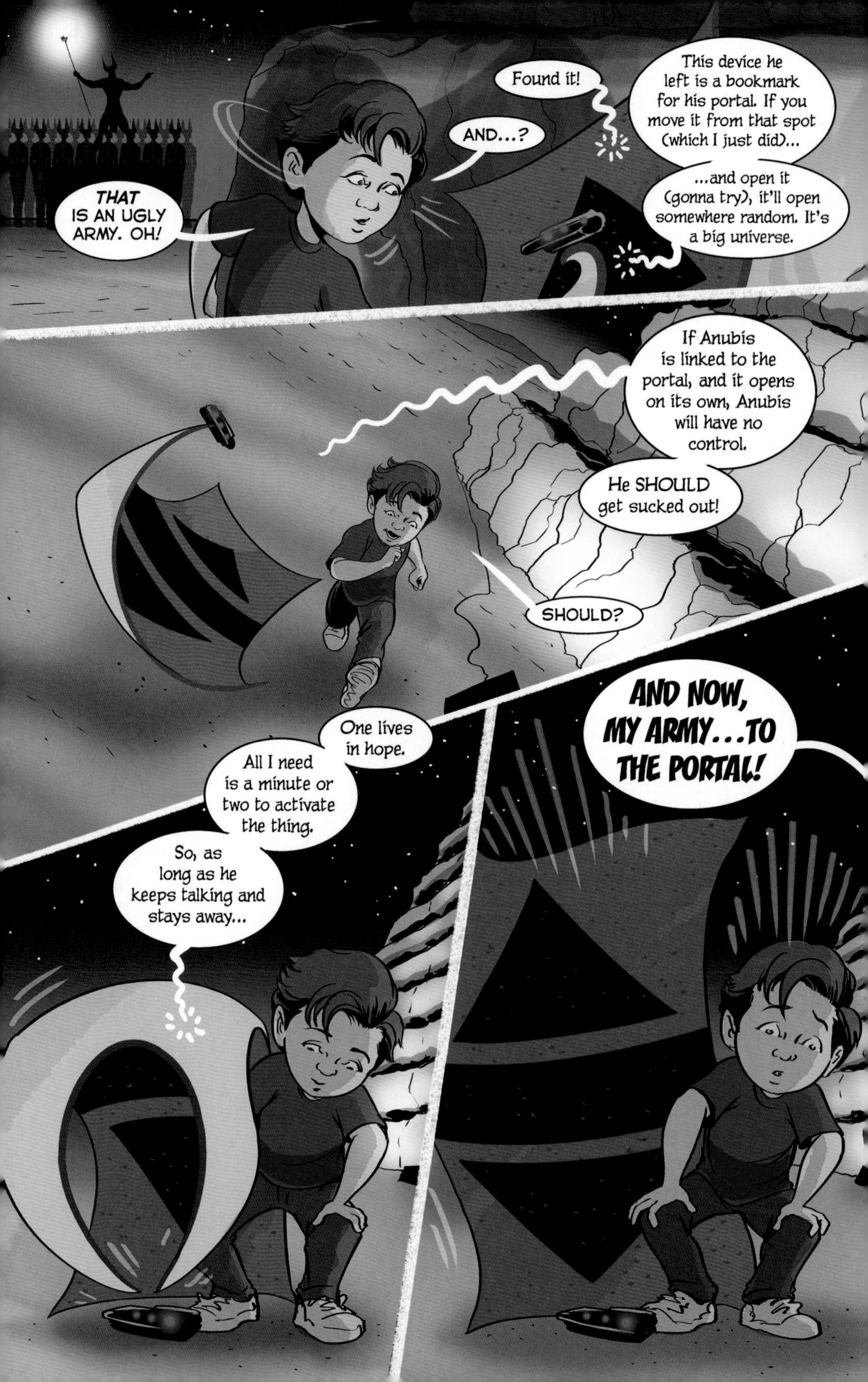
THAT IS AN UGLY ARMY. OH!
AND...?
Found it!
This device he left is a bookmark for his portal. If you move it from that spot (which I just did)...
...and open it (gonna try), it'll open somewhere random. It's a big universe.
If Anubis is linked to the portal, and it opens on its own, Anubis will have no control.
He SHOULD get sucked out!
SHOULD?
One lives in hope.
All I need is a minute or two to activate the thing.
So, as long as he keeps talking and stays away...
AND NOW, MY ARMY...TO THE PORTAL!

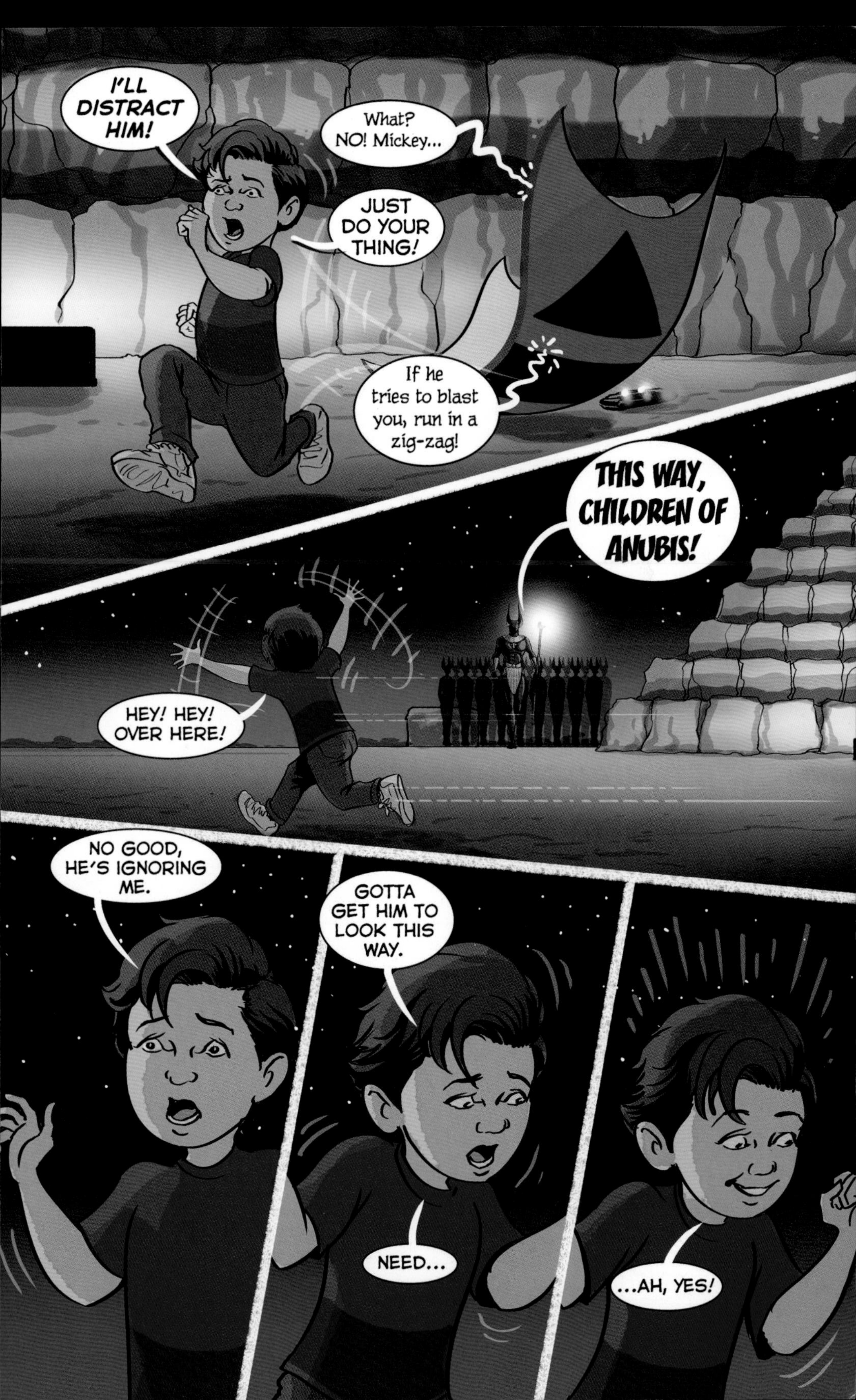
I'LL DISTRACT HIM!
What? NO! Mickey...
JUST DO YOUR THING!
If he tries to blast you, run in a zig-zag!
THIS WAY, CHILDREN OF ANUBIS!
HEY! HEY! OVER HERE!
NO GOOD, HE'S IGNORING ME.
GOTTA GET HIM TO LOOK THIS WAY.
NEED...
...AH, YES!

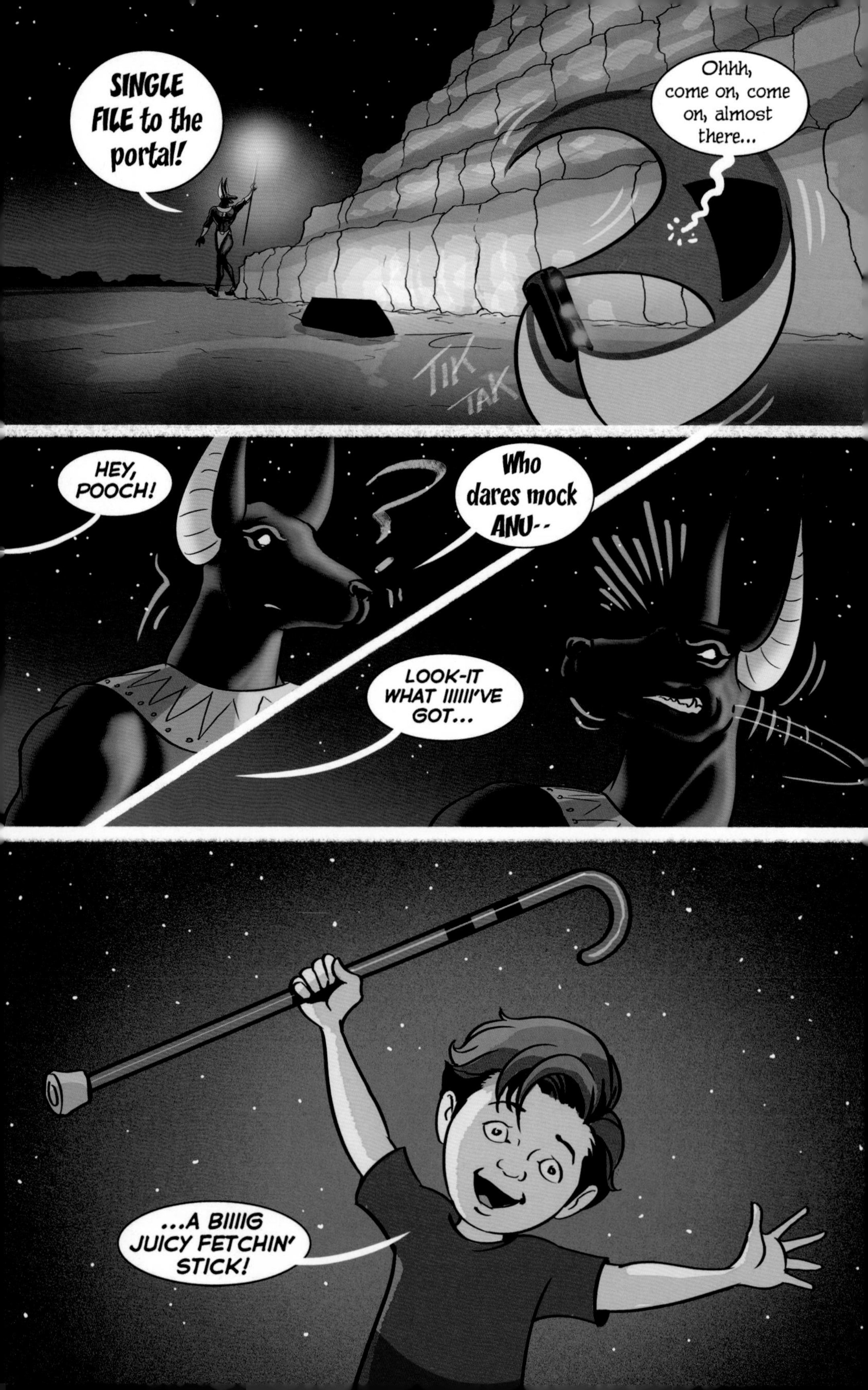
SINGLE FILE to the portal!
Ohhh, come on, come on, almost there...
TIK TAK
HEY, POOCH!
Who dares mock ANU--
LOOK-IT WHAT IIIIII'VE GOT...
...A BIIIIG JUICY FETCHIN' STICK!

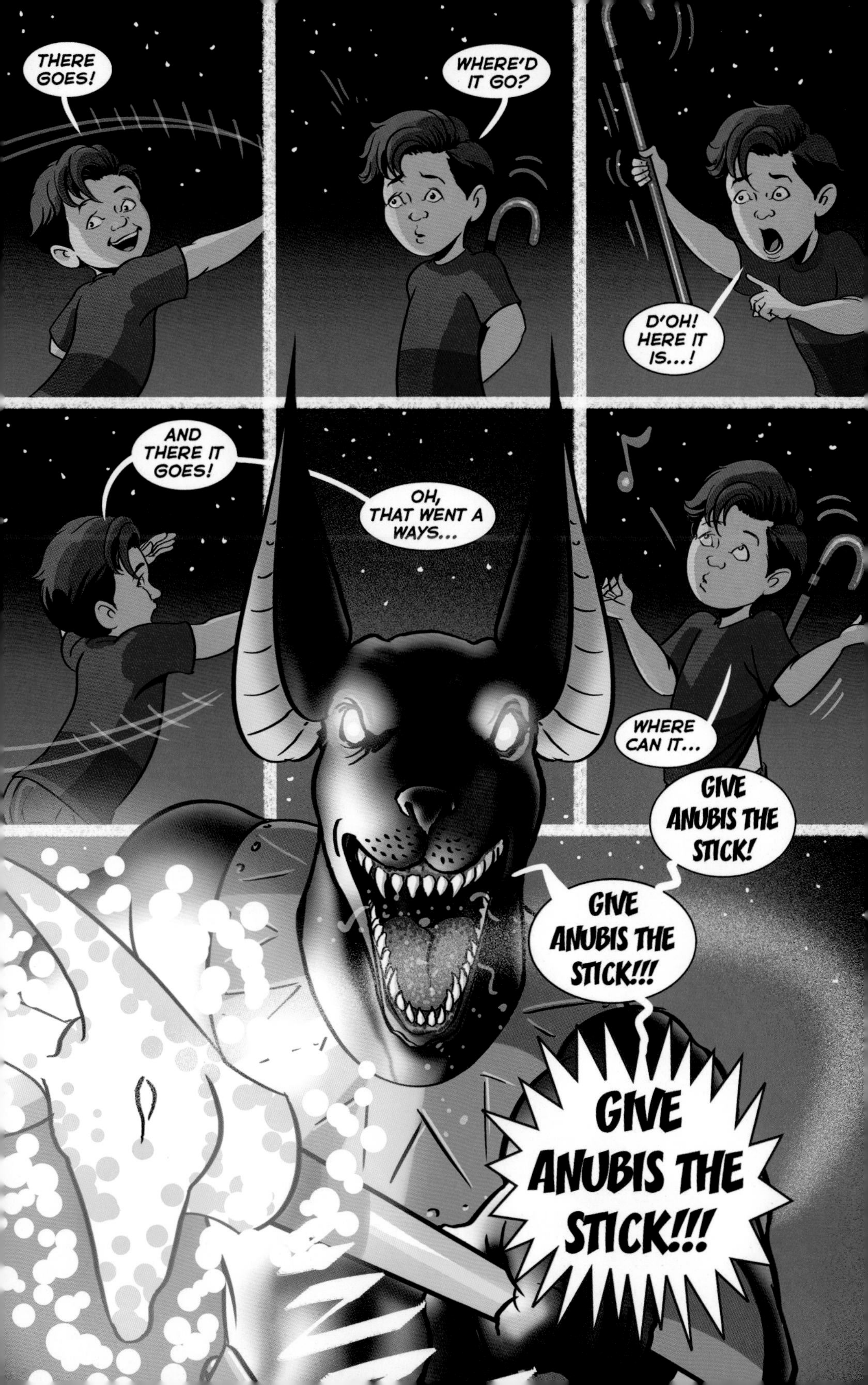
THERE GOES!
WHERE'D IT GO?
D'OH! HERE IT IS...!
AND THERE IT GOES!
OH, THAT WENT A WAYS...
WHERE CAN IT...
GIVE ANUBIS THE STICK!
GIVE ANUBIS THE STICK!!!
GIVE ANUBIS THE STICK!!!

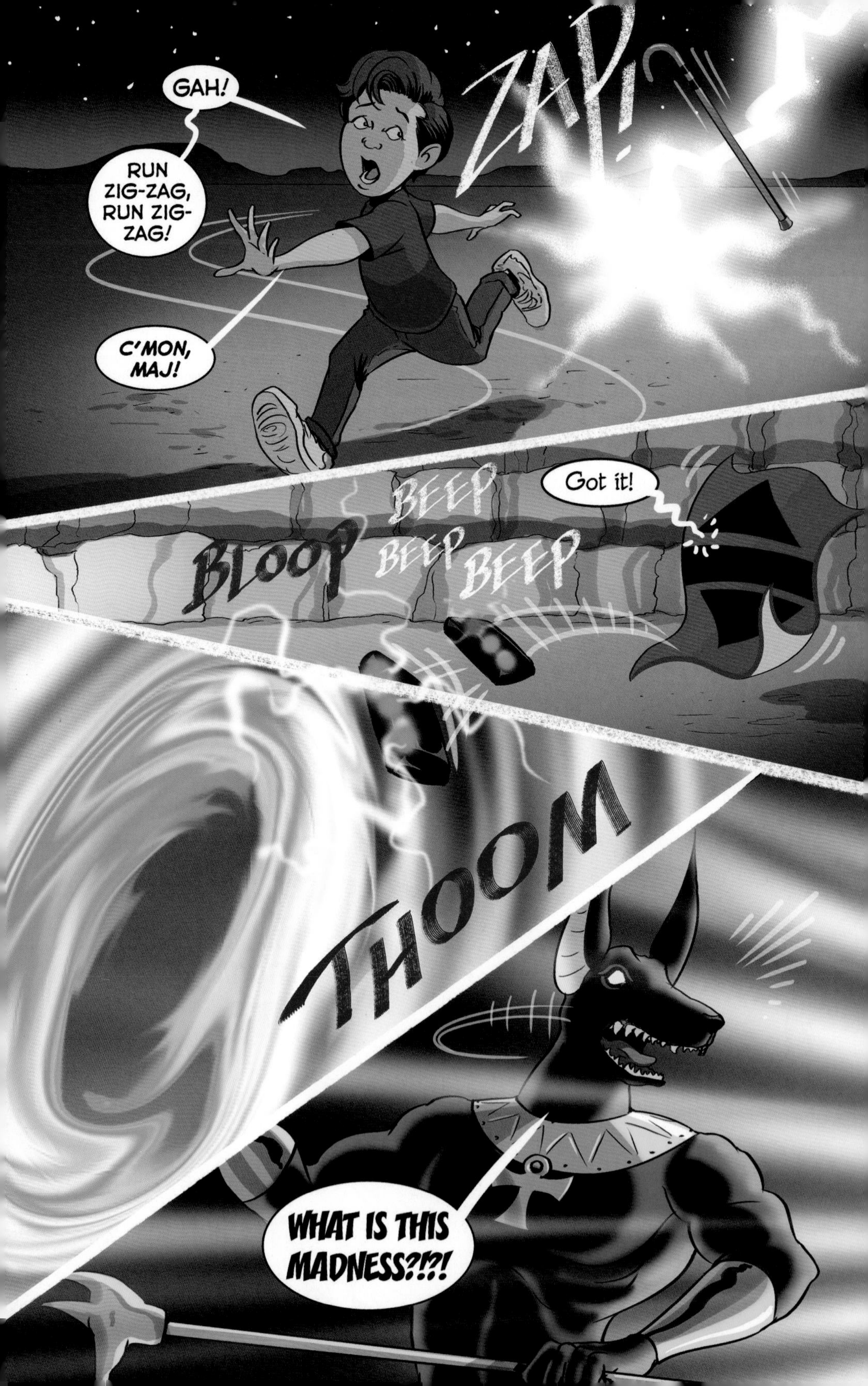
GAH!
RUN ZIG-ZAG, RUN ZIG-ZAG!
C'MON, MAJ!
ZAP!
Got it!
BLOOP
BEEP
BEEP
BEEP
THOOM
WHAT IS THIS MADNESS?!?!

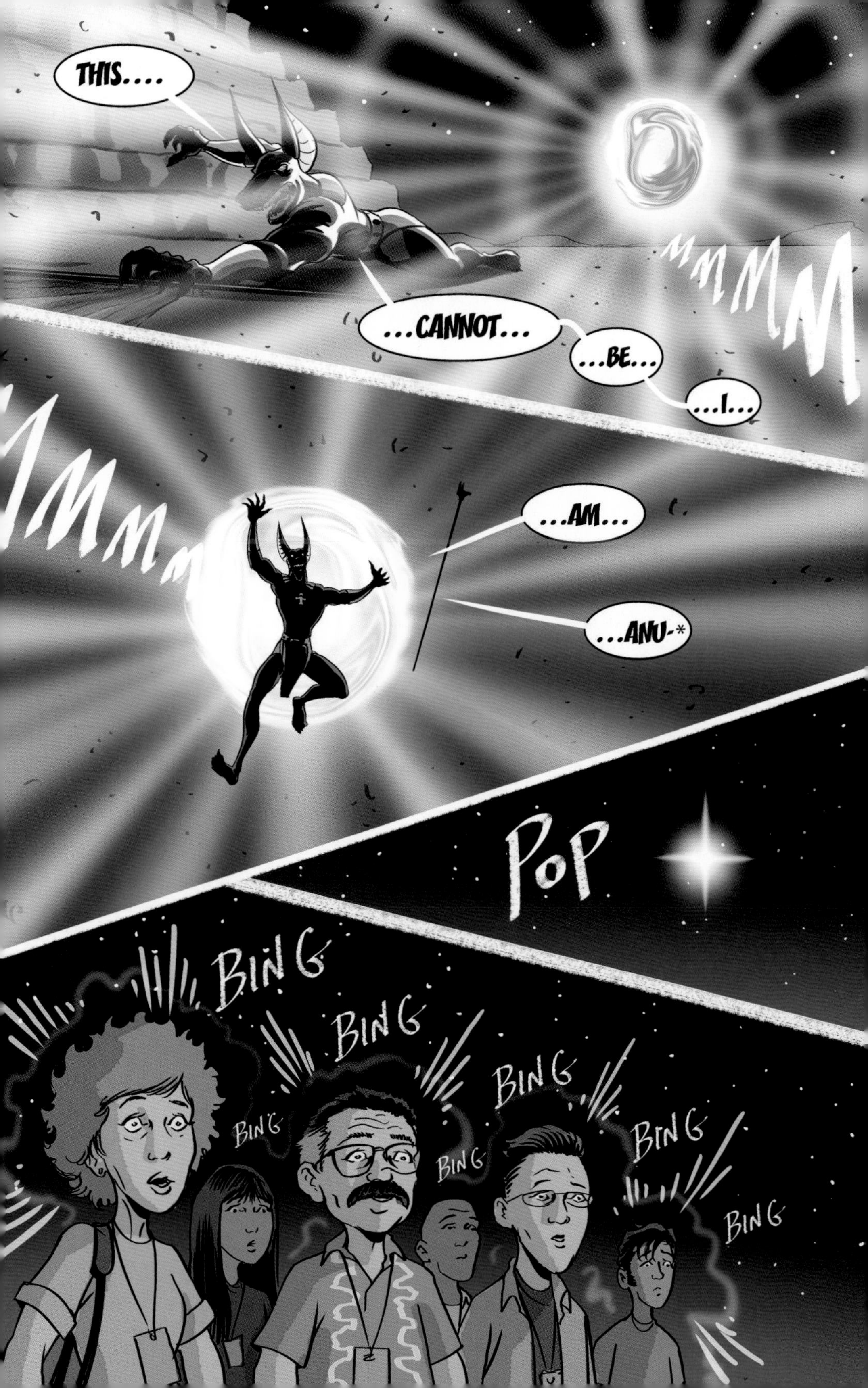
THIS....
...CANNOT...
...BE...
...I...
MMMM
MMMM
...AM...
...ANU-*
POP
BING
BING
BING
BING
BING
BING
BING

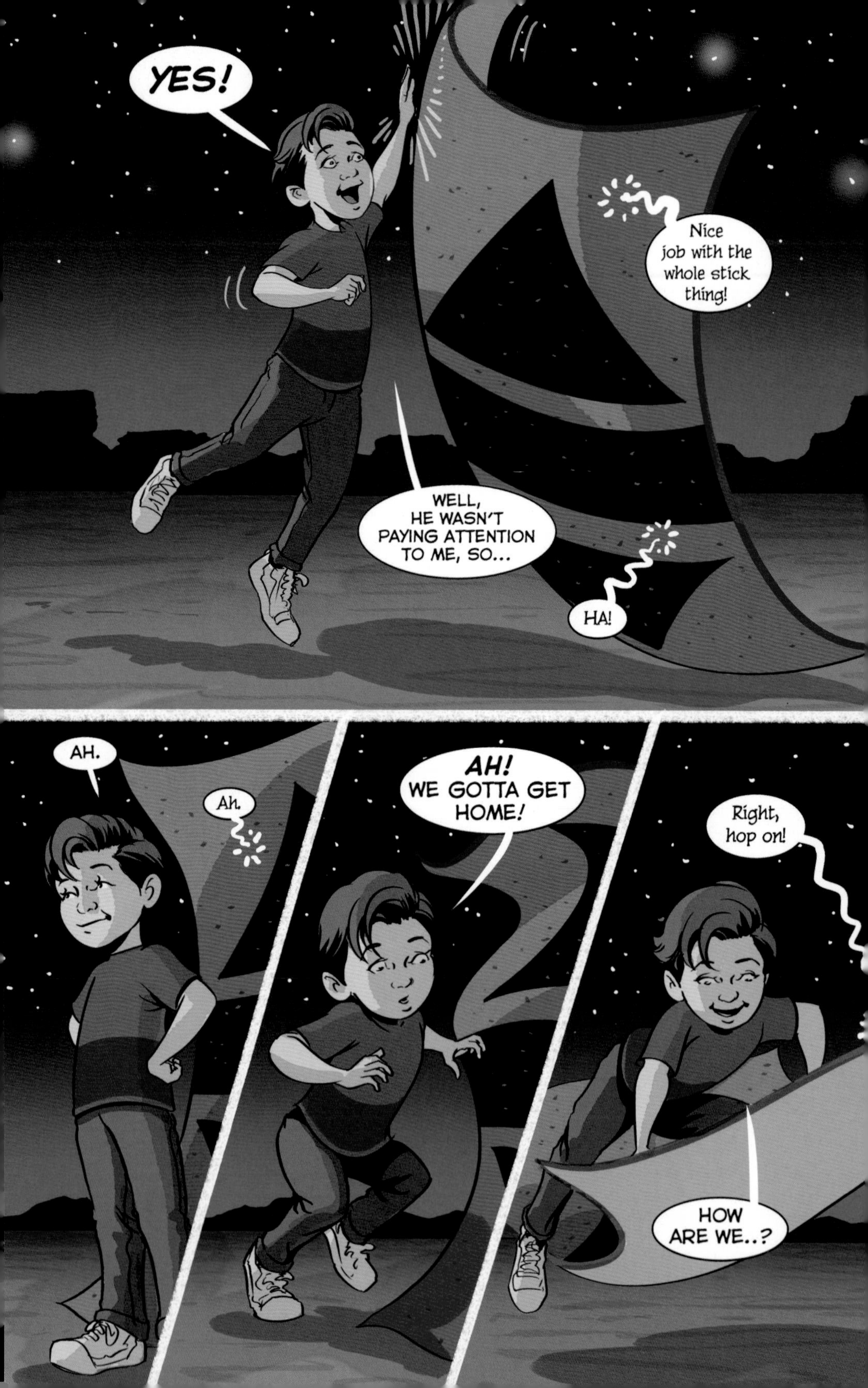
YES!
Nice job with the whole stick thing!
WELL, HE WASN'T PAYING ATTENTION TO ME, SO...
HA!
AH.
Ah.
AH! WE GOTTA GET HOME!
Right, hop on!
HOW ARE WE..?

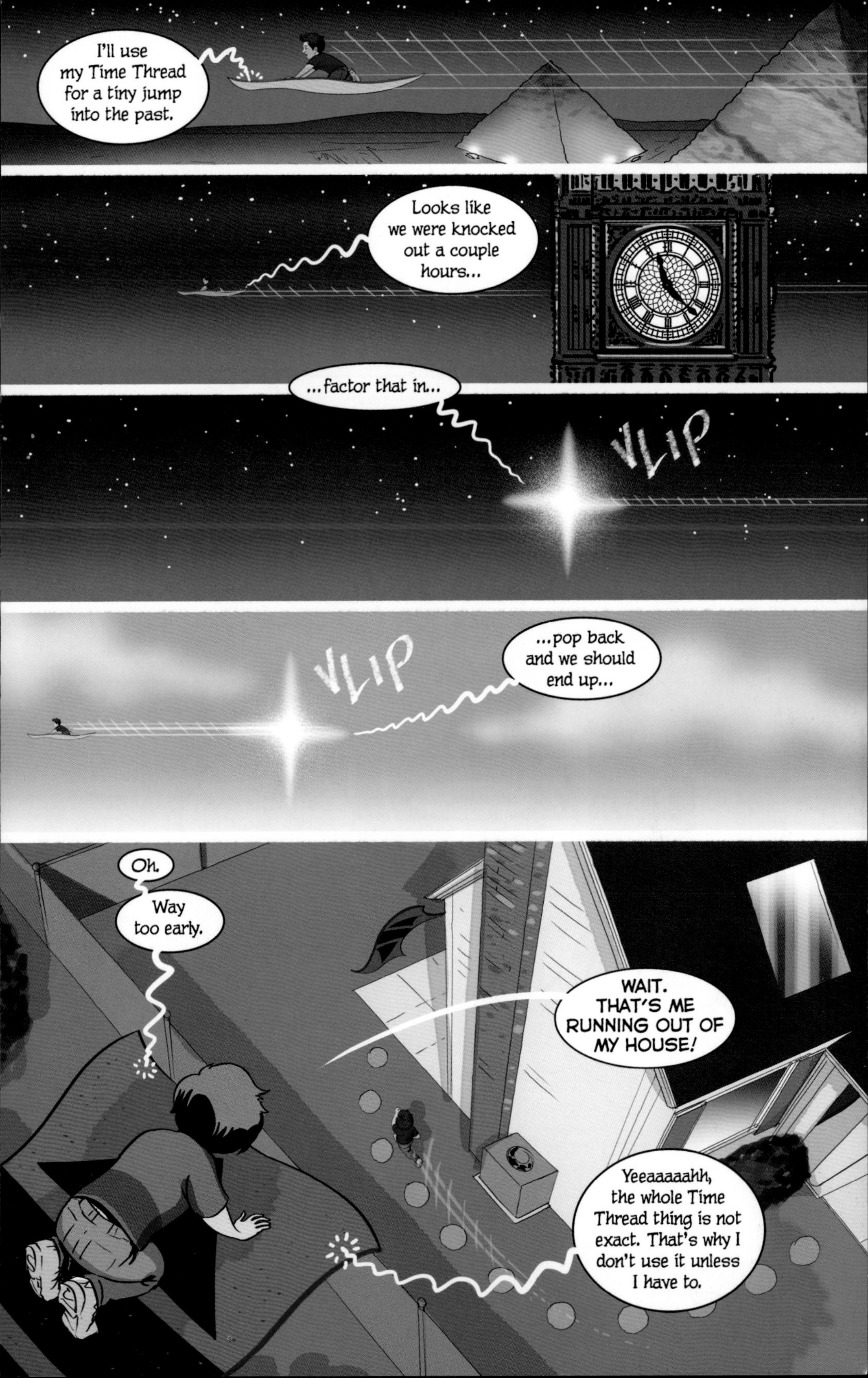
I'll use my Time Thread for a tiny jump into the past.
Looks like we were knocked out a couple hours...
...factor that in...
VLIP
VLIP
...pop back and we should end up...
Oh.
Way too early.
WAIT. THAT'S ME RUNNING OUT OF MY HOUSE!
Yeeaaaaahh, the whole Time Thread thing is not exact. That's why I don't use it unless I have to.

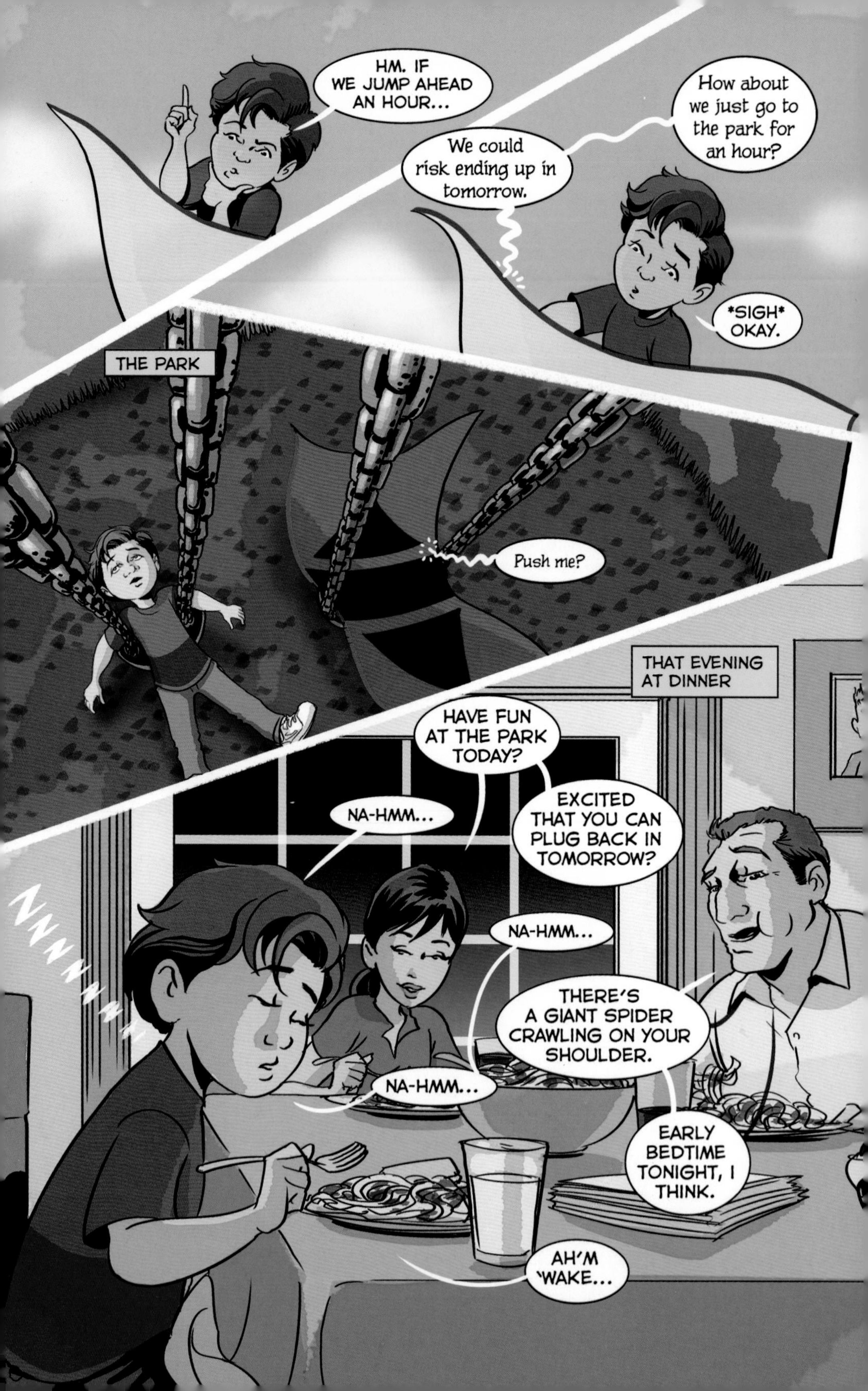
HM. IF WE JUMP AHEAD AN HOUR...
We could risk ending up in tomorrow.
How about we just go to the park for an hour?
SIGH OKAY.
THE PARK
Push me?
THAT EVENING AT DINNER
HAVE FUN AT THE PARK TODAY?
NA-HMM...
EXCITED THAT YOU CAN PLUG BACK IN TOMORROW?
NA-HMM...
THERE'S A GIANT SPIDER CRAWLING ON YOUR SHOULDER.
NA-HMM...
EARLY BEDTIME TONIGHT, I THINK.
AH'M 'WAKE...

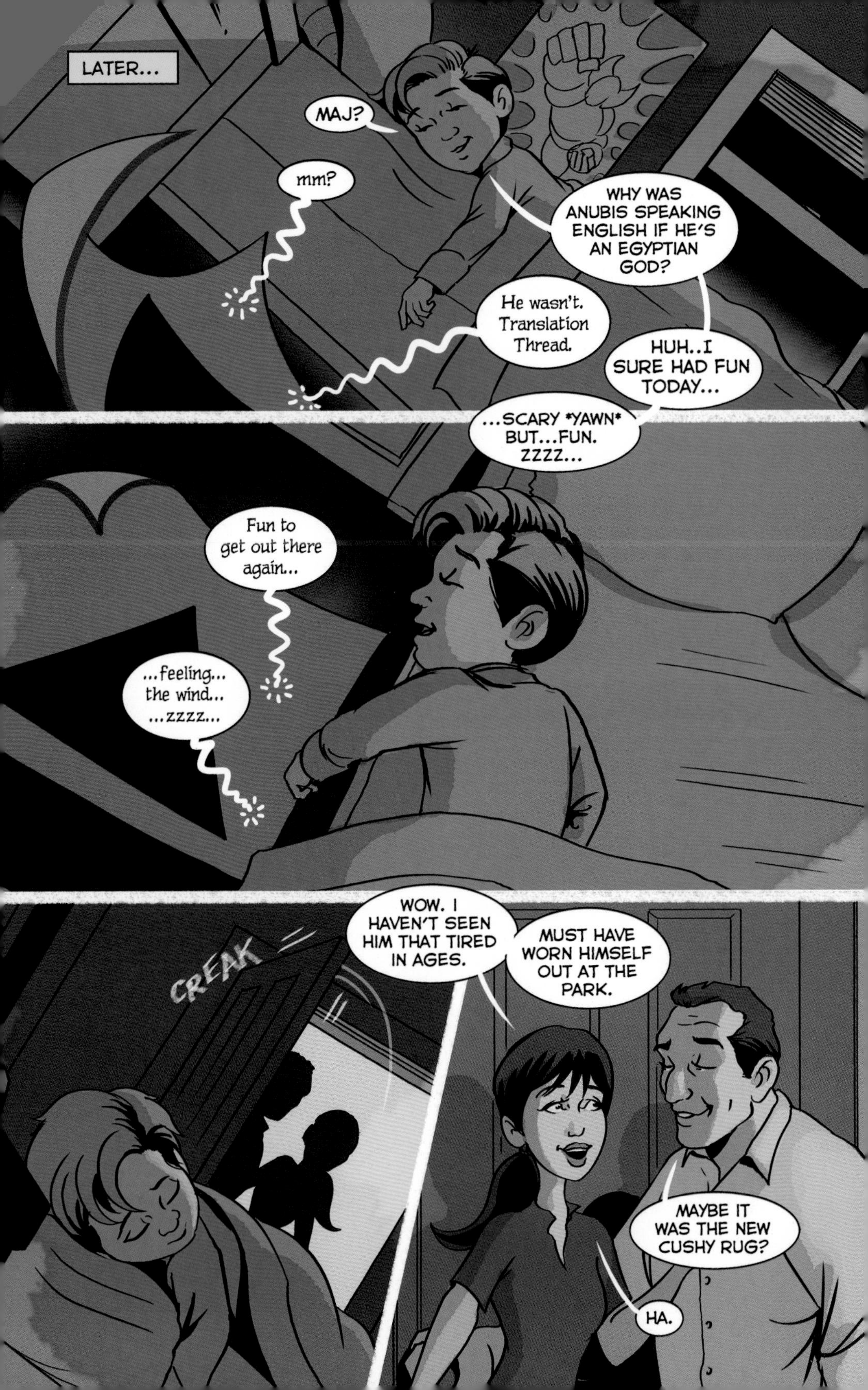
LATER...
MAJ?
mm?
WHY WAS ANUBIS SPEAKING ENGLISH IF HE'S AN EGYPTIAN GOD?
He wasn't. Translation Thread.
HUH..I SURE HAD FUN TODAY...
...SCARY *YAWN* BUT...FUN. ZZZZ...
Fun to get out there again...
...feeling... the wind... ...zzzz...
CREAK
WOW. I HAVEN'T SEEN HIM THAT TIRED IN AGES.
MUST HAVE WORN HIMSELF OUT AT THE PARK.
MAYBE IT WAS THE NEW CUSHY RUG?
HA.

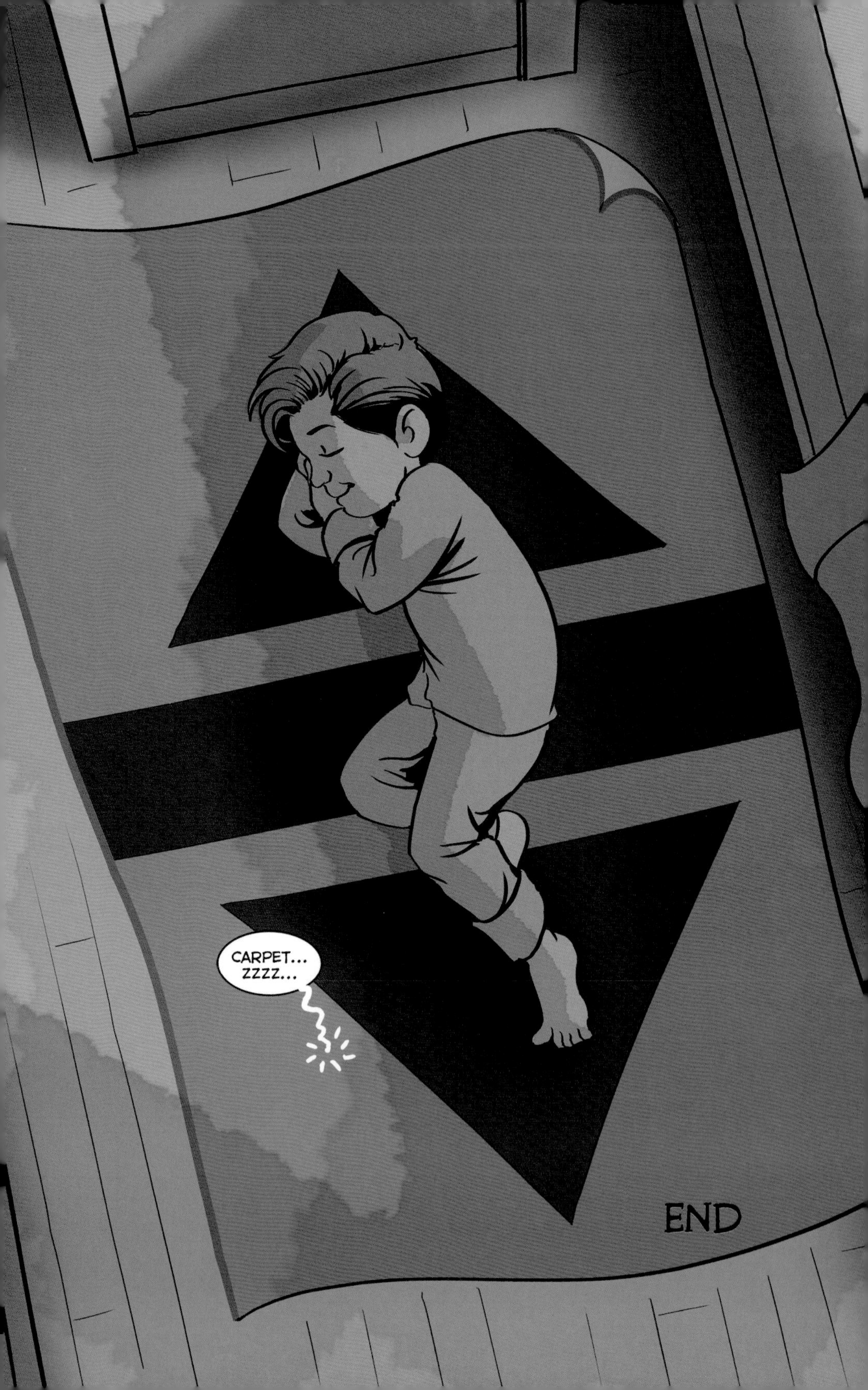
CARPET...
ZZZZ...
END

BOOK TWO

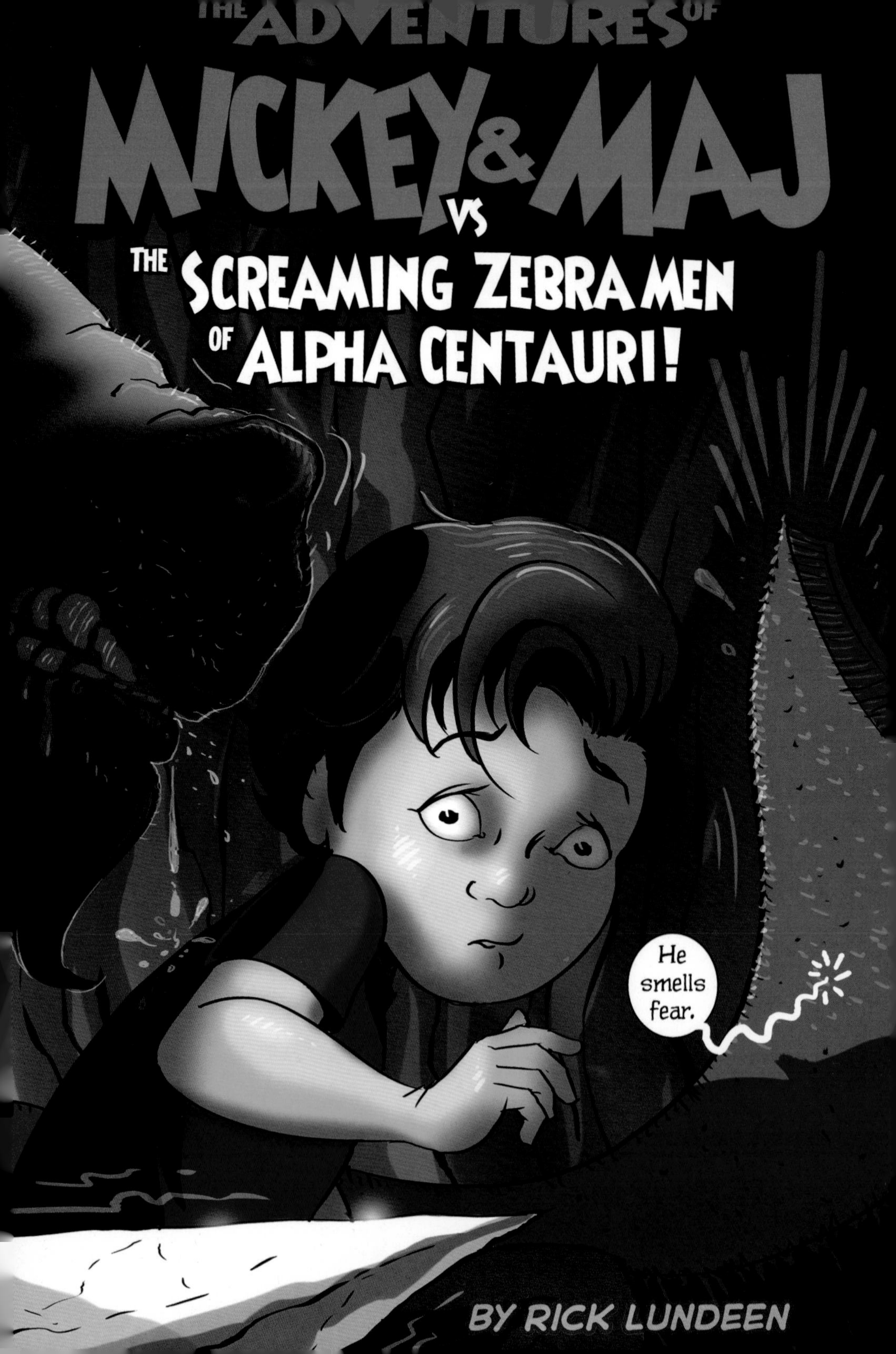
THE ADVENTURES OF
MICKEY & MAJ
VS
THE SCREAMING ZEBRA MEN
OF ALPHA CENTAURI!
He smells fear.
BY RICK LUNDEEN

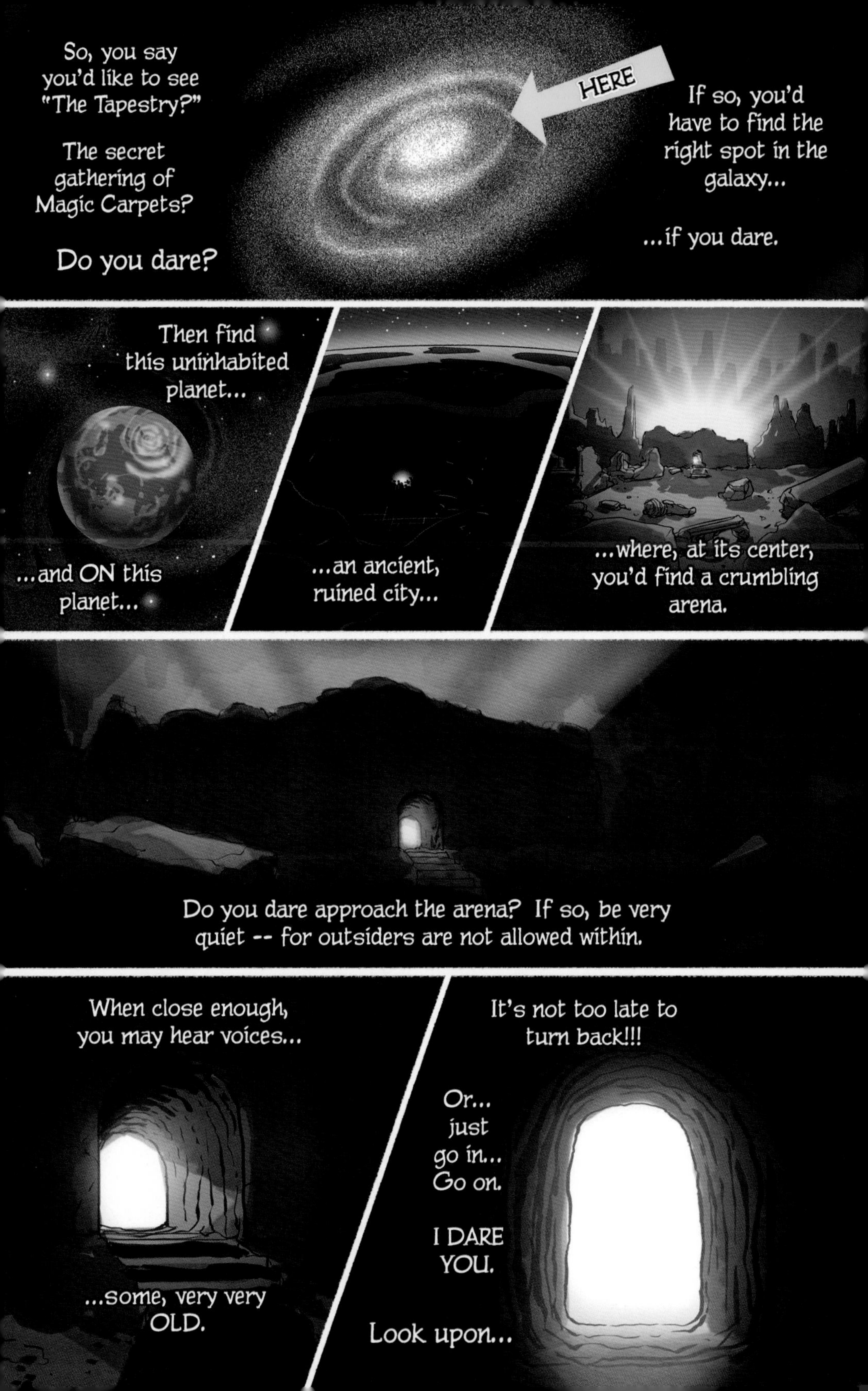
So, you say you'd like to see "The Tapestry?"
The secret gathering of Magic Carpets?
Do you dare?
HERE
If so, you'd have to find the right spot in the galaxy...
...if you dare.
Then find this uninhabited planet...
...and ON this planet...
...an ancient, ruined city...
...where, at its center, you'd find a crumbling arena.
Do you dare approach the arena? If so, be very quiet -- for outsiders are not allowed within.
When close enough, you may hear voices...
...some, very very OLD.
It's not too late to turn back!!!
Or... just go in... Go on.
I DARE YOU.
Look upon...

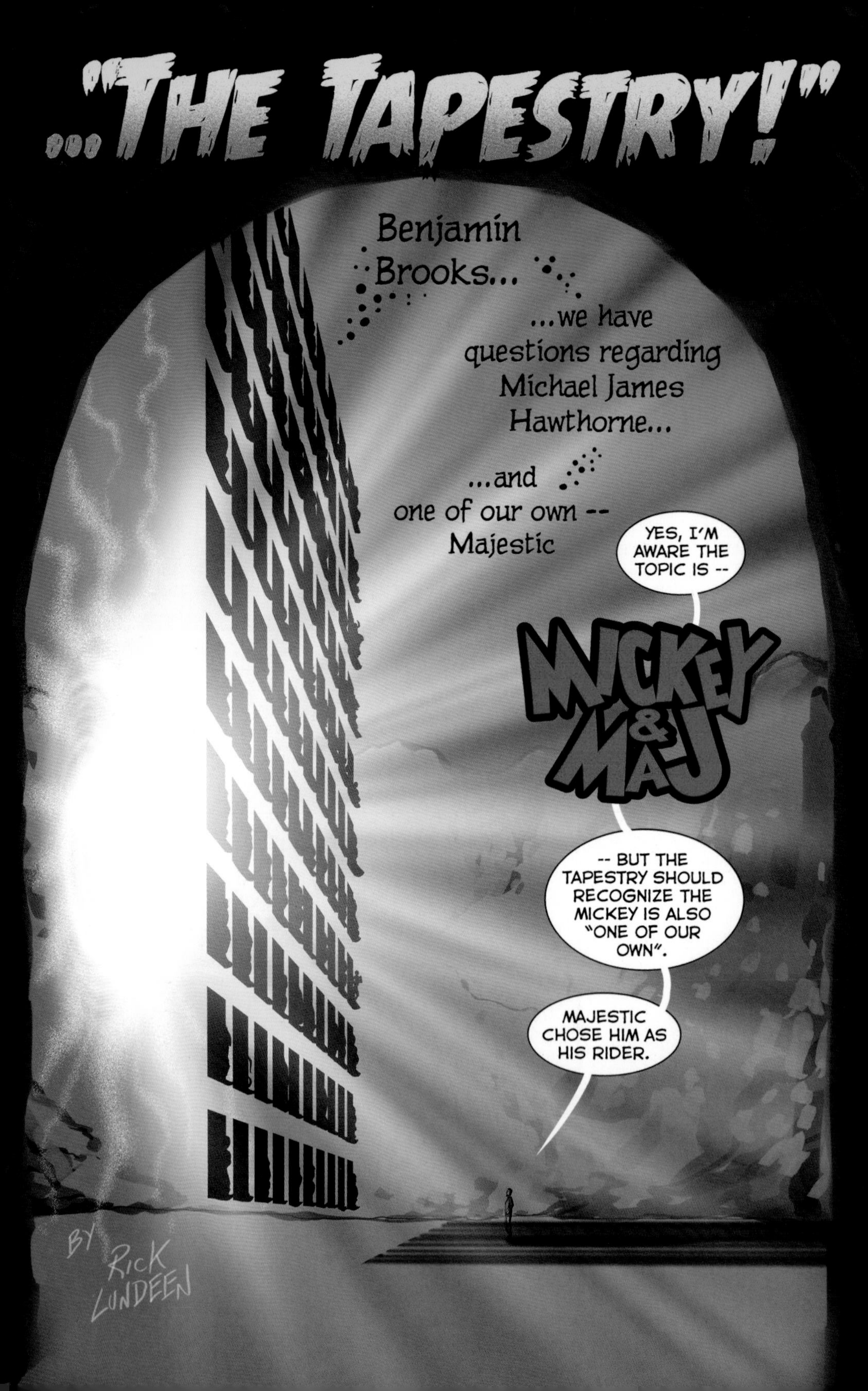
..."THE TAPESTRY!"
Benjamin Brooks...
...we have questions regarding Michael James Hawthorne...
...and one of our own -- Majestic
YES, I'M AWARE THE TOPIC IS --
MICKEY & MAJ
-- BUT THE TAPESTRY SHOULD RECOGNIZE THE MICKEY IS ALSO "ONE OF OUR OWN".
MAJESTIC CHOSE HIM AS HIS RIDER.
BY RICK LUNDEEN

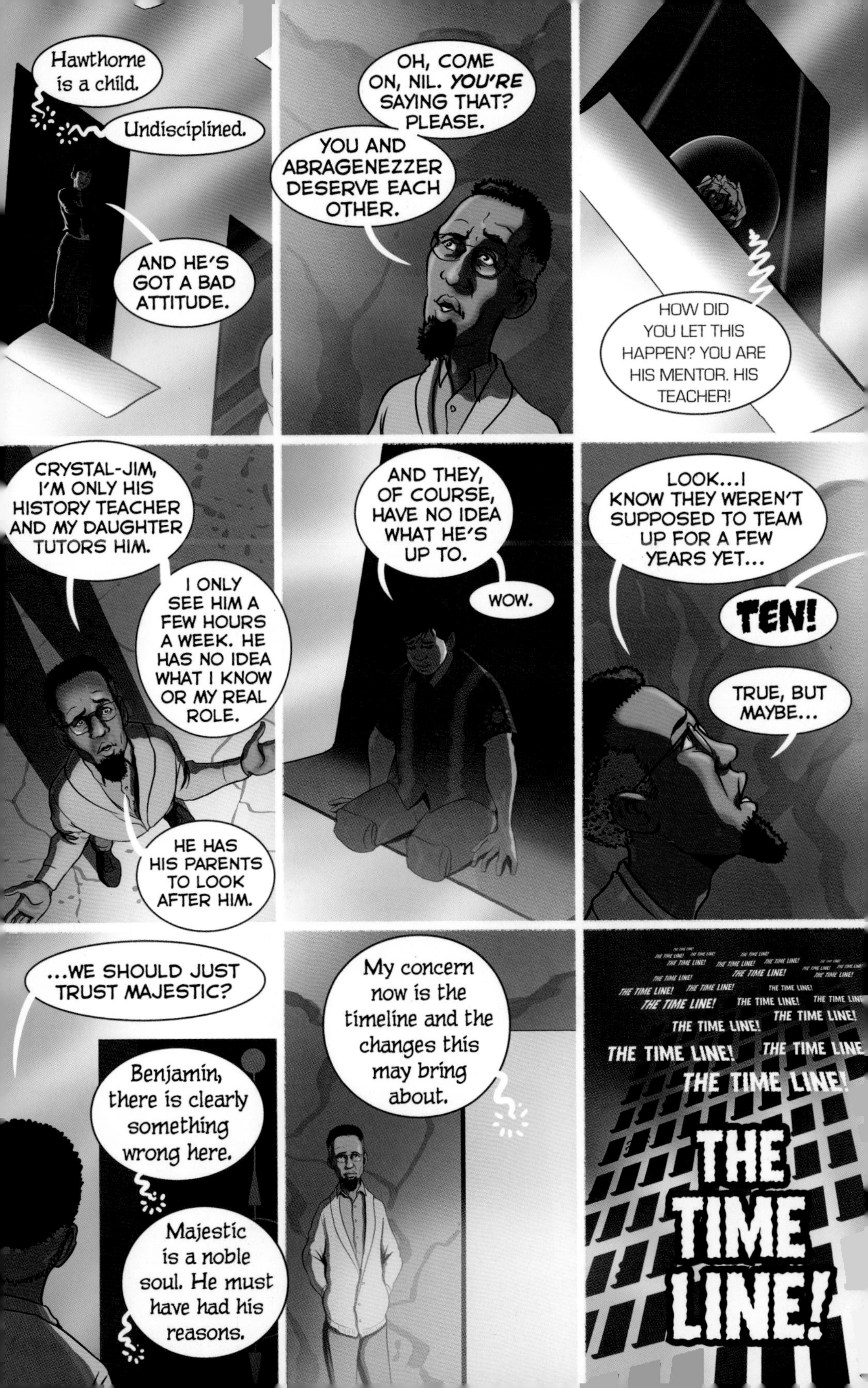
Hawthorne is a child.
Undisciplined.
AND HE'S GOT A BAD ATTITUDE.
OH, COME ON, NIL. *YOU'RE* SAYING THAT? PLEASE.
YOU AND ABRAGENEZZER DESERVE EACH OTHER.
HOW DID YOU LET THIS HAPPEN? YOU ARE HIS MENTOR. HIS TEACHER!
CRYSTAL-JIM, I'M ONLY HIS HISTORY TEACHER AND MY DAUGHTER TUTORS HIM.
I ONLY SEE HIM A FEW HOURS A WEEK. HE HAS NO IDEA WHAT I KNOW OR MY REAL ROLE.
HE HAS HIS PARENTS TO LOOK AFTER HIM.
AND THEY, OF COURSE, HAVE NO IDEA WHAT HE'S UP TO.
WOW.
LOOK...I KNOW THEY WEREN'T SUPPOSED TO TEAM UP FOR A FEW YEARS YET...
TEN!
TRUE, BUT MAYBE...
...WE SHOULD JUST TRUST MAJESTIC?
Benjamin, there is clearly something wrong here.
Majestic is a noble soul. He must have had his reasons.
My concern now is the timeline and the changes this may bring about.
THE TIME LINE! THE TIME LINE! THE TIME LINE! THE TIME LINE! THE TIME LINE! THE TIME LINE! THE TIME LINE!
THE TIME LINE!

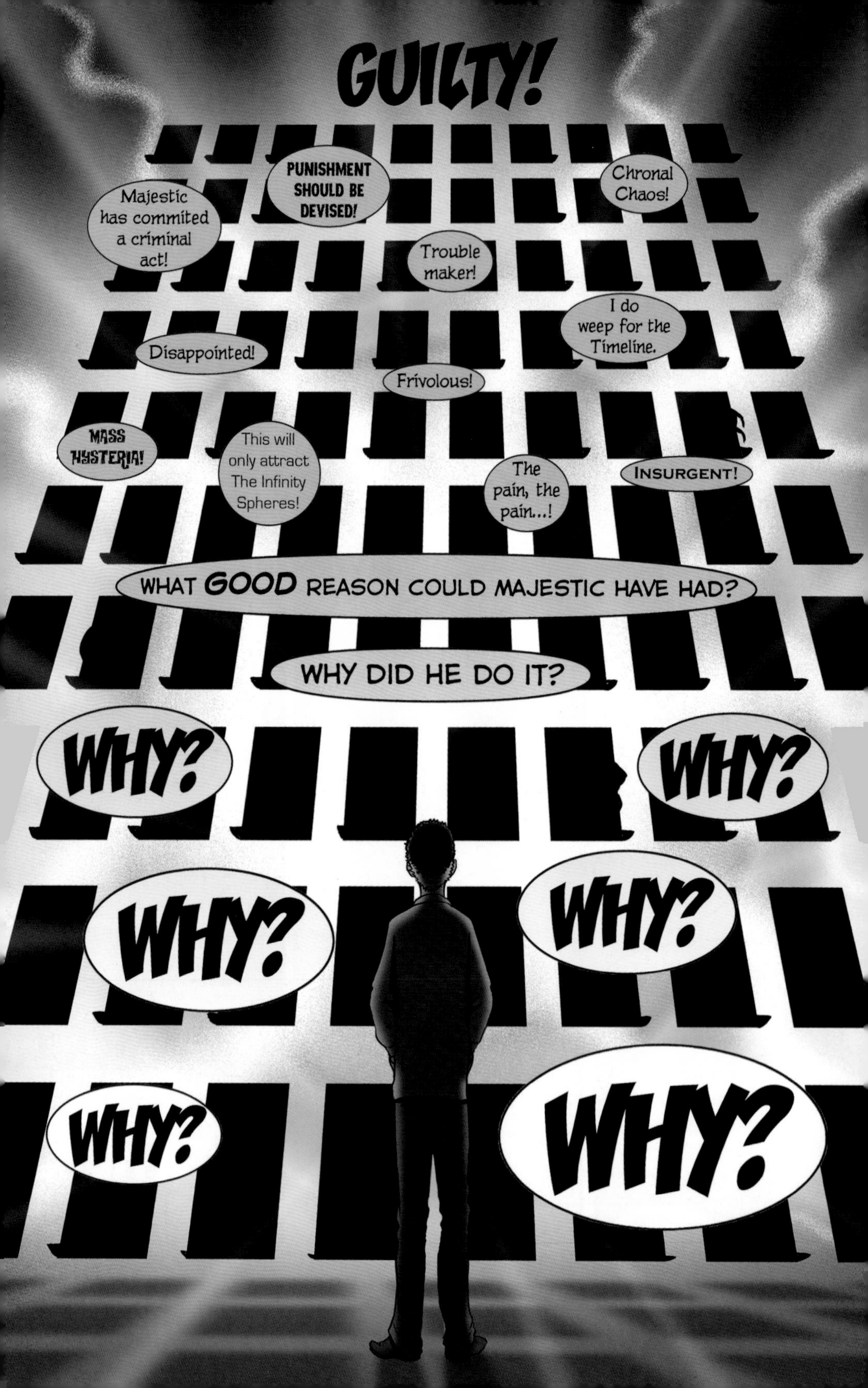
GUILTY!
Majestic has commited a criminal act!
PUNISHMENT SHOULD BE DEVISED!
Chronal Chaos!
Trouble maker!
I do weep for the Timeline.
Disappointed!
Frivolous!
MASS HYSTERIA!
This will only attract The Infinity Spheres!
The pain, the pain...!
INSURGENT!
WHAT GOOD REASON COULD MAJESTIC HAVE HAD?
WHY DID HE DO IT?
WHY?
WHY?
WHY?
WHY?
WHY?
WHY?

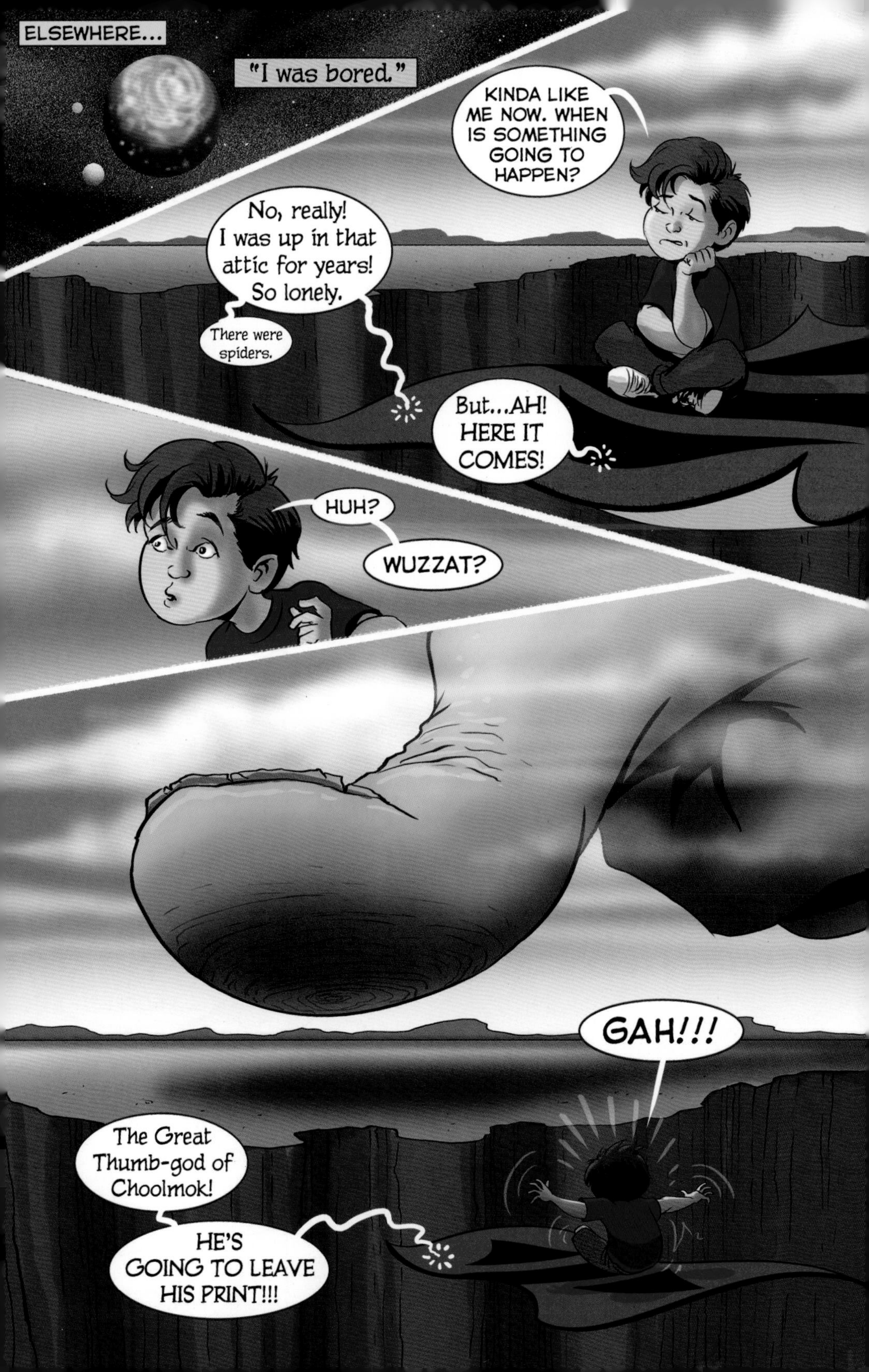
ELSEWHERE...
"I was bored."
KINDA LIKE ME NOW. WHEN IS SOMETHING GOING TO HAPPEN?
No, really! I was up in that attic for years! So lonely.
There were spiders.
But...AH! HERE IT COMES!
HUH?
WUZZAT?
GAH!!!
The Great Thumb-god of Choolmok!
HE'S GOING TO LEAVE HIS PRINT!!!

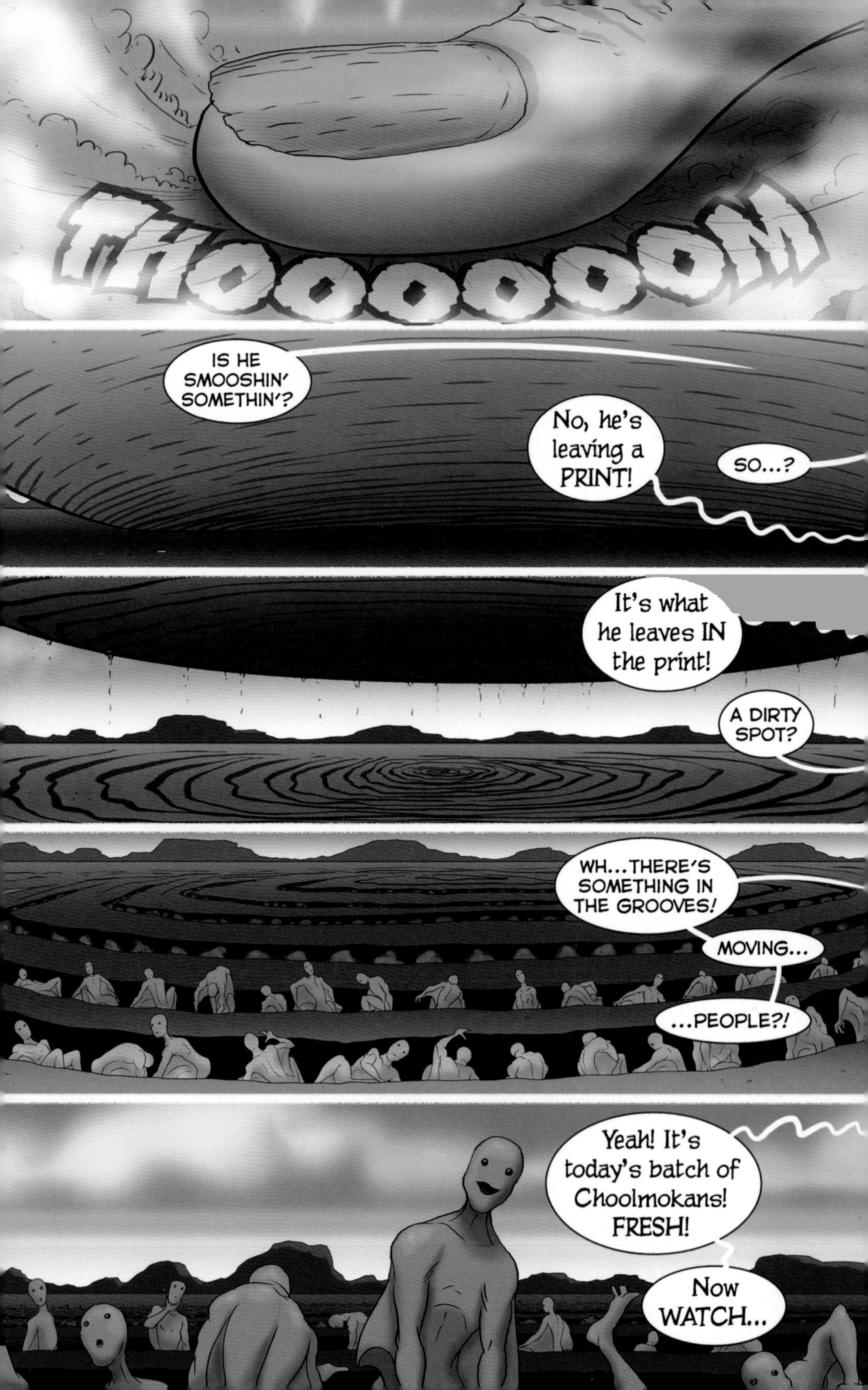
THOOOOOOM
IS HE SMOOSHIN' SOMETHIN'?
No, he's leaving a PRINT!
SO...?
It's what he leaves IN the print!
A DIRTY SPOT?
WH...THERE'S SOMETHING IN THE GROOVES!
MOVING...
...PEOPLE?!
Yeah! It's today's batch of Choolmokans! FRESH!
Now WATCH...

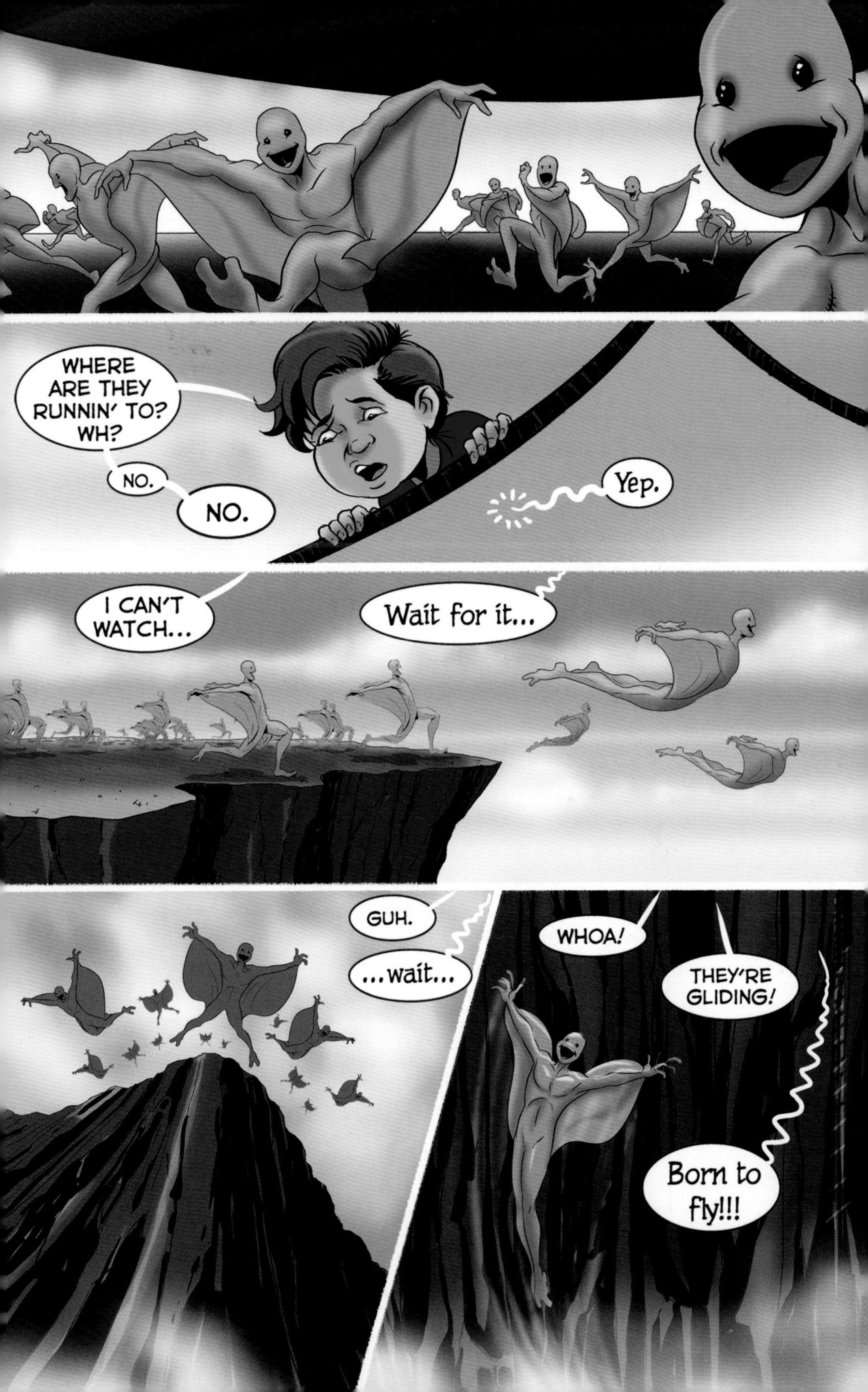
WHERE ARE THEY RUNNIN' TO? WH?
NO.
NO.
Yep.
I CAN'T WATCH...
Wait for it...
GUH.
...wait...
WHOA!
THEY'RE GLIDING!
Born to fly!!!

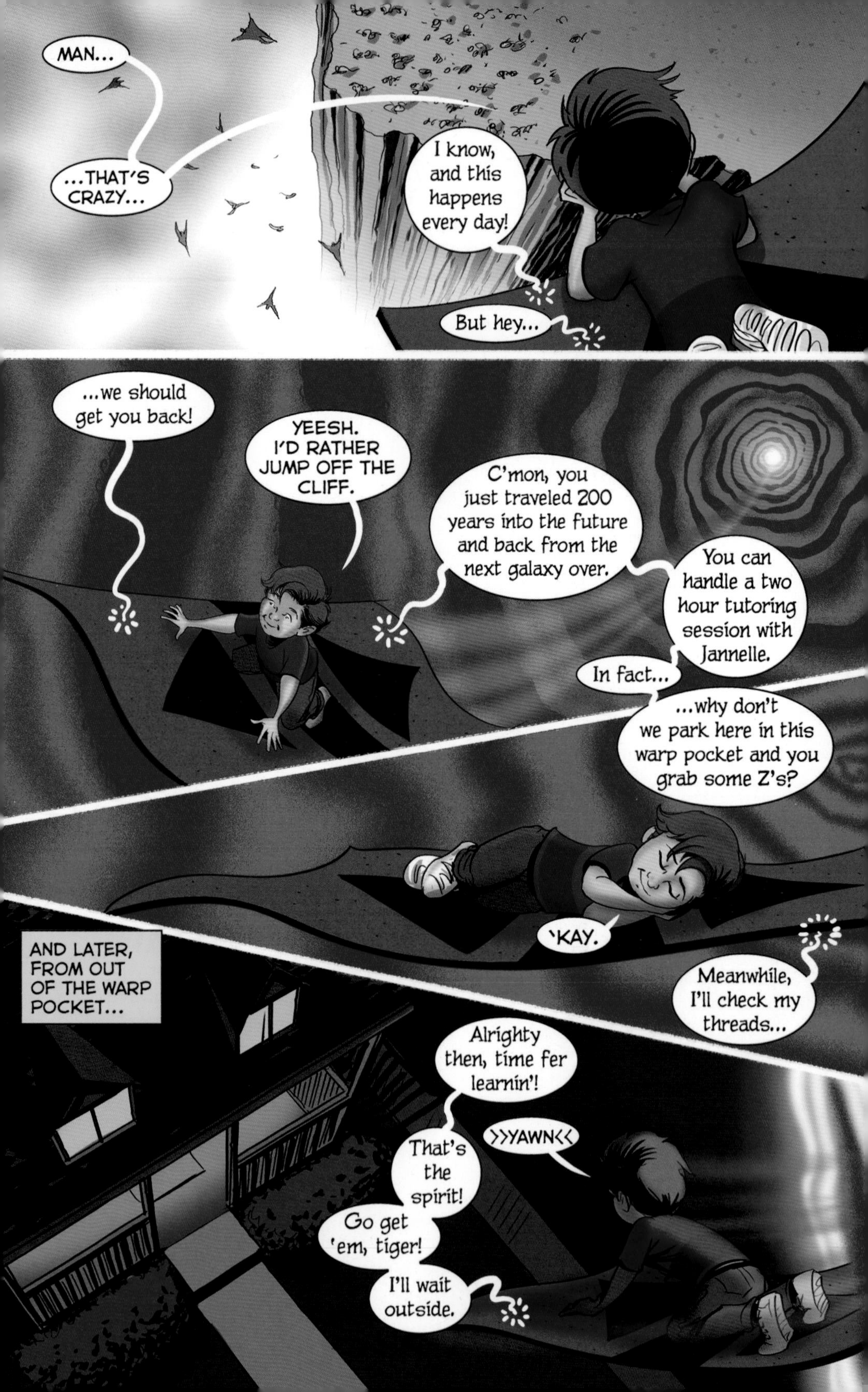
MAN...
...THAT'S CRAZY...
I know, and this happens every day!
But hey...
...we should get you back!
YEESH. I'D RATHER JUMP OFF THE CLIFF.
C'mon, you just traveled 200 years into the future and back from the next galaxy over.
You can handle a two hour tutoring session with Jannelle.
In fact...
...why don't we park here in this warp pocket and you grab some Z's?
'KAY.
Meanwhile, I'll check my threads...
AND LATER, FROM OUT OF THE WARP POCKET...
Alrighty then, time fer learnin'!
>>YAWN<<
That's the spirit!
Go get 'em, tiger!
I'll wait outside.

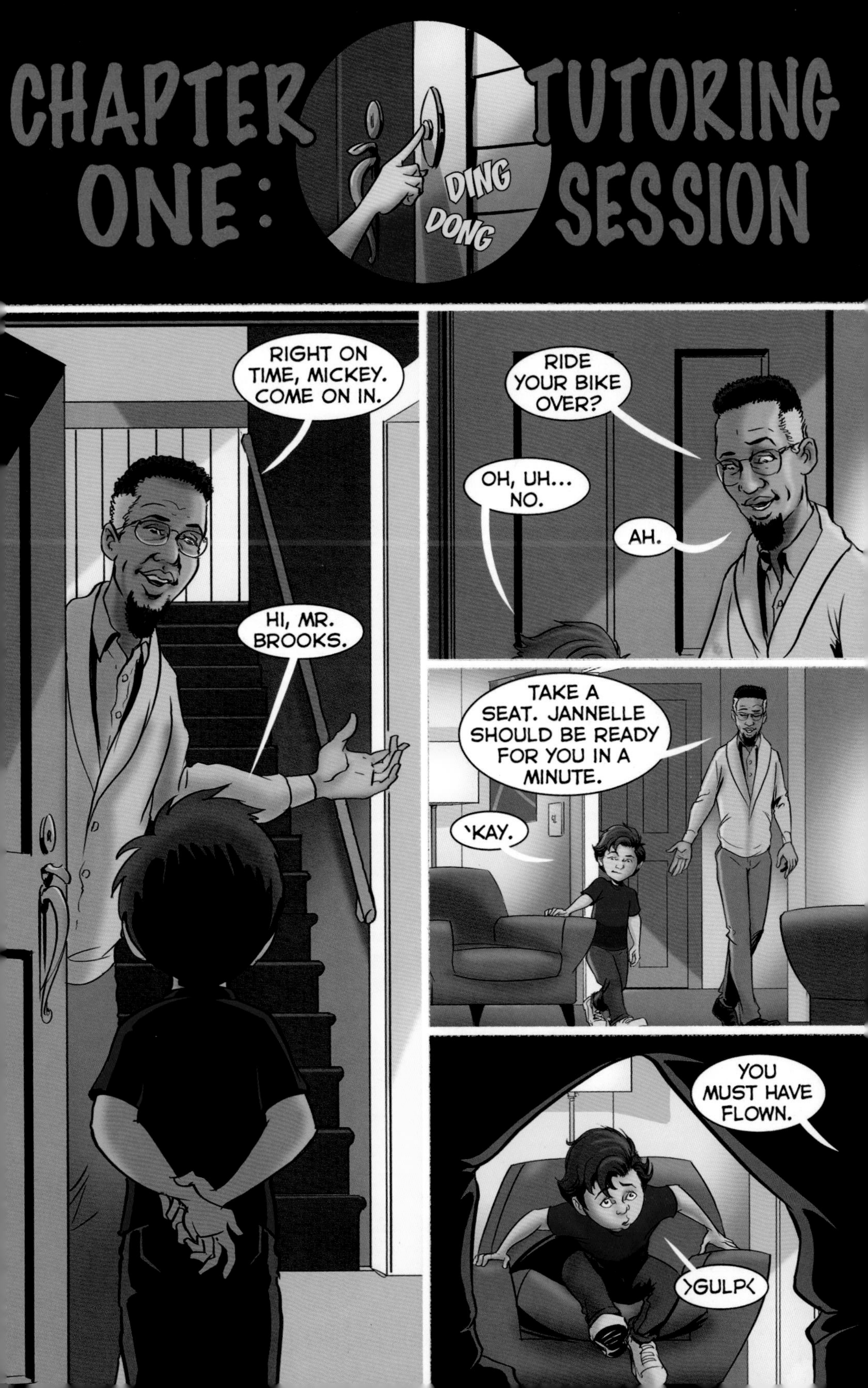
CHAPTER ONE: TUTORING SESSION
DING
DONG
RIGHT ON TIME, MICKEY. COME ON IN.
HI, MR. BROOKS.
RIDE YOUR BIKE OVER?
OH, UH... NO.
AH.
TAKE A SEAT. JANNELLE SHOULD BE READY FOR YOU IN A MINUTE.
'KAY.
YOU MUST HAVE FLOWN.
>GULP<

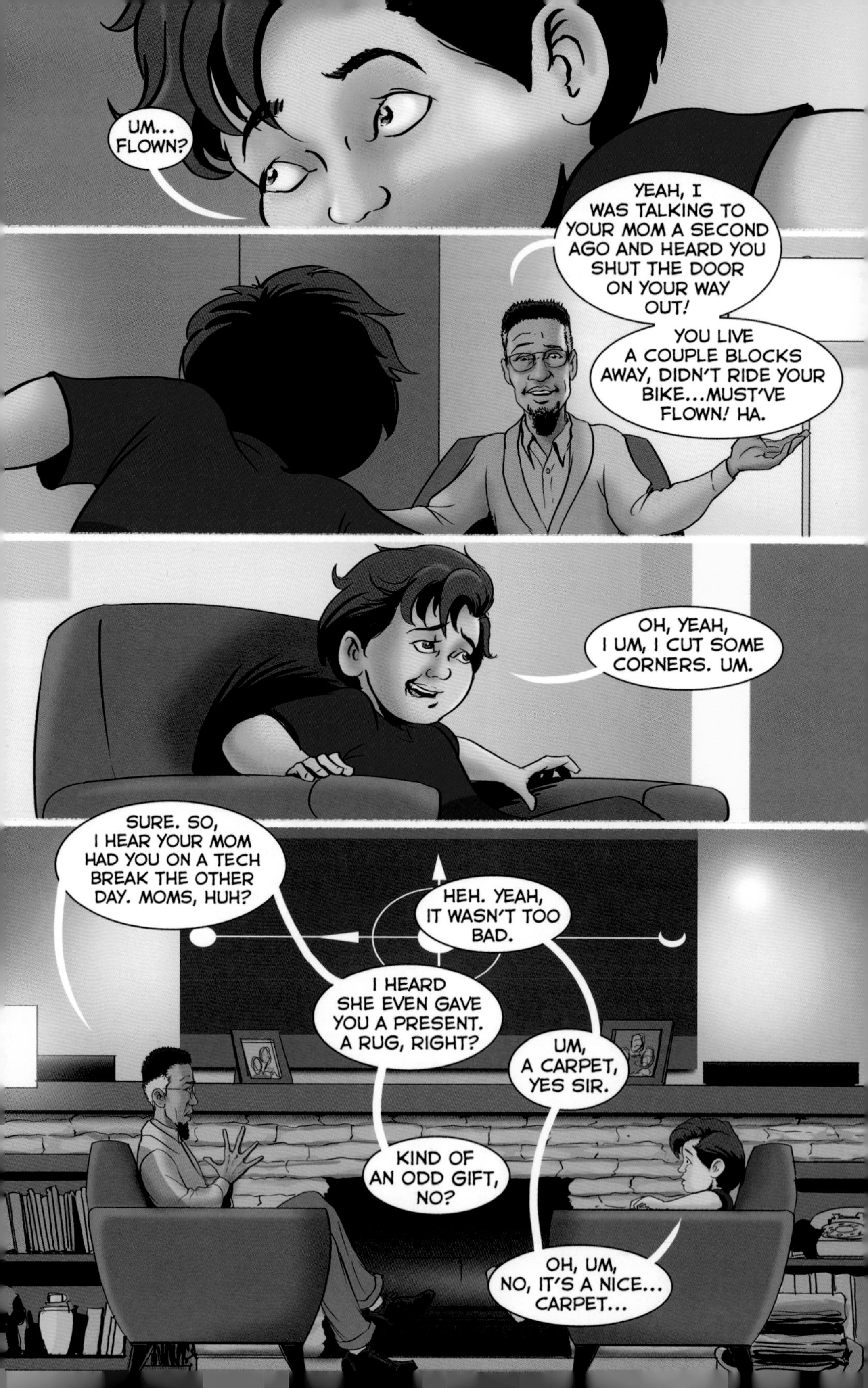
UM... FLOWN?
YEAH, I WAS TALKING TO YOUR MOM A SECOND AGO AND HEARD YOU SHUT THE DOOR ON YOUR WAY OUT!
YOU LIVE A COUPLE BLOCKS AWAY, DIDN'T RIDE YOUR BIKE...MUST'VE FLOWN! HA.
OH, YEAH, I UM, I CUT SOME CORNERS. UM.
SURE. SO, I HEAR YOUR MOM HAD YOU ON A TECH BREAK THE OTHER DAY. MOMS, HUH?
HEH. YEAH, IT WASN'T TOO BAD.
I HEARD SHE EVEN GAVE YOU A PRESENT. A RUG, RIGHT?
UM, A CARPET, YES SIR.
KIND OF AN ODD GIFT, NO?
OH, UM, NO, IT'S A NICE... CARPET...

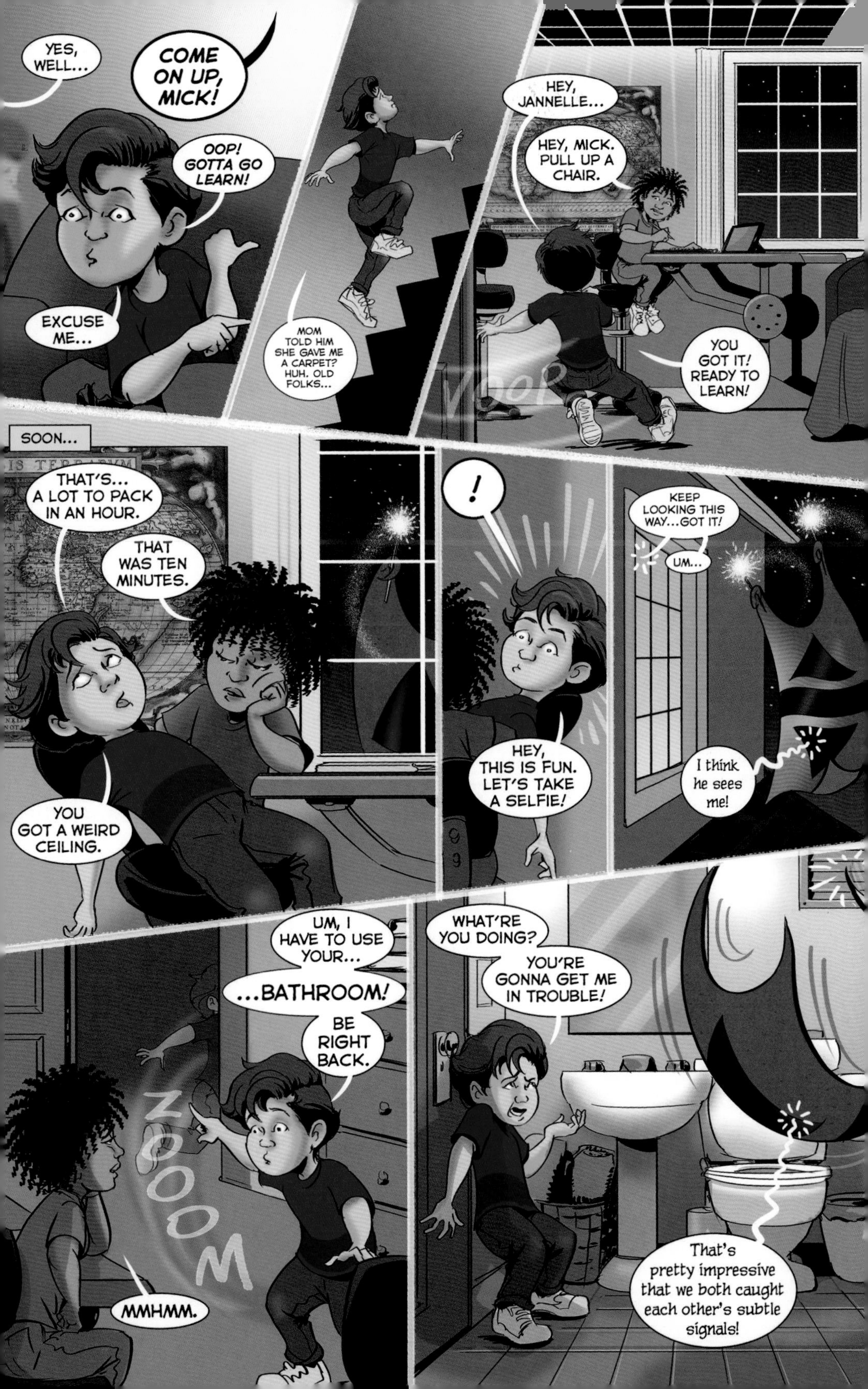
YES, WELL...
COME ON UP, MICK!
OOP! GOTTA GO LEARN!
EXCUSE ME...
MOM TOLD HIM SHE GAVE ME A CARPET? HUH. OLD FOLKS...
HEY, JANNELLE...
HEY, MICK. PULL UP A CHAIR.
VOOP
YOU GOT IT! READY TO LEARN!
SOON...
THAT'S... A LOT TO PACK IN AN HOUR.
THAT WAS TEN MINUTES.
YOU GOT A WEIRD CEILING.
!
HEY, THIS IS FUN. LET'S TAKE A SELFIE!
KEEP LOOKING THIS WAY...GOT IT!
UM...
I think he sees me!
UM, I HAVE TO USE YOUR...
...BATHROOM!
BE RIGHT BACK.
ZOOOOM
MMHMM.
WHAT'RE YOU DOING?
YOU'RE GONNA GET ME IN TROUBLE!
That's pretty impressive that we both caught each other's subtle signals!

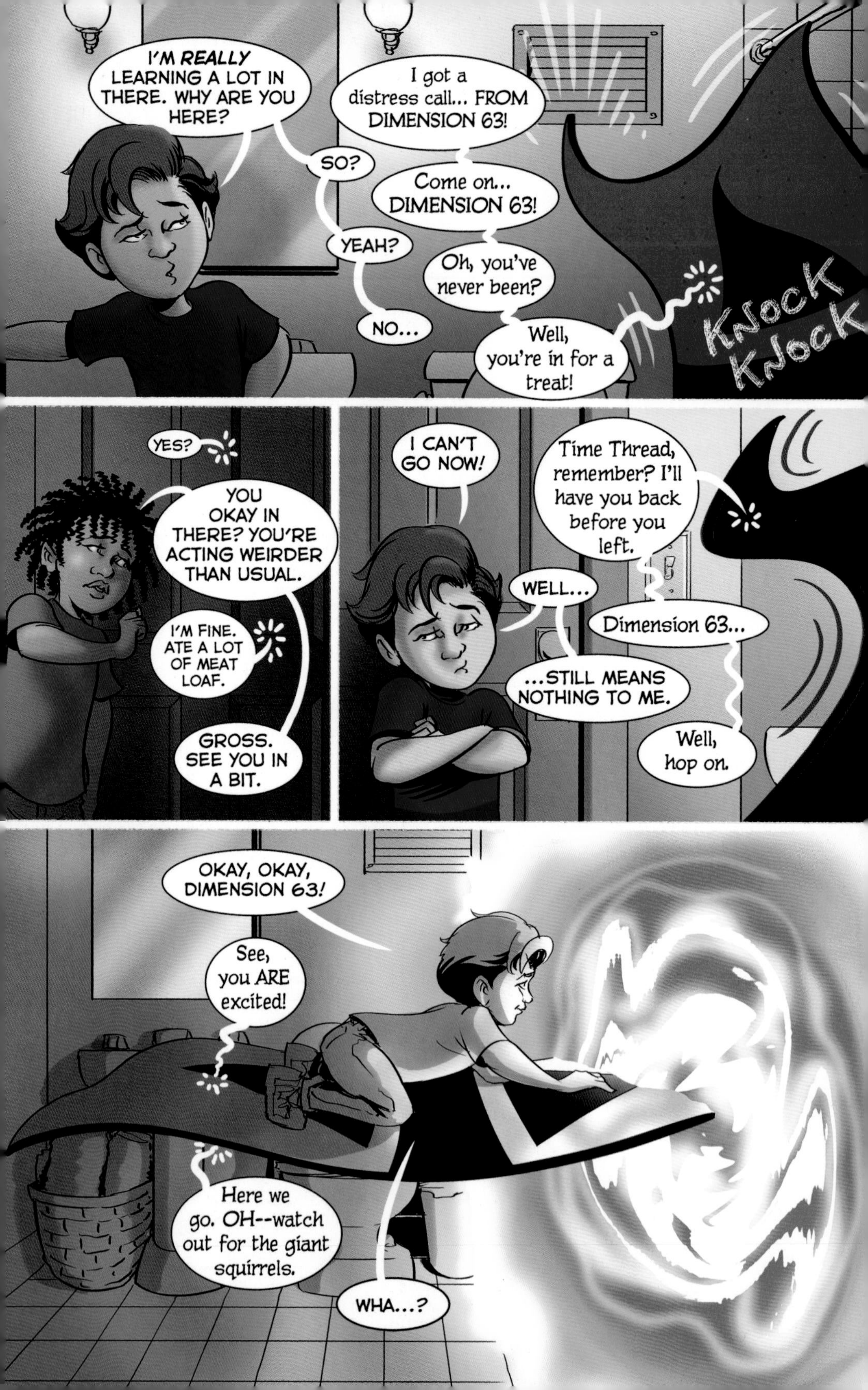
I'M *REALLY* LEARNING A LOT IN THERE. WHY ARE YOU HERE?
I got a distress call... FROM DIMENSION 63!
SO?
Come on... DIMENSION 63!
YEAH?
Oh, you've never been?
NO...
Well, you're in for a treat!
KNOCK KNOCK
YES?
YOU OKAY IN THERE? YOU'RE ACTING WEIRDER THAN USUAL.
I'M FINE. ATE A LOT OF MEAT LOAF.
GROSS. SEE YOU IN A BIT.
I CAN'T GO NOW!
Time Thread, remember? I'll have you back before you left.
WELL...
Dimension 63...
...STILL MEANS NOTHING TO ME.
Well, hop on.
OKAY, OKAY, DIMENSION 63!
See, you ARE excited!
Here we go. OH--watch out for the giant squirrels.
WHA...?

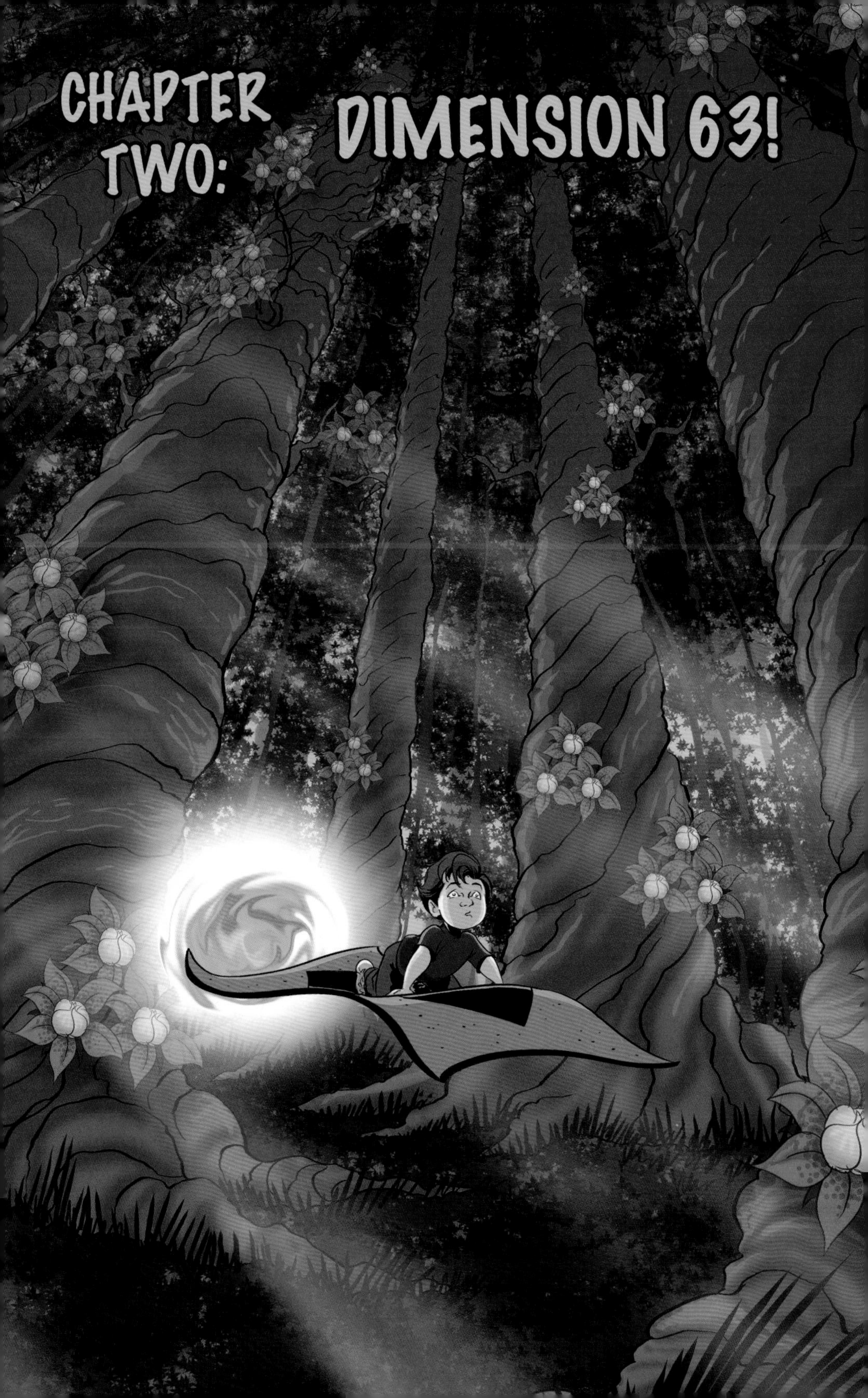
CHAPTER TWO:
DIMENSION 63!

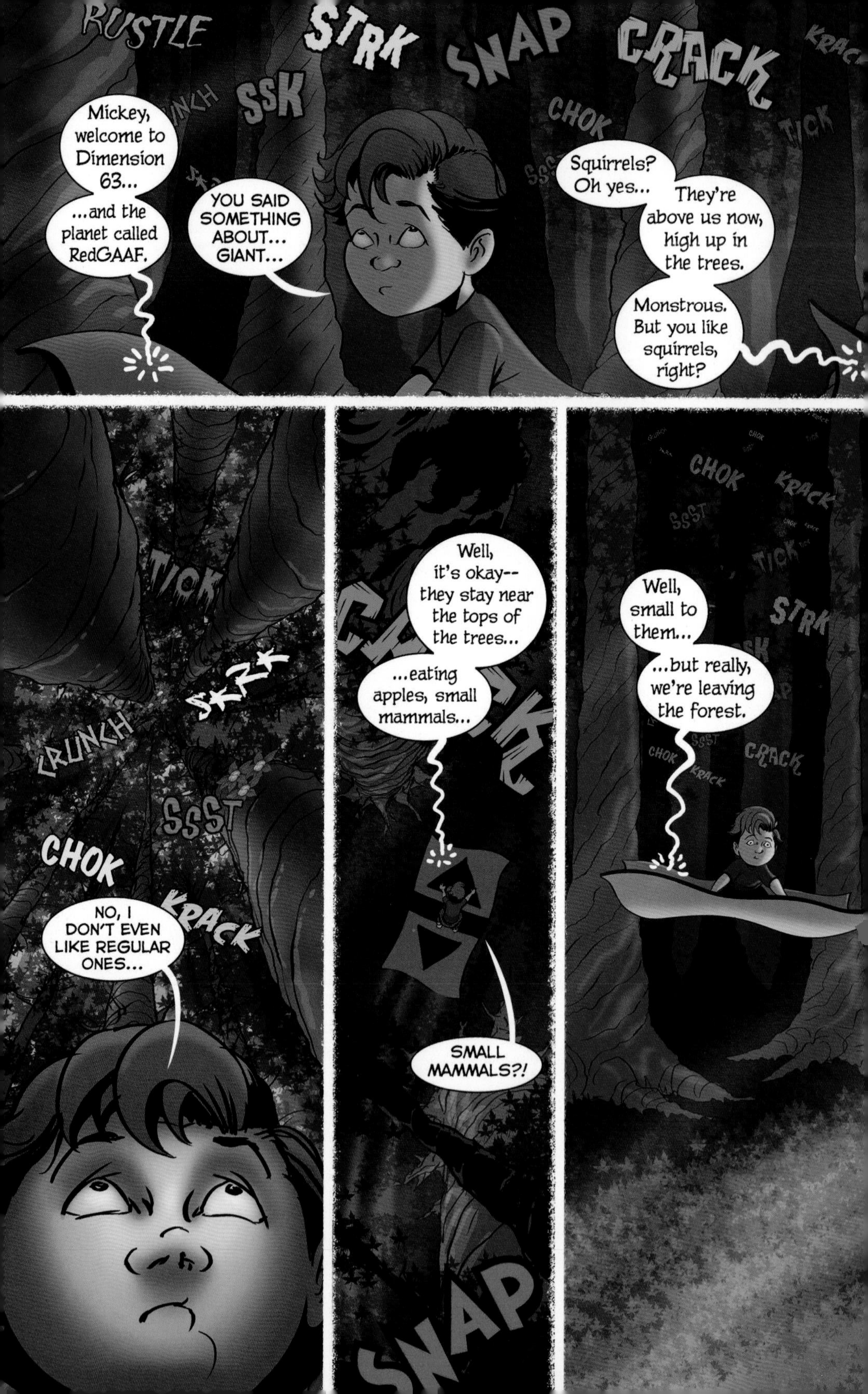
RUSTLE
STRK
SNAP
CRACK
KRACK
CRUNCH
SSK
CHOK
TICK
Mickey, welcome to Dimension 63...
...and the planet called RedGAAF.
YOU SAID SOMETHING ABOUT... GIANT...
Squirrels? Oh yes...
They're above us now, high up in the trees.
Monstrous. But you like squirrels, right?
TICK
SKZK
CRUNCH
SSST
CHOK
KRACK
NO, I DON'T EVEN LIKE REGULAR ONES...
CRACK
Well, it's okay--they stay near the tops of the trees...
...eating apples, small mammals...
SMALL MAMMALS?!
SNAP
CHOK
KRACK
SSST
TICK
STRK
Well, small to them...
...but really, we're leaving the forest.
SSST
CHOK
CRACK
KRACK

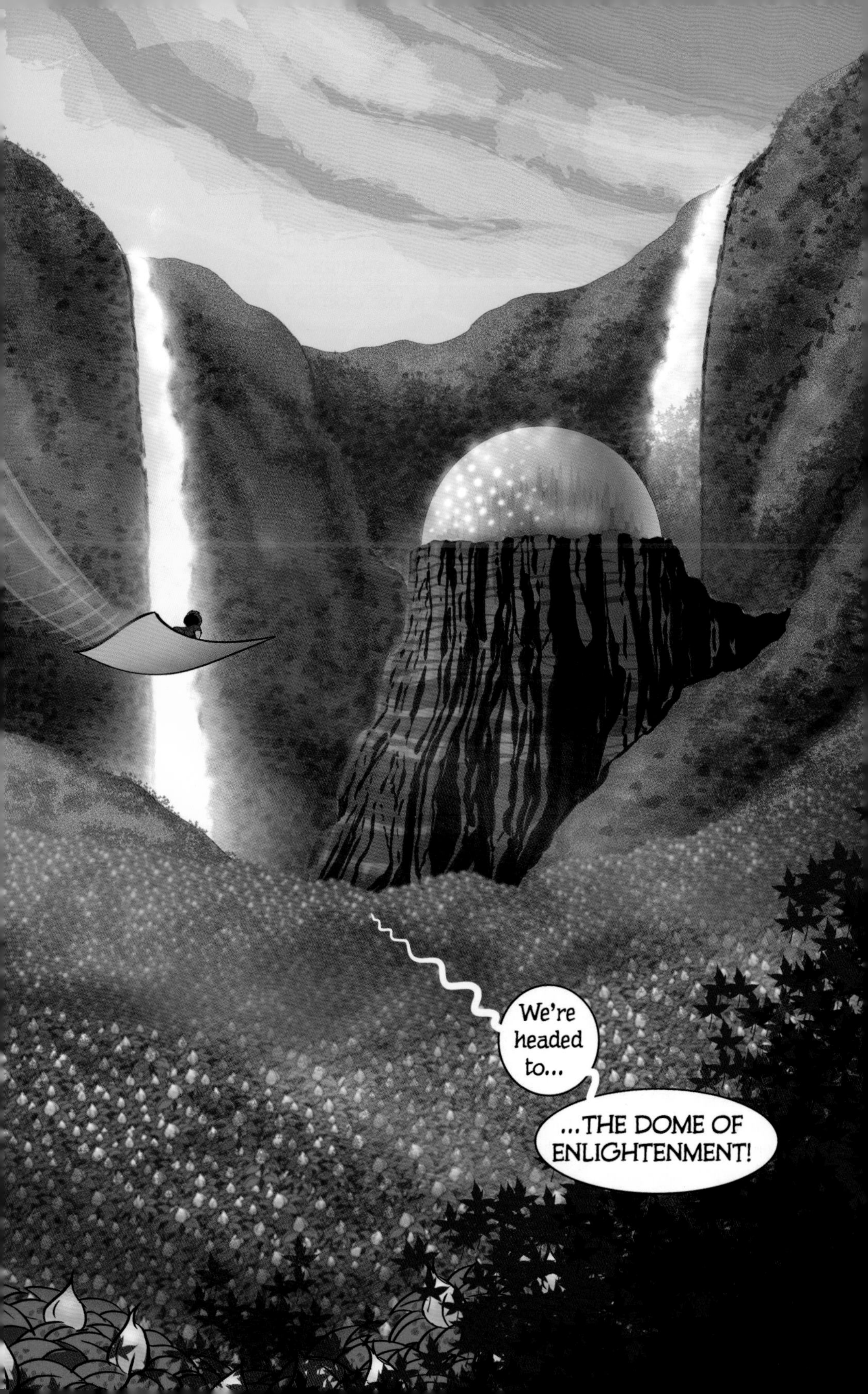
We're headed to...
...THE DOME OF ENLIGHTENMENT!

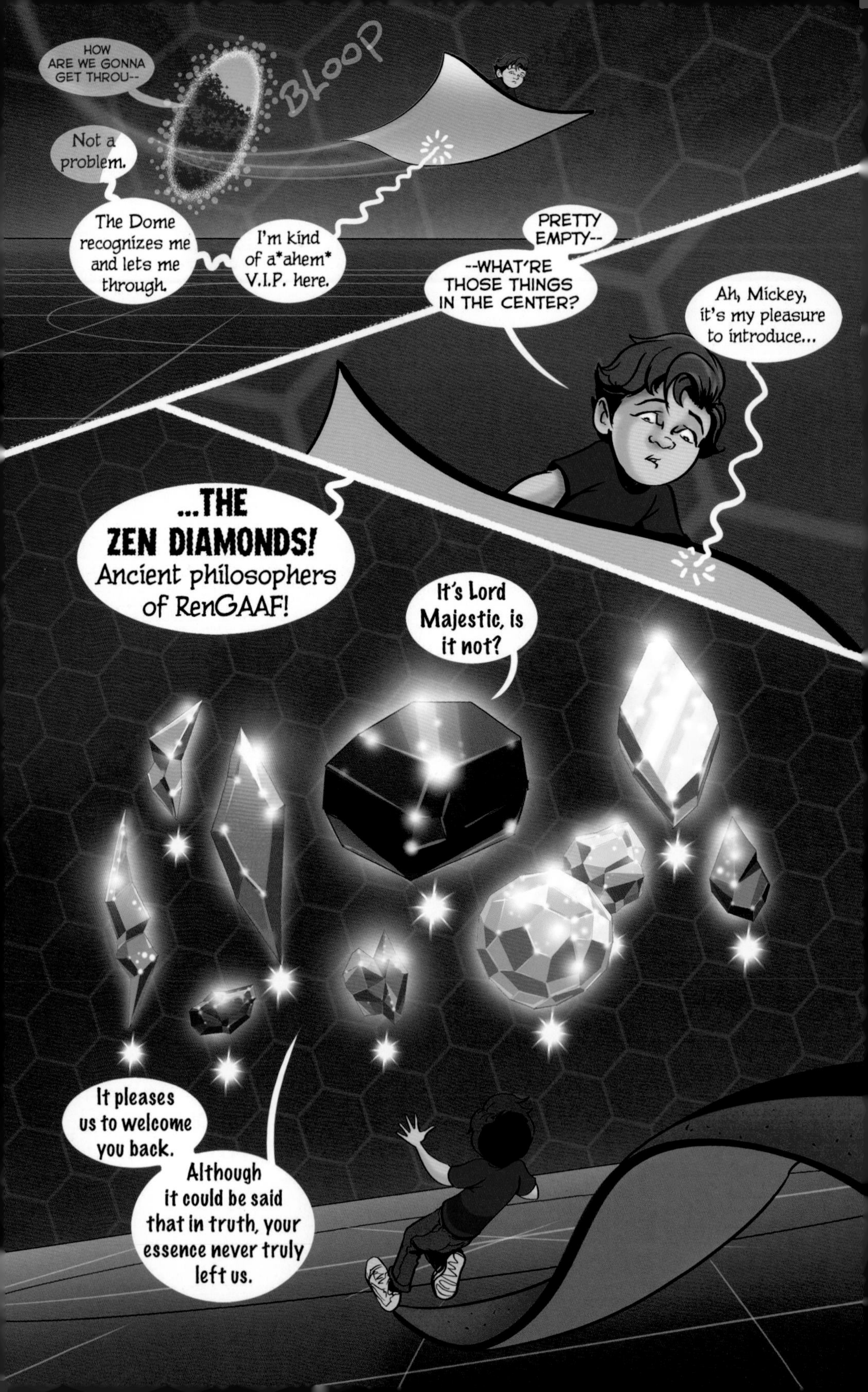
HOW ARE WE GONNA GET THROU--
BLOOP
Not a problem.
The Dome recognizes me and lets me through.
I'm kind of a*ahem* V.I.P. here.
PRETTY EMPTY--
--WHAT'RE THOSE THINGS IN THE CENTER?
Ah, Mickey, it's my pleasure to introduce...
...THE ZEN DIAMONDS! Ancient philosophers of RenGAAF!
It's Lord Majestic, is it not?
It pleases us to welcome you back.
Although it could be said that in truth, your essence never truly left us.

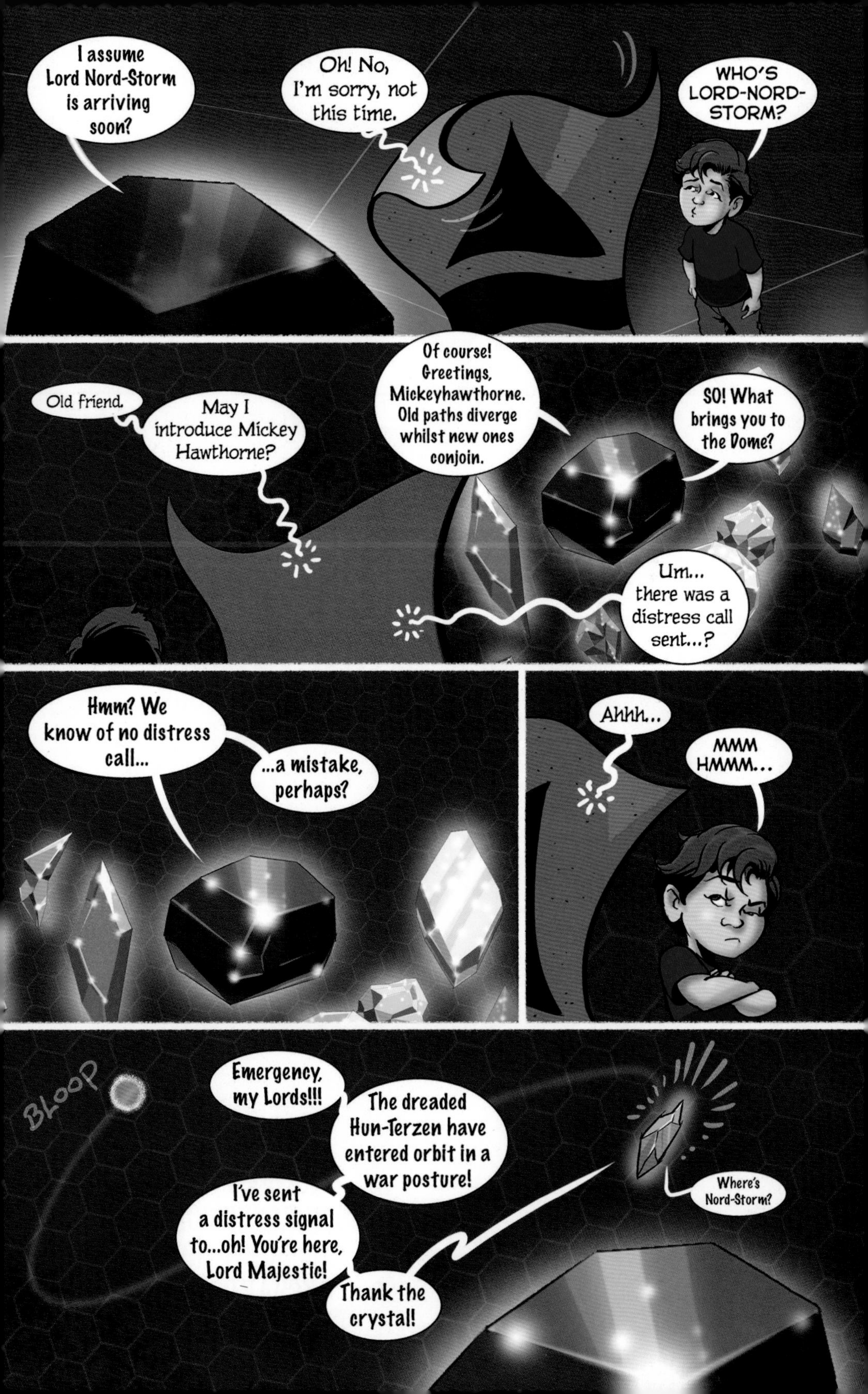
I assume Lord Nord-Storm is arriving soon?
Oh! No, I'm sorry, not this time.
WHO'S LORD-NORD-STORM?
Old friend.
May I introduce Mickey Hawthorne?
Of course! Greetings, Mickeyhawthorne. Old paths diverge whilst new ones conjoin.
SO! What brings you to the Dome?
Um... there was a distress call sent...?
Hmm? We know of no distress call...
...a mistake, perhaps?
Ahhh...
MMM HMMM...
BLOOP
Emergency, my Lords!!!
The dreaded Hun-Terzen have entered orbit in a war posture!
I've sent a distress signal to...oh! You're here, Lord Majestic!
Thank the crystal!
Where's Nord-Storm?

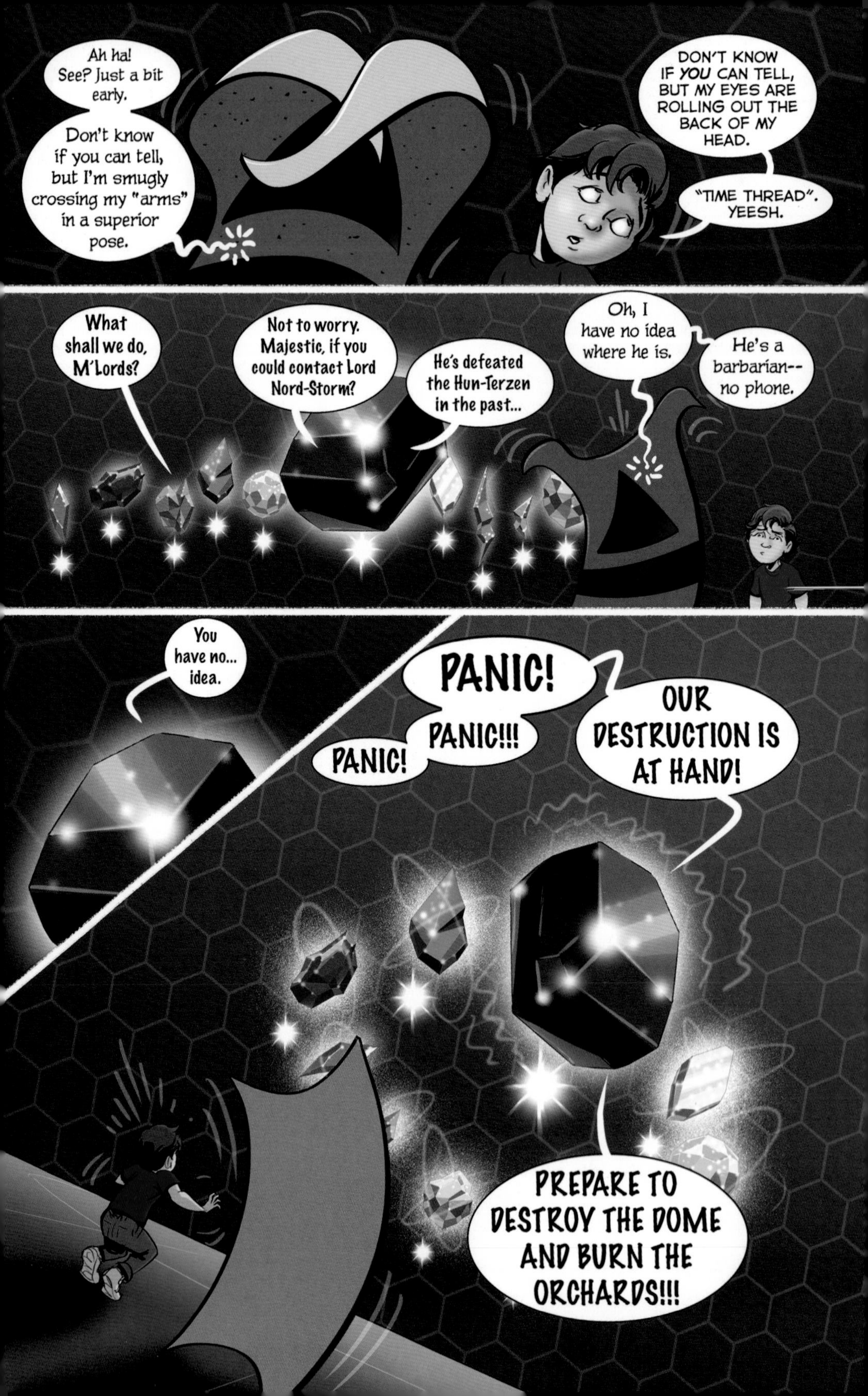
Ah ha! See? Just a bit early.
Don't know if you can tell, but I'm smugly crossing my "arms" in a superior pose.
DON'T KNOW IF *YOU* CAN TELL, BUT MY EYES ARE ROLLING OUT THE BACK OF MY HEAD.
"TIME THREAD". YEESH.
What shall we do, M'Lords?
Not to worry. Majestic, if you could contact Lord Nord-Storm?
He's defeated the Hun-Terzen in the past...
Oh, I have no idea where he is.
He's a barbarian-- no phone.
You have no... idea.
PANIC!
PANIC!!!
PANIC!
OUR DESTRUCTION IS AT HAND!
PREPARE TO DESTROY THE DOME AND BURN THE ORCHARDS!!!

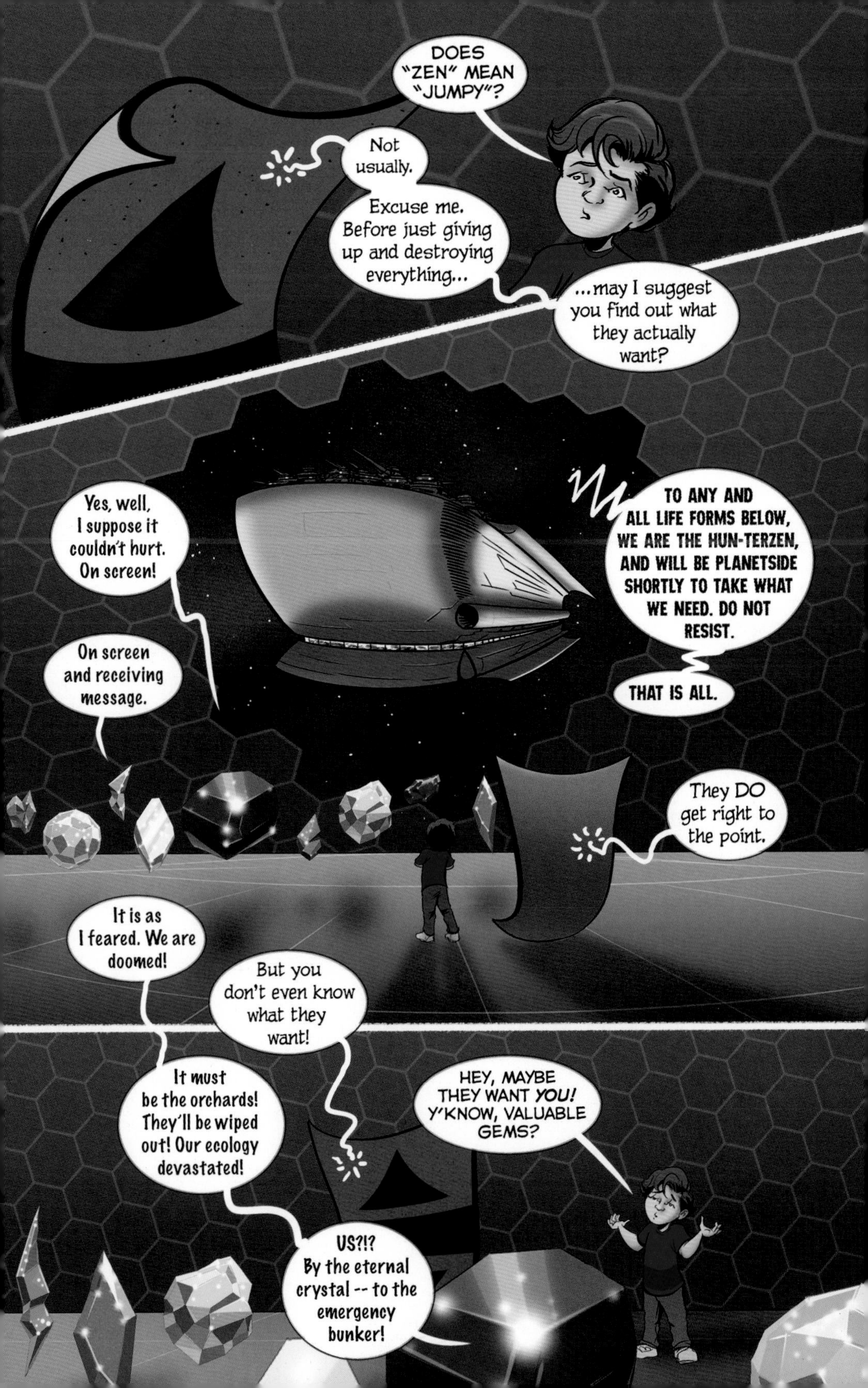
DOES "ZEN" MEAN "JUMPY"?
Not usually.
Excuse me. Before just giving up and destroying everything...
...may I suggest you find out what they actually want?
Yes, well, I suppose it couldn't hurt. On screen!
On screen and receiving message.
TO ANY AND ALL LIFE FORMS BELOW, WE ARE THE HUN-TERZEN, AND WILL BE PLANETSIDE SHORTLY TO TAKE WHAT WE NEED. DO NOT RESIST.
THAT IS ALL.
They DO get right to the point.
It is as I feared. We are doomed!
But you don't even know what they want!
It must be the orchards! They'll be wiped out! Our ecology devastated!
HEY, MAYBE THEY WANT *YOU!* Y'KNOW, VALUABLE GEMS?
US?!? By the eternal crystal -- to the emergency bunker!

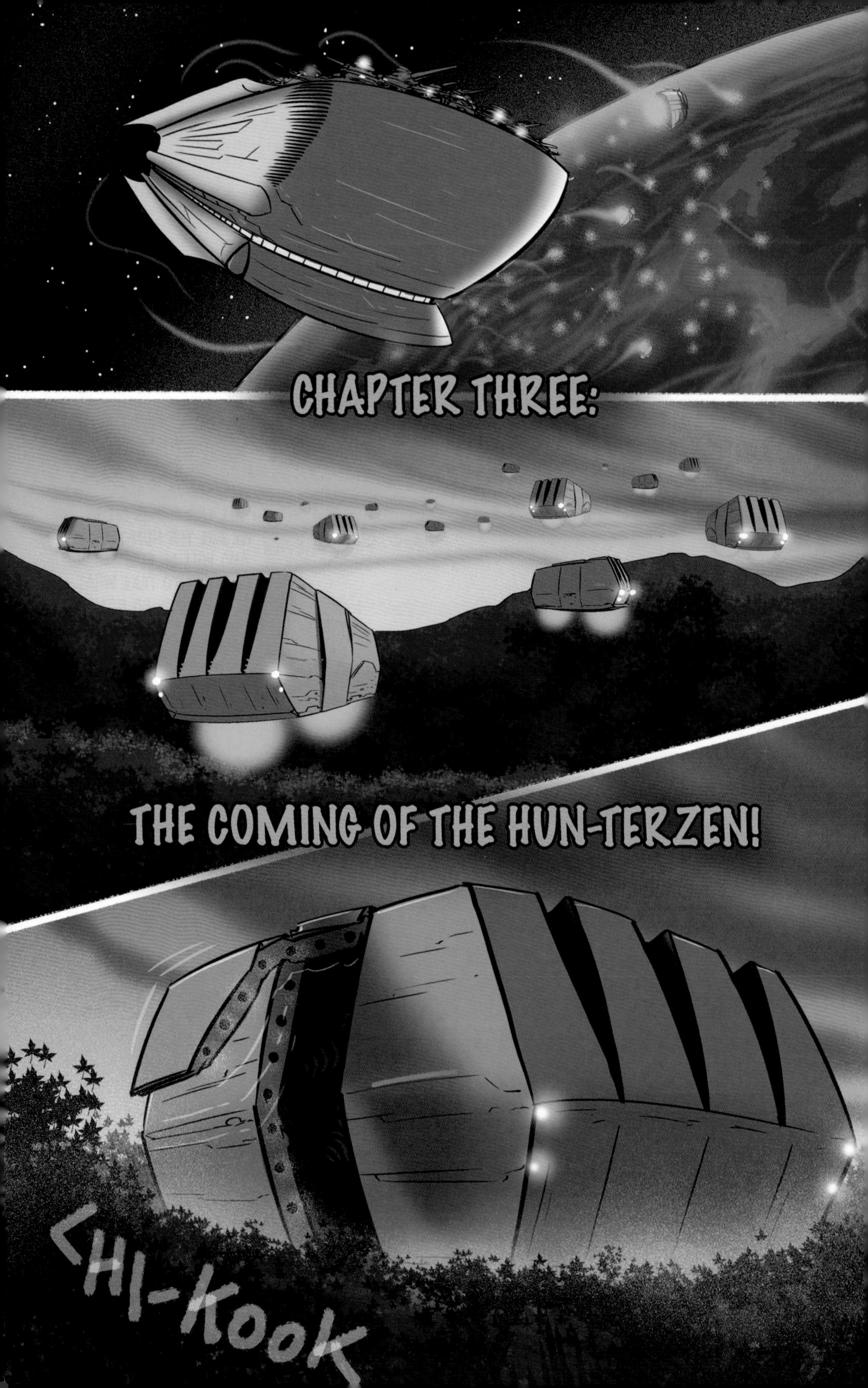
CHAPTER THREE:
THE COMING OF THE HUN-TERZEN!
CHI-KOOK

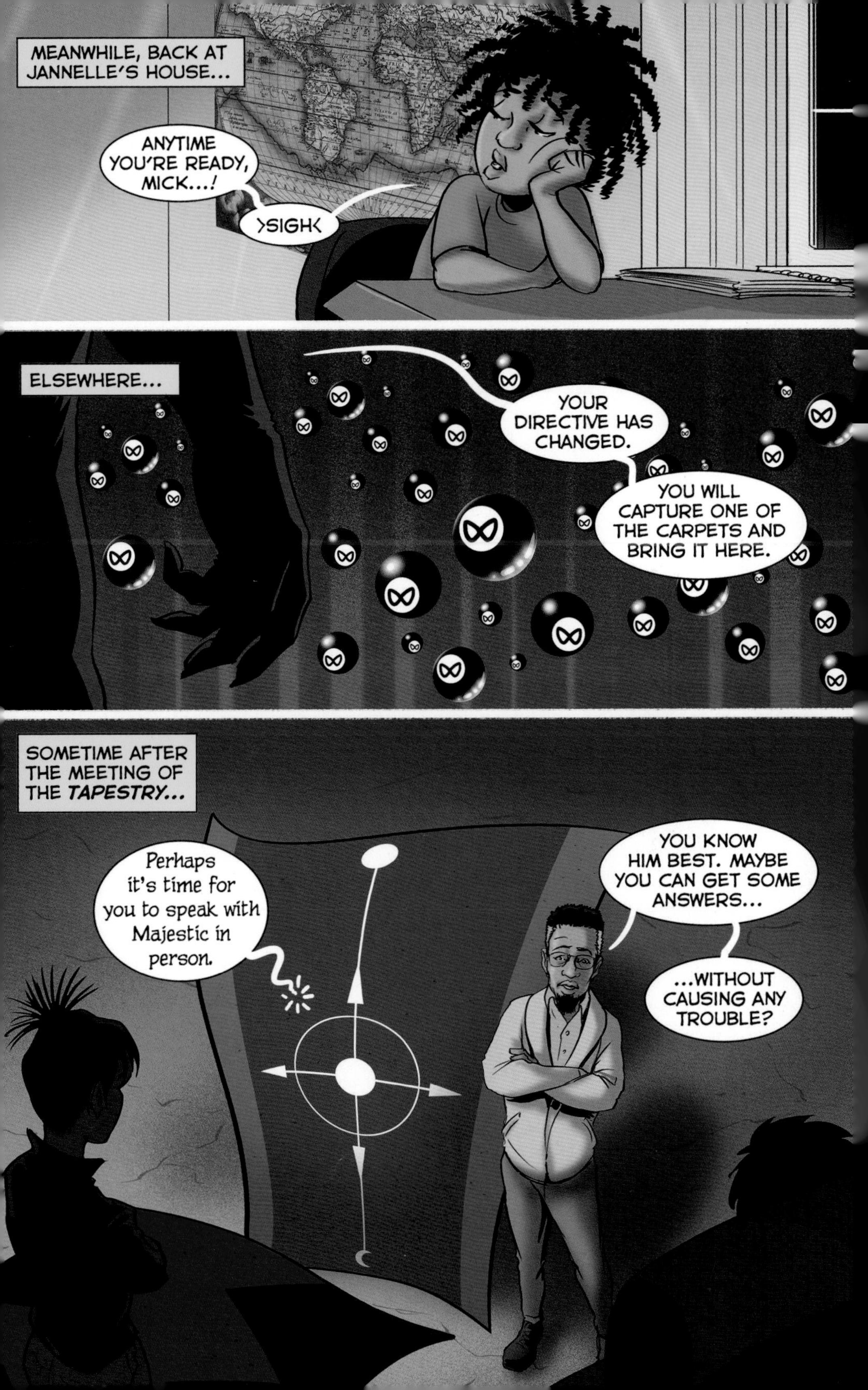
MEANWHILE, BACK AT JANNELLE'S HOUSE...
ANYTIME YOU'RE READY, MICK...!
>SIGH<
ELSEWHERE...
YOUR DIRECTIVE HAS CHANGED.
YOU WILL CAPTURE ONE OF THE CARPETS AND BRING IT HERE.
SOMETIME AFTER THE MEETING OF THE *TAPESTRY*...
Perhaps it's time for you to speak with Majestic in person.
YOU KNOW HIM BEST. MAYBE YOU CAN GET SOME ANSWERS...
...WITHOUT CAUSING ANY TROUBLE?

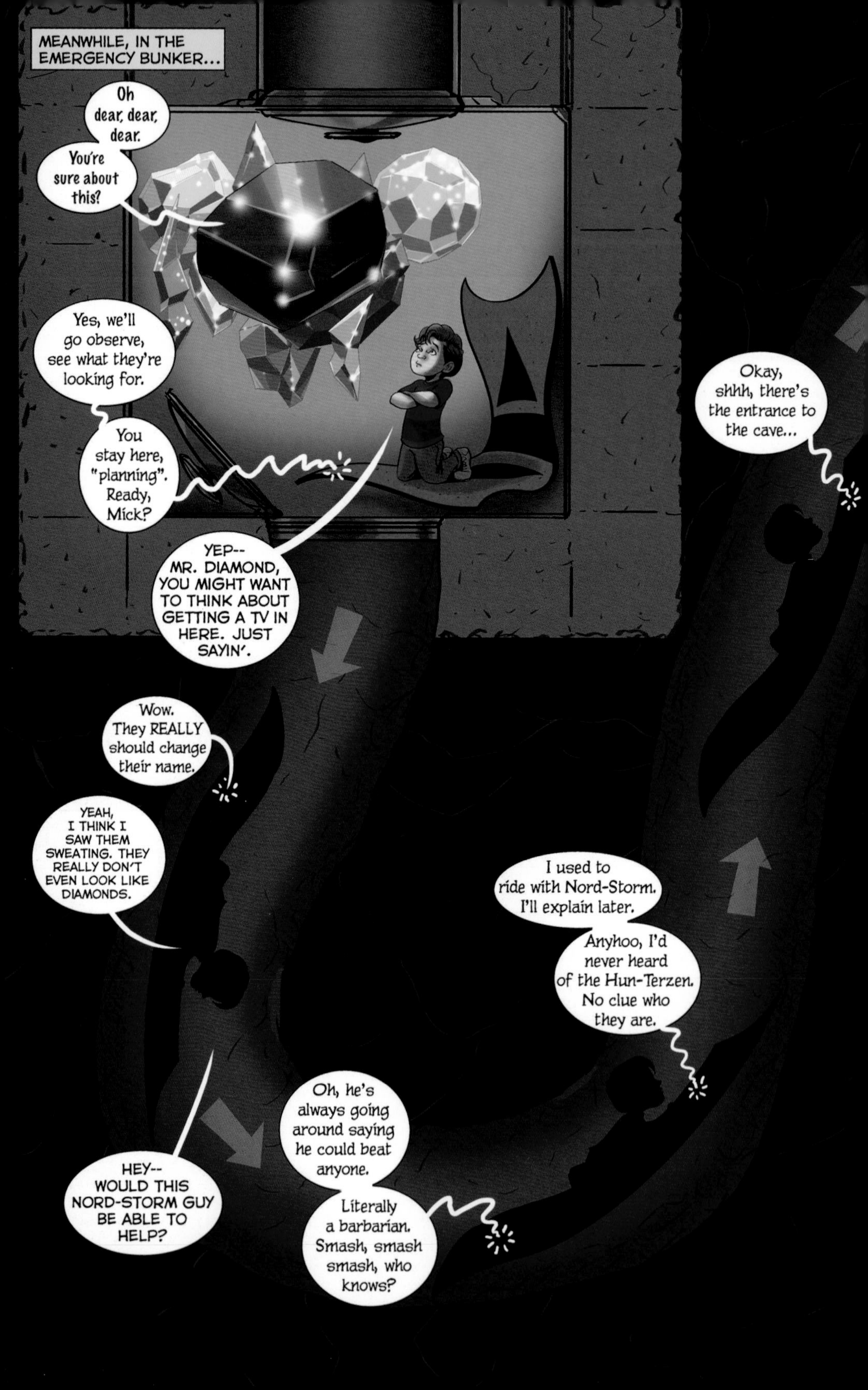
MEANWHILE, IN THE EMERGENCY BUNKER...
Oh dear, dear, dear.
You're sure about this?
Yes, we'll go observe, see what they're looking for.
You stay here, "planning". Ready, Mick?
YEP-- MR. DIAMOND, YOU MIGHT WANT TO THINK ABOUT GETTING A TV IN HERE. JUST SAYIN'.
Wow. They REALLY should change their name.
YEAH, I THINK I SAW THEM SWEATING. THEY REALLY DON'T EVEN LOOK LIKE DIAMONDS.
HEY-- WOULD THIS NORD-STORM GUY BE ABLE TO HELP?
Oh, he's always going around saying he could beat anyone.
Literally a barbarian. Smash, smash smash, who knows?
I used to ride with Nord-Storm. I'll explain later.
Anyhoo, I'd never heard of the Hun-Terzen. No clue who they are.
Okay, shhh, there's the entrance to the cave...

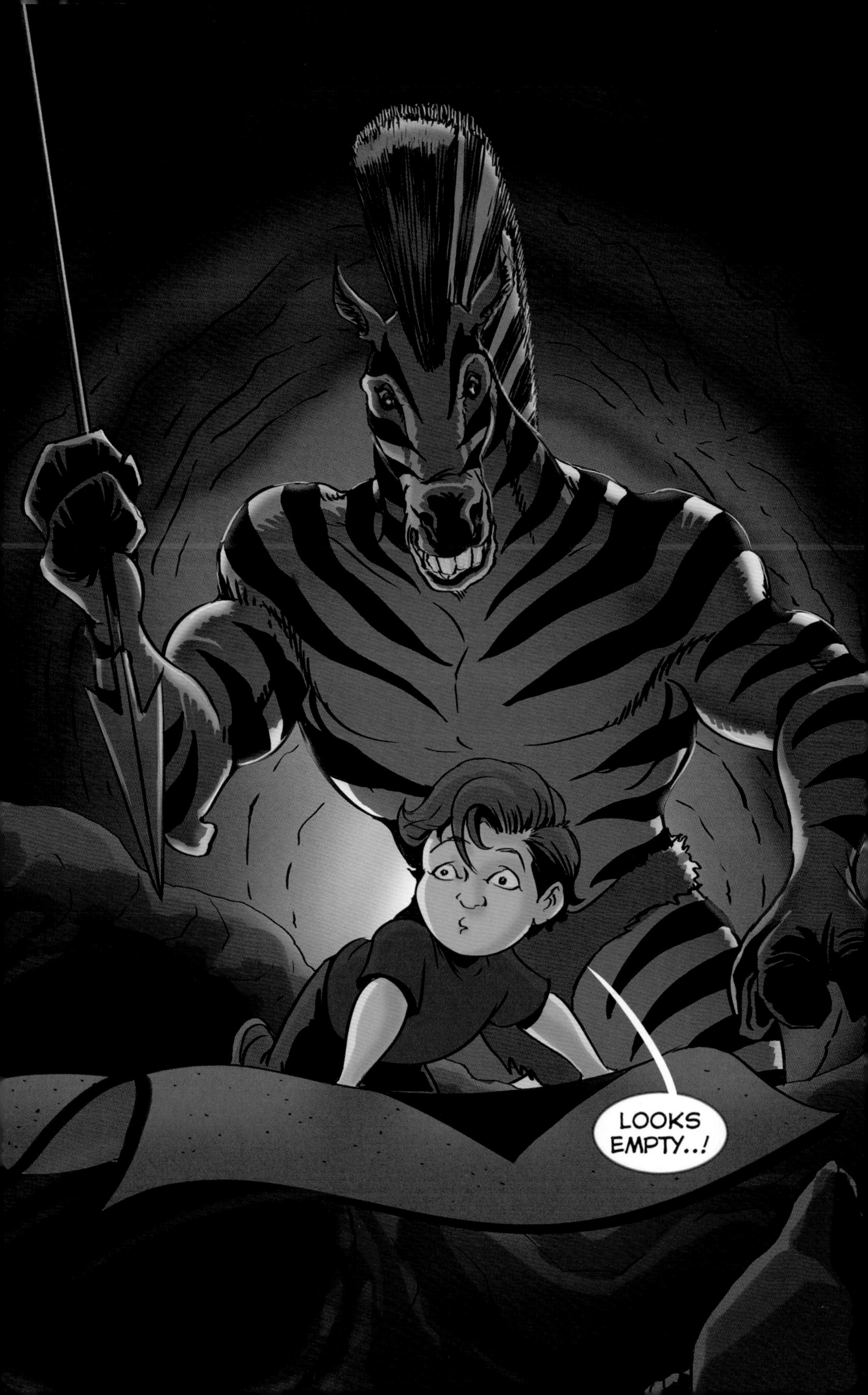
LOOKS EMPTY..!

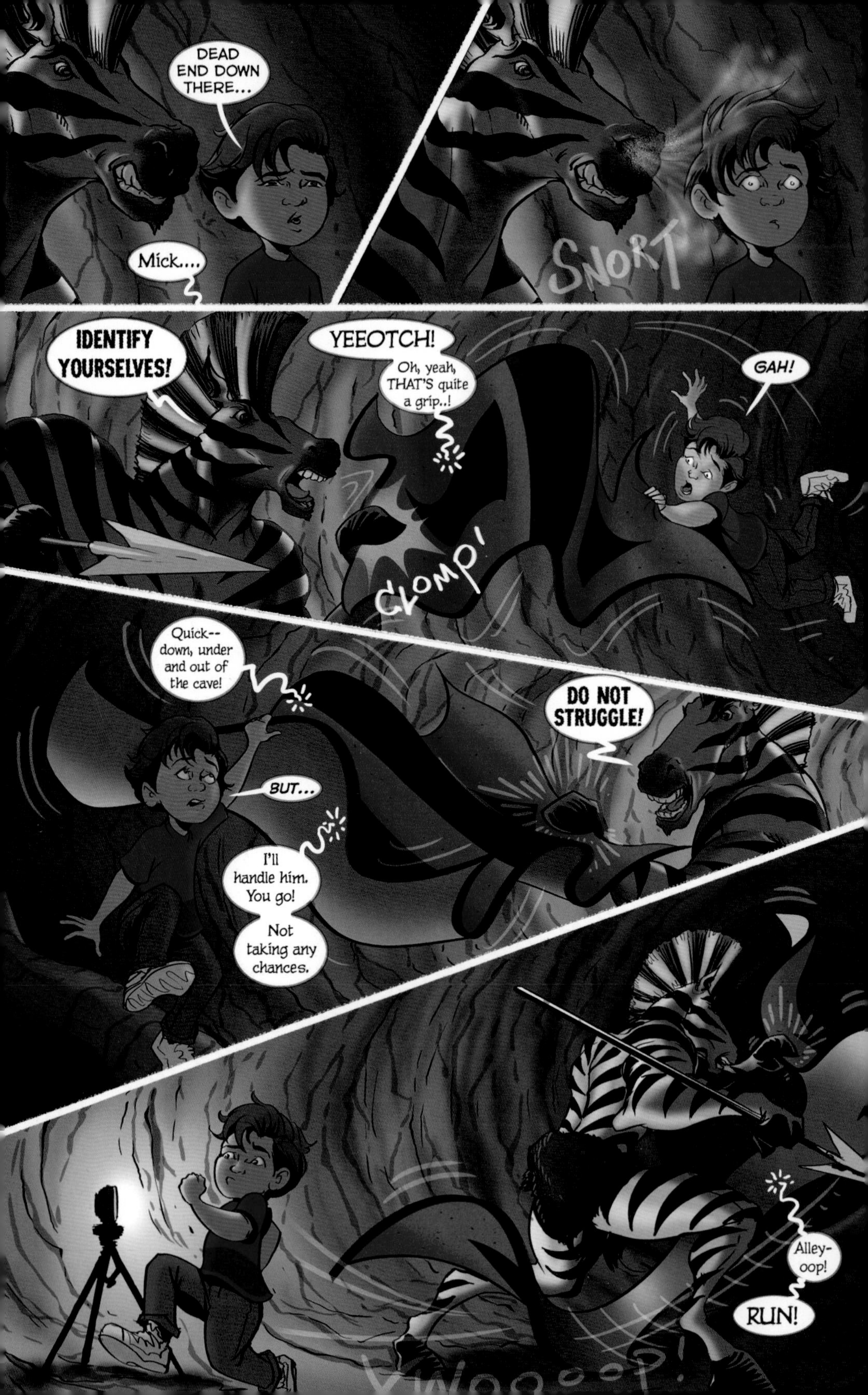
DEAD END DOWN THERE...
Mick....
SNORT
IDENTIFY YOURSELVES!
YEEOTCH!
Oh, yeah, THAT'S quite a grip..!
GAH!
CLOMP!
Quick-- down, under and out of the cave!
DO NOT STRUGGLE!
BUT...
I'll handle him. You go!
Not taking any chances.
Alley-oop!
RUN!

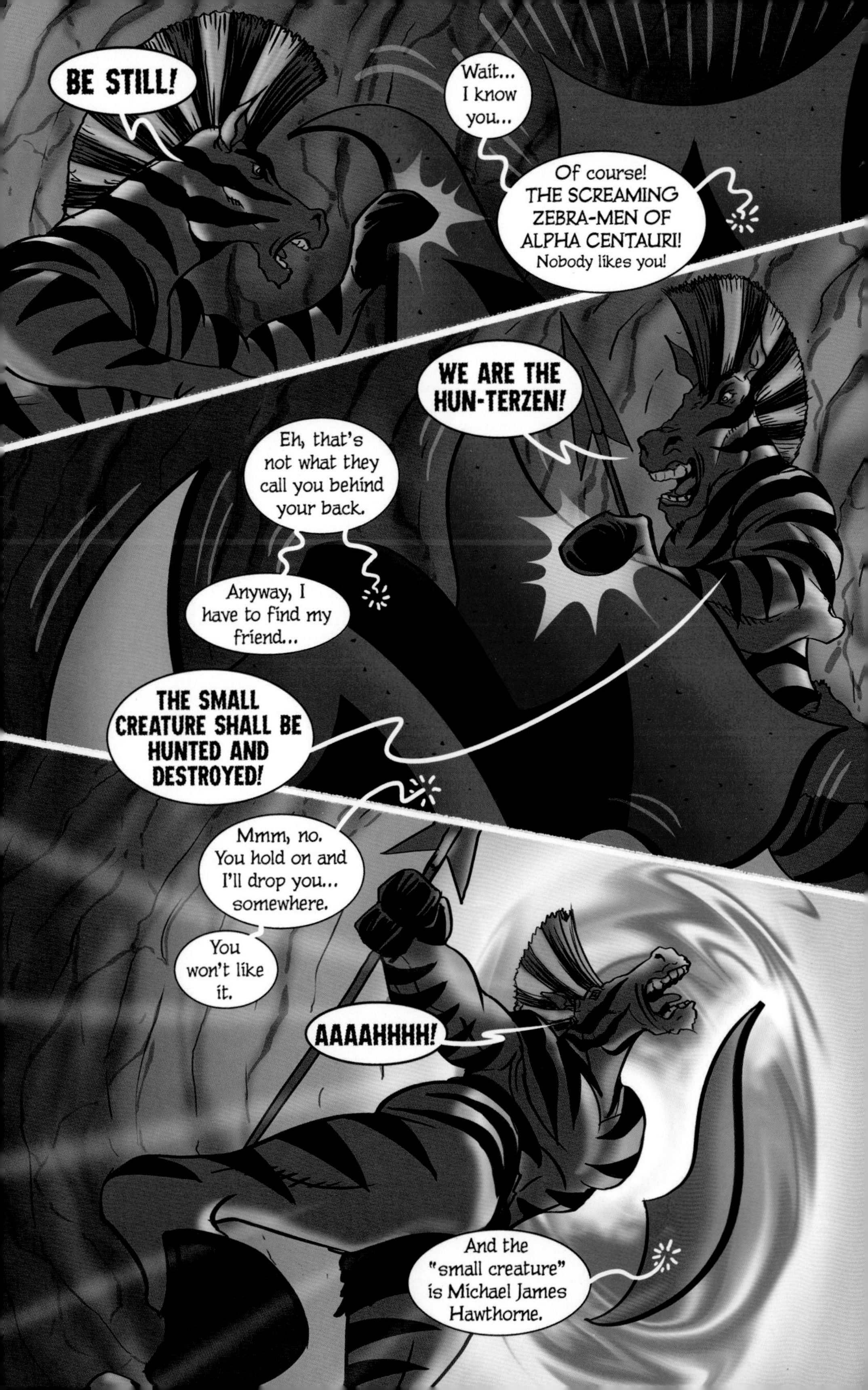
BE STILL!
Wait... I know you...
Of course! THE SCREAMING ZEBRA-MEN OF ALPHA CENTAURI! Nobody likes you!
WE ARE THE HUN-TERZEN!
Eh, that's not what they call you behind your back.
Anyway, I have to find my friend...
THE SMALL CREATURE SHALL BE HUNTED AND DESTROYED!
Mmm, no. You hold on and I'll drop you... somewhere.
You won't like it.
AAAAHHHH!
And the "small creature" is Michael James Hawthorne.

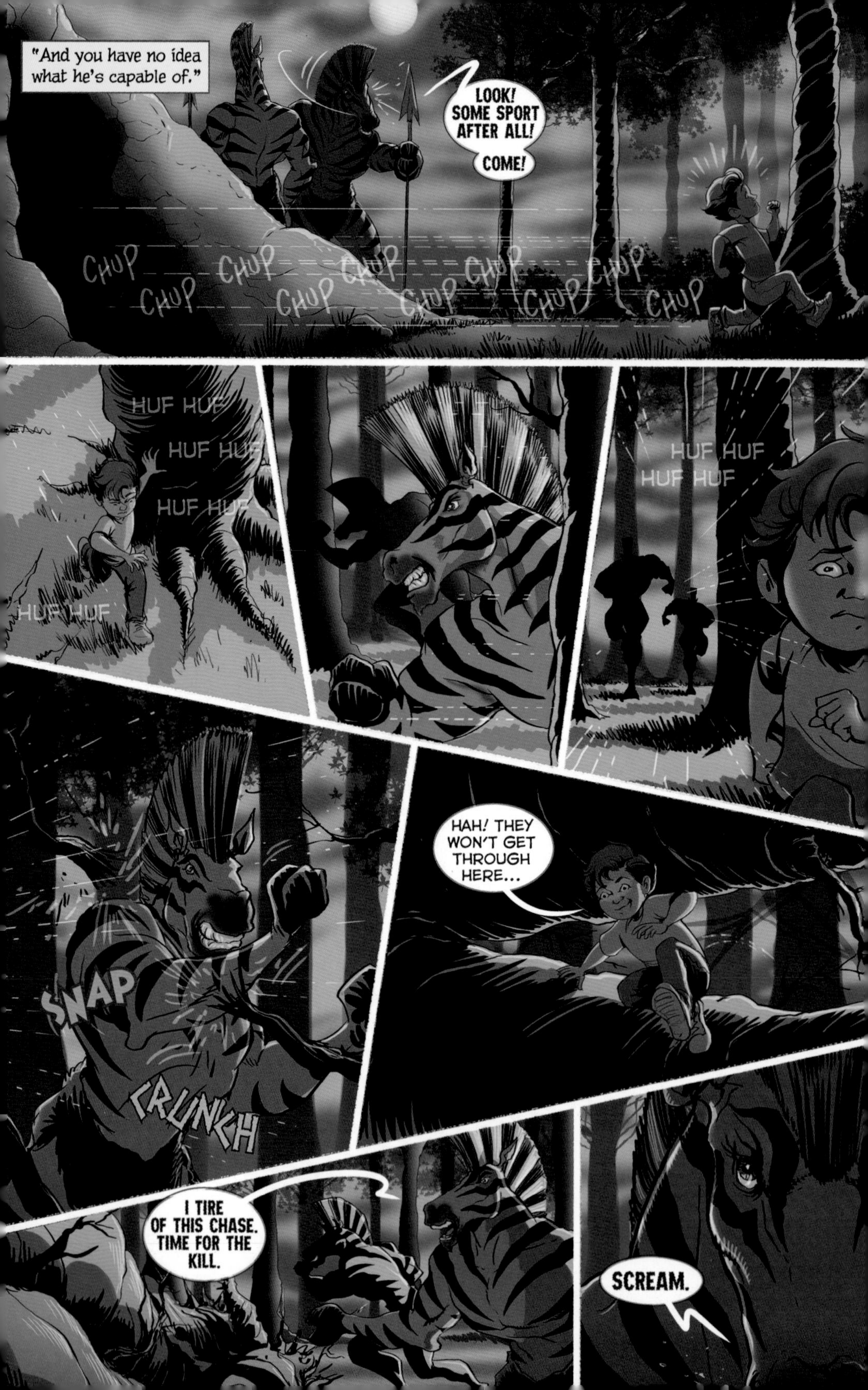
"And you have no idea what he's capable of."
LOOK! SOME SPORT AFTER ALL!
COME!
CHUP CHUP CHUP CHUP CHUP CHUP CHUP CHUP CHUP CHUP
HUF HUF
HUF HUF
HUF HUF
HUF HUF
HUF HUF
HUF HUF
SNAP
CRUNCH
HAH! THEY WON'T GET THROUGH HERE...
I TIRE OF THIS CHASE. TIME FOR THE KILL.
SCREAM.

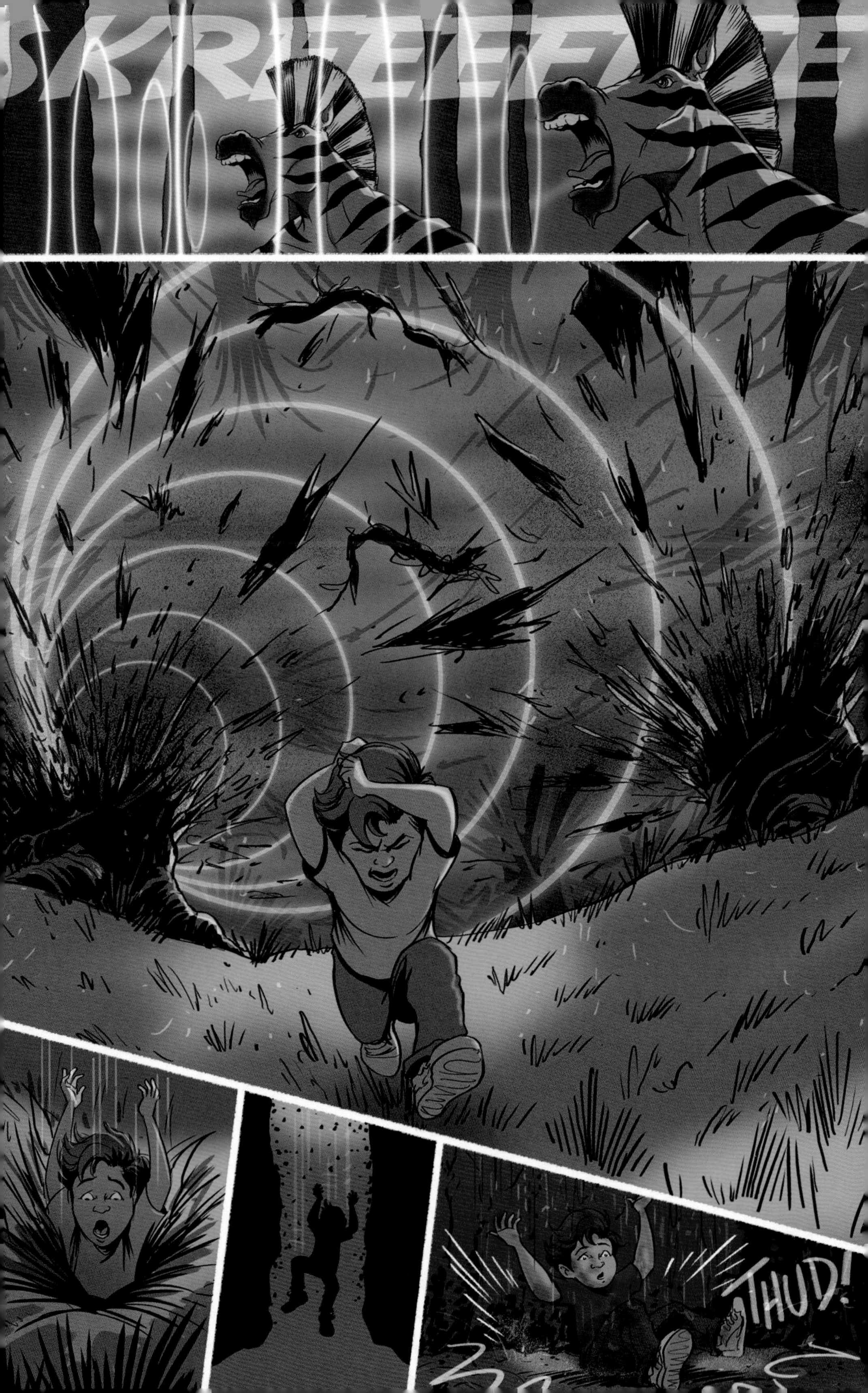
THUD!

CHAPTER FOUR:

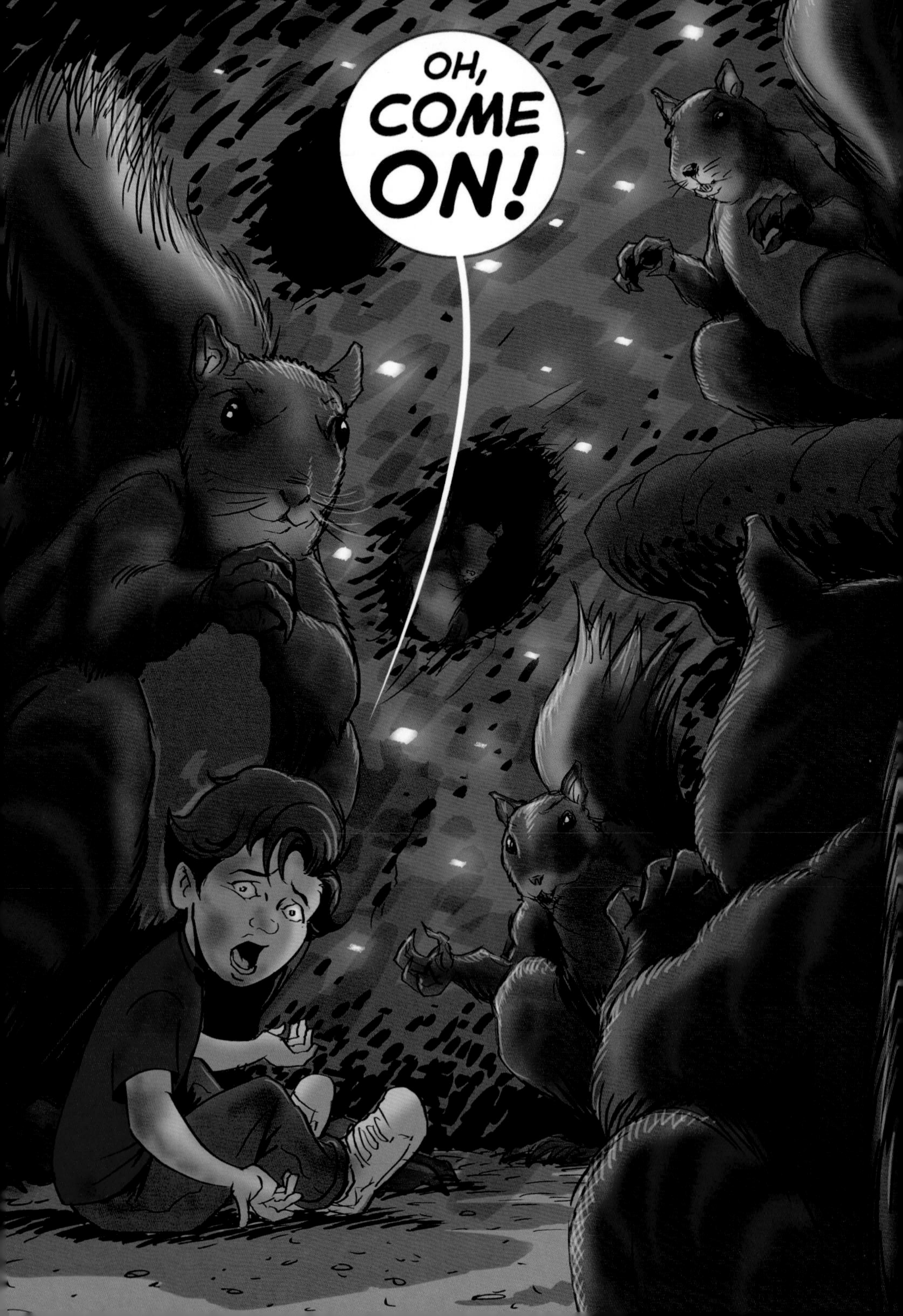
OH, COME ON!

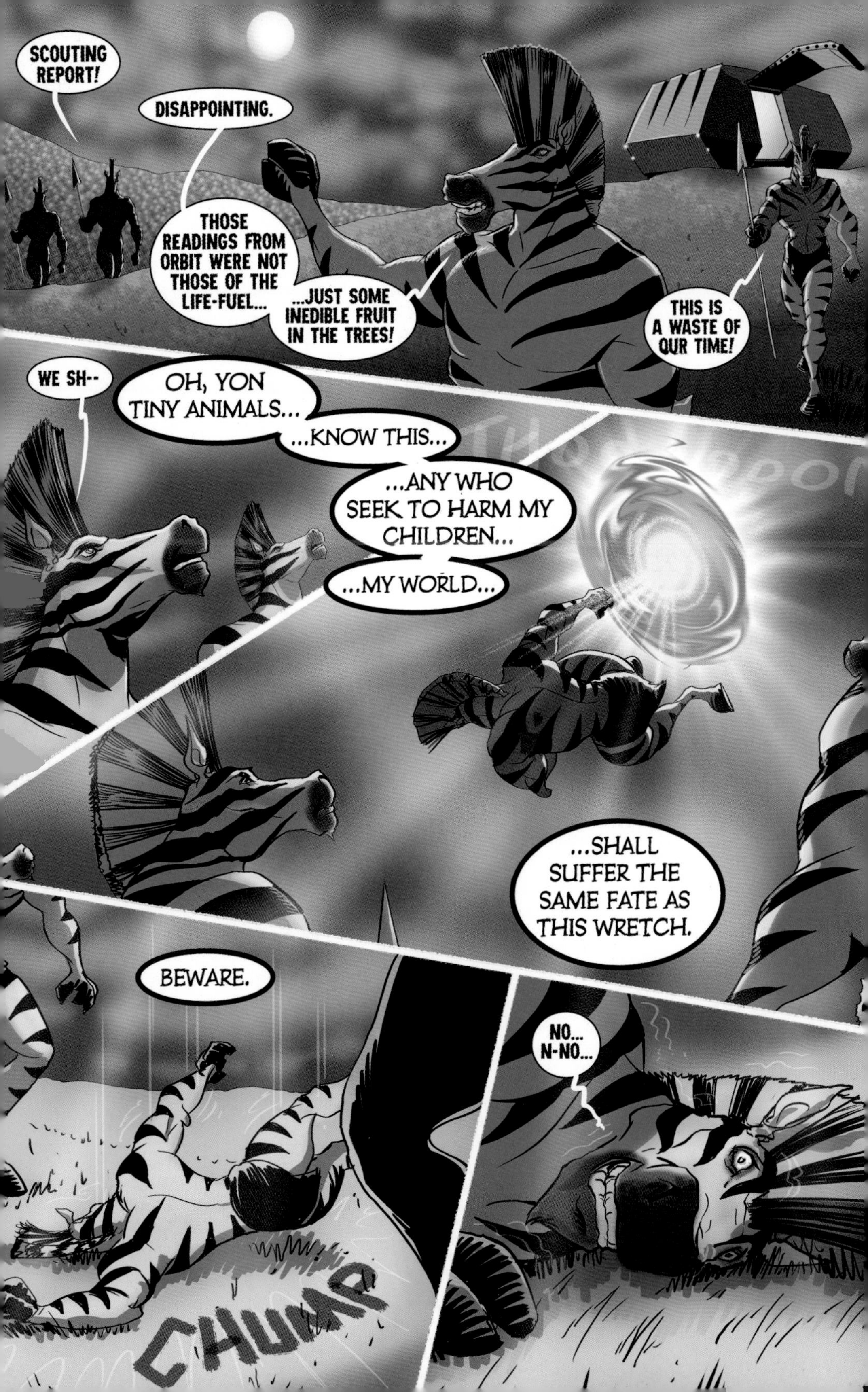
SCOUTING REPORT!
DISAPPOINTING.
THOSE READINGS FROM ORBIT WERE NOT THOSE OF THE LIFE-FUEL...
...JUST SOME INEDIBLE FRUIT IN THE TREES!
THIS IS A WASTE OF OUR TIME!
WE SH--
OH, YON TINY ANIMALS...
...KNOW THIS...
...ANY WHO SEEK TO HARM MY CHILDREN...
...MY WORLD...
...SHALL SUFFER THE SAME FATE AS THIS WRETCH.
BEWARE.
NO... N-NO...

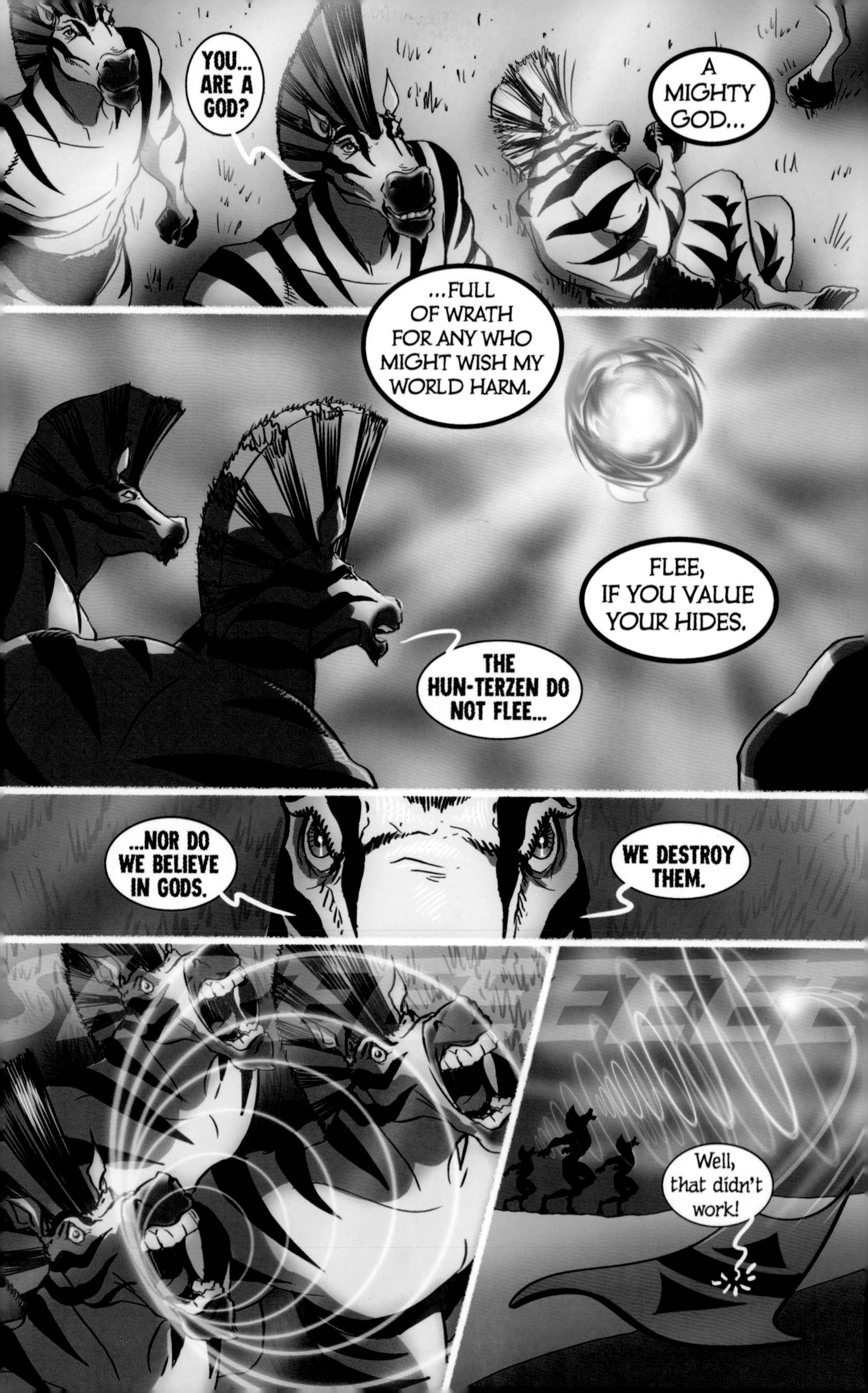
YOU... ARE A GOD?
A MIGHTY GOD...
...FULL OF WRATH FOR ANY WHO MIGHT WISH MY WORLD HARM.
FLEE, IF YOU VALUE YOUR HIDES.
THE HUN-TERZEN DO NOT FLEE...
...NOR DO WE BELIEVE IN GODS.
WE DESTROY THEM.
Well, that didn't work!

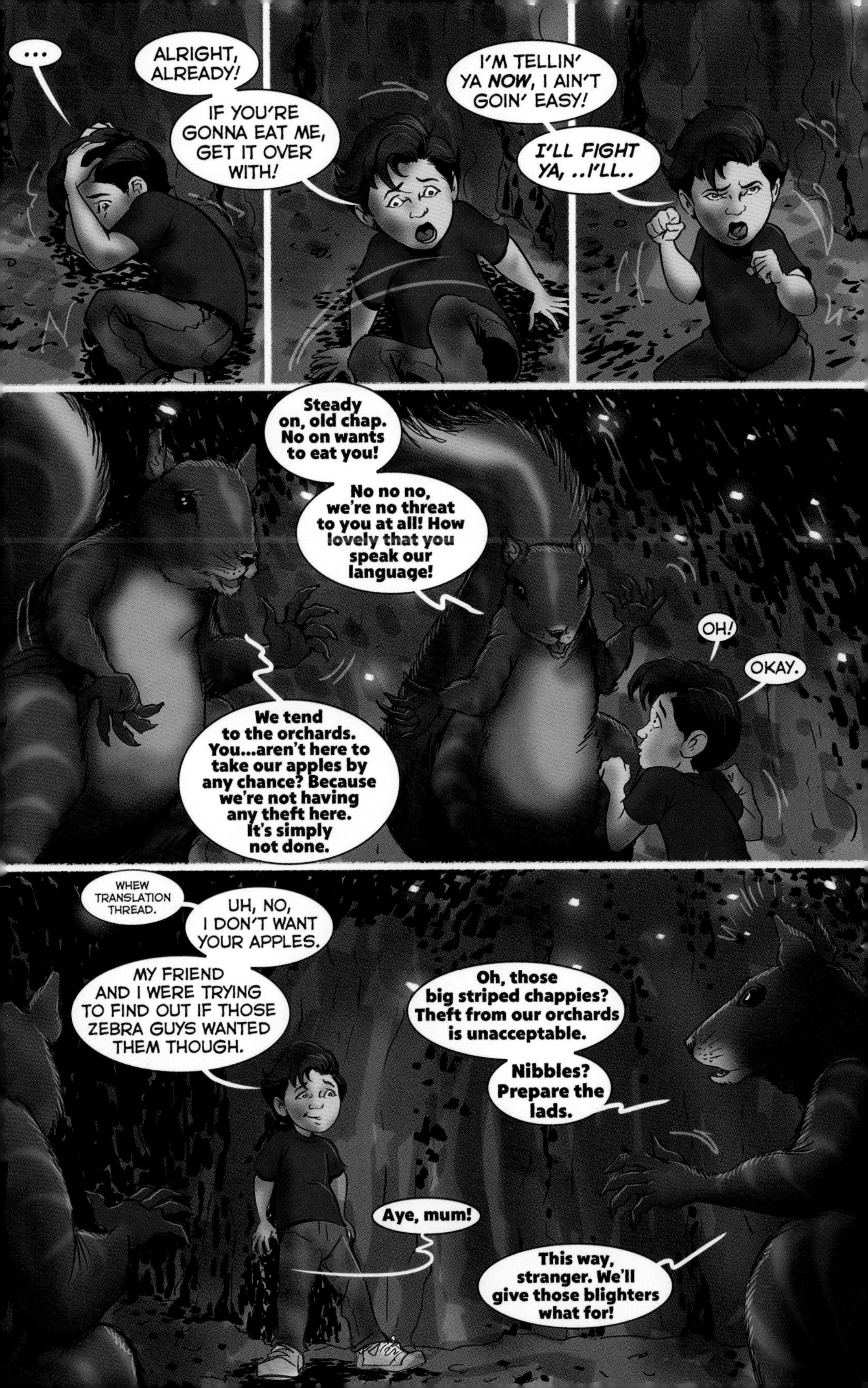
...
ALRIGHT, ALREADY!
IF YOU'RE GONNA EAT ME, GET IT OVER WITH!
I'M TELLIN' YA NOW, I AIN'T GOIN' EASY!
I'LL FIGHT YA, ..I'LL..
Steady on, old chap. No on wants to eat you!
No no no, we're no threat to you at all! How lovely that you speak our language!
We tend to the orchards. You...aren't here to take our apples by any chance? Because we're not having any theft here. It's simply not done.
OH!
OKAY.
WHEW TRANSLATION THREAD.
UH, NO, I DON'T WANT YOUR APPLES.
MY FRIEND AND I WERE TRYING TO FIND OUT IF THOSE ZEBRA GUYS WANTED THEM THOUGH.
Oh, those big striped chappies? Theft from our orchards is unacceptable.
Nibbles? Prepare the lads.
Aye, mum!
This way, stranger. We'll give those blighters what for!

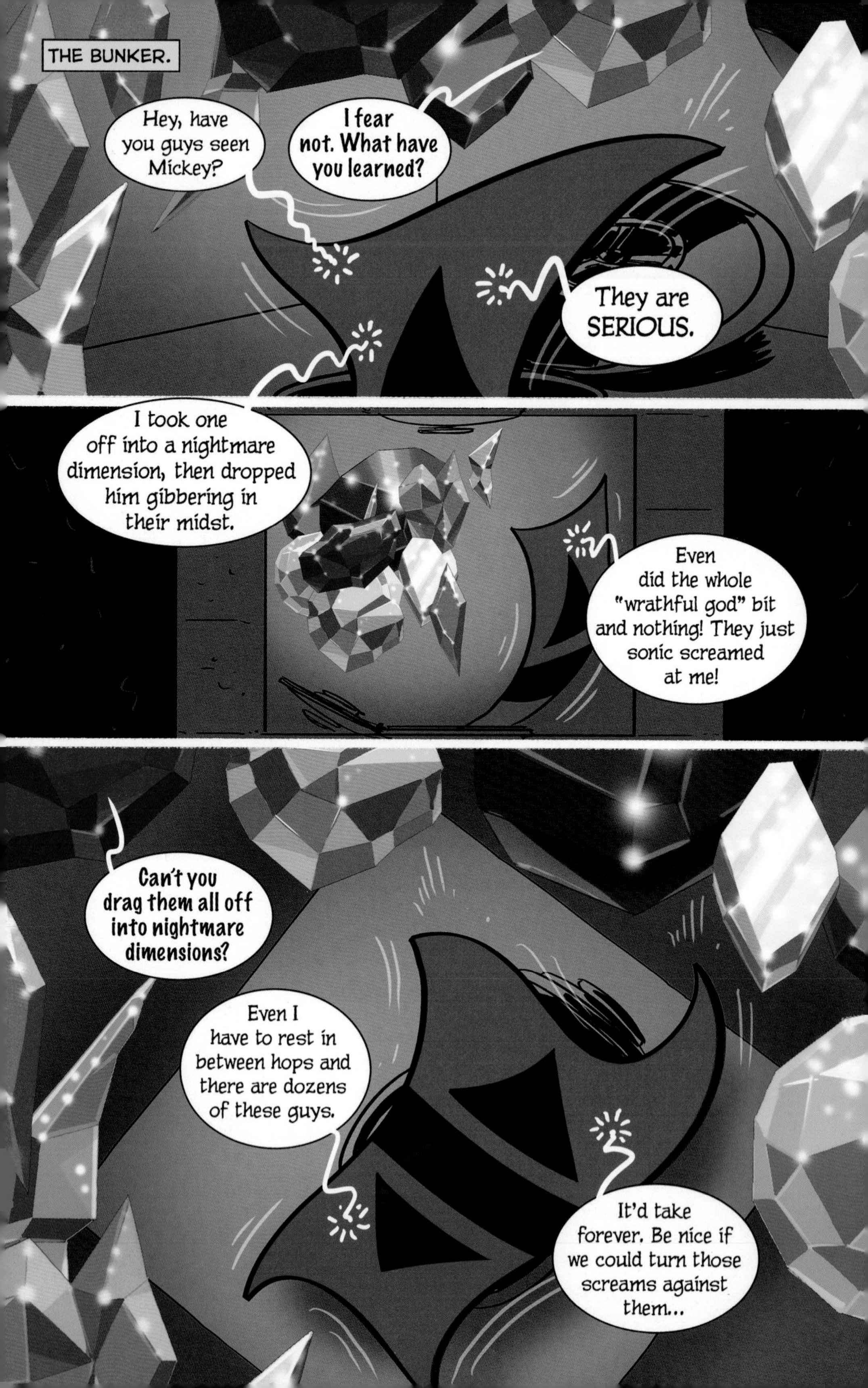
THE BUNKER.
Hey, have you guys seen Mickey?
I fear not. What have you learned?
They are SERIOUS.
I took one off into a nightmare dimension, then dropped him gibbering in their midst.
Even did the whole "wrathful god" bit and nothing! They just sonic screamed at me!
Can't you drag them all off into nightmare dimensions?
Even I have to rest in between hops and there are dozens of these guys.
It'd take forever. Be nice if we could turn those screams against them...

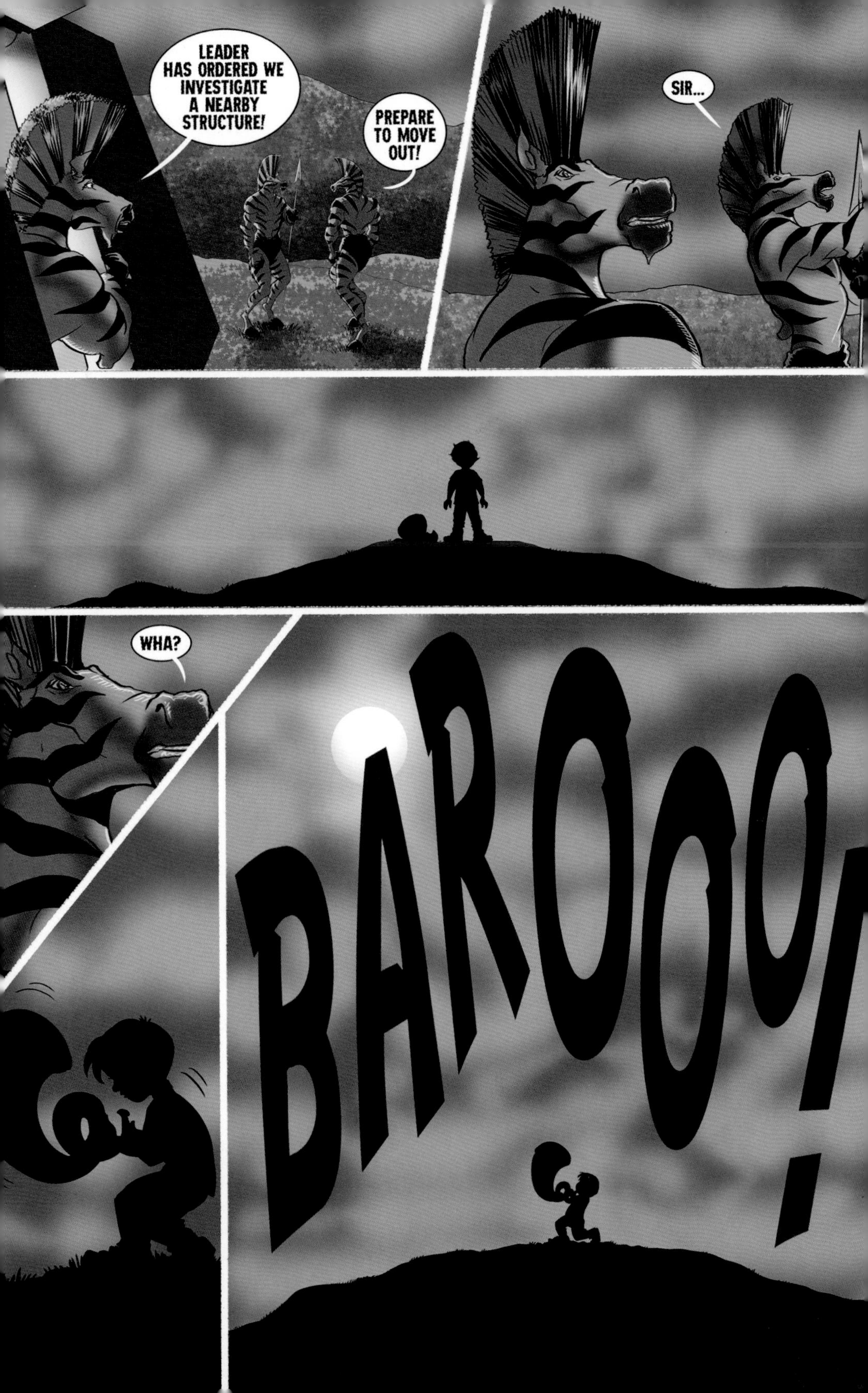
LEADER HAS ORDERED WE INVESTIGATE A NEARBY STRUCTURE!
PREPARE TO MOVE OUT!
SIR...
WHA?
BAROOO!

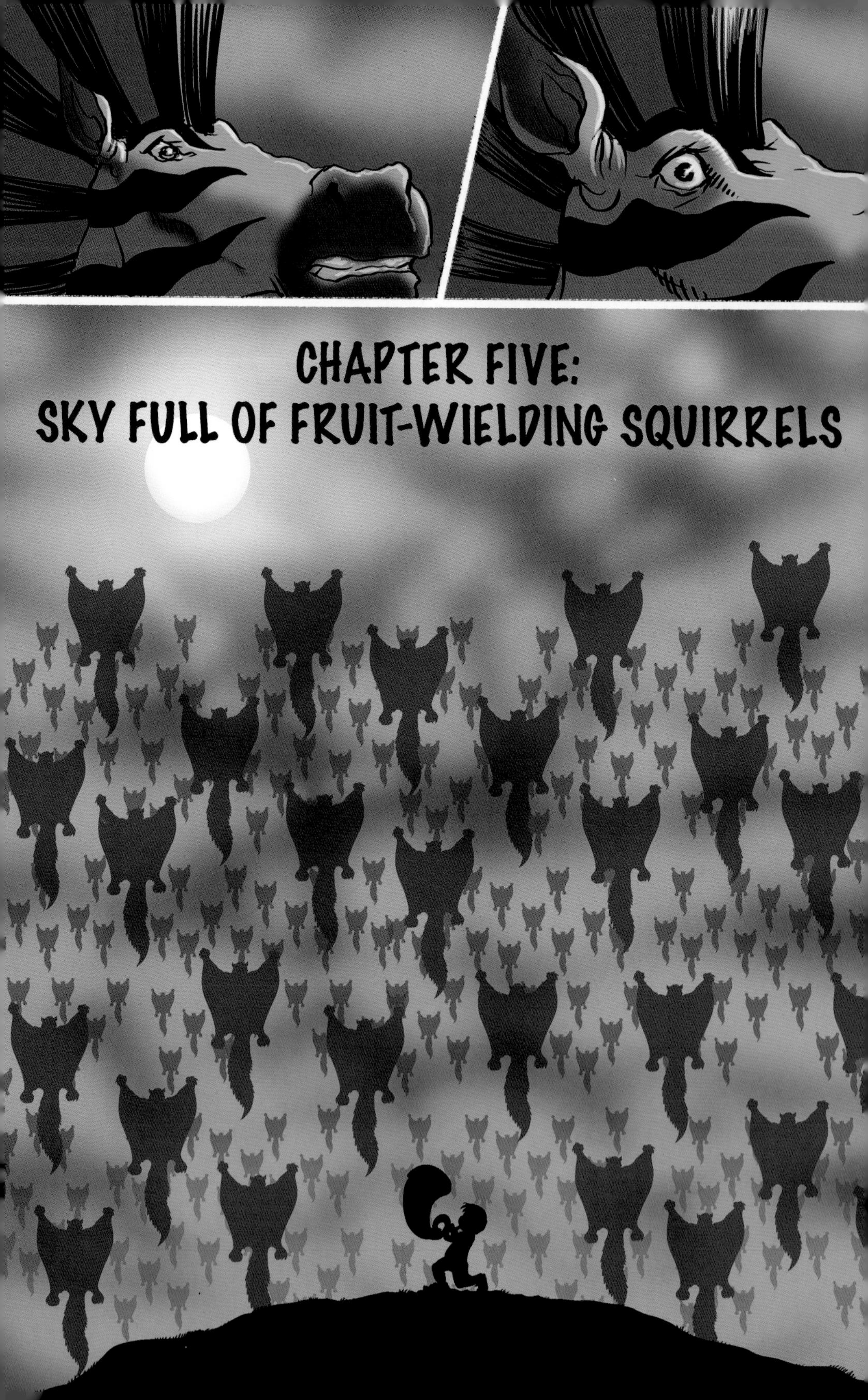
CHAPTER FIVE:
SKY FULL OF FRUIT-WIELDING SQUIRRELS

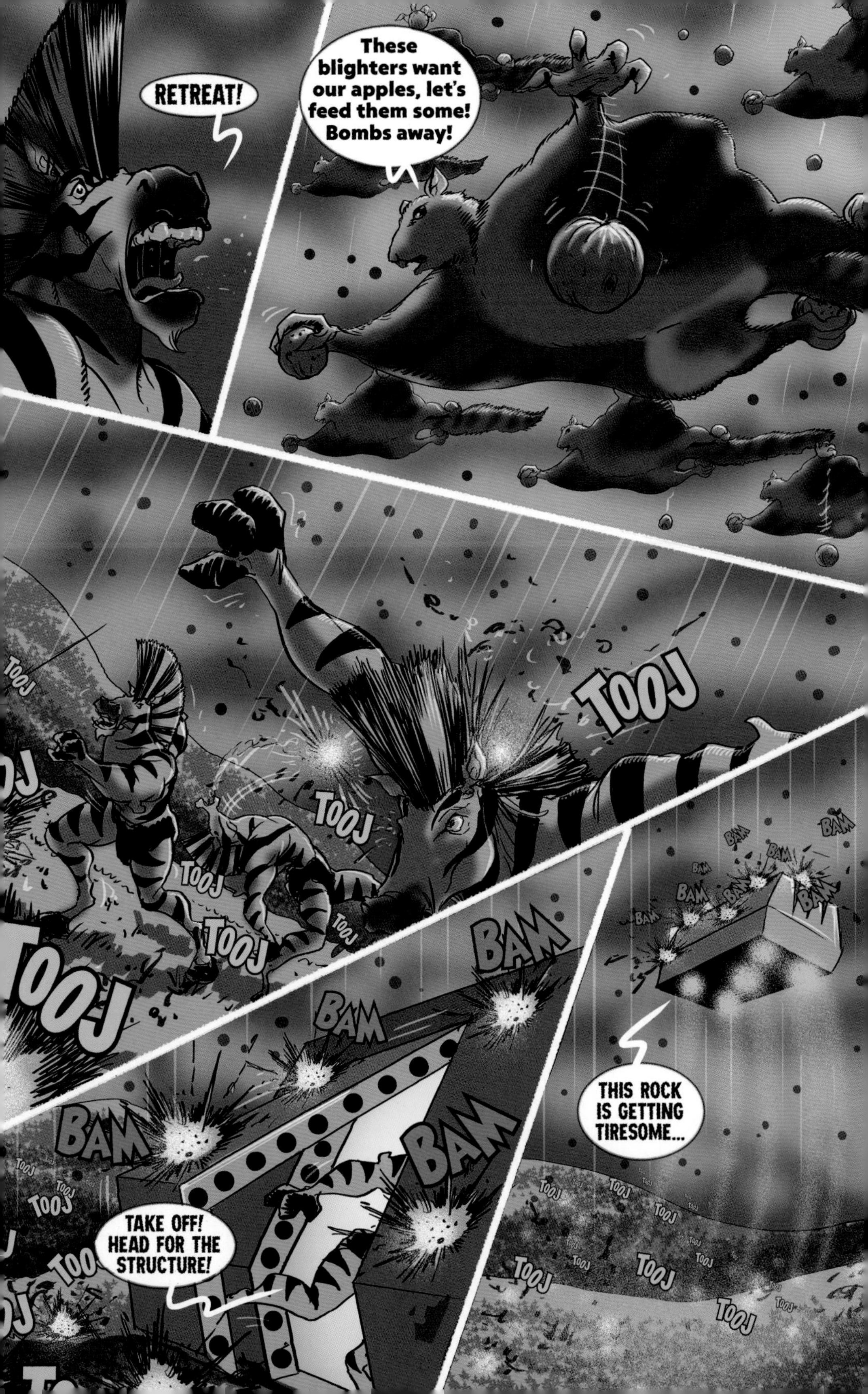
RETREAT!
These blighters want our apples, let's feed them some! Bombs away!
TOOJ
TOOJ
TOOJ
TOOJ
TOOJ
TOOJ
BAM
BAM
BAM
BAM
THIS ROCK IS GETTING TIRESOME...
TAKE OFF! HEAD FOR THE STRUCTURE!
TOOJ
TOOJ
TOOJ

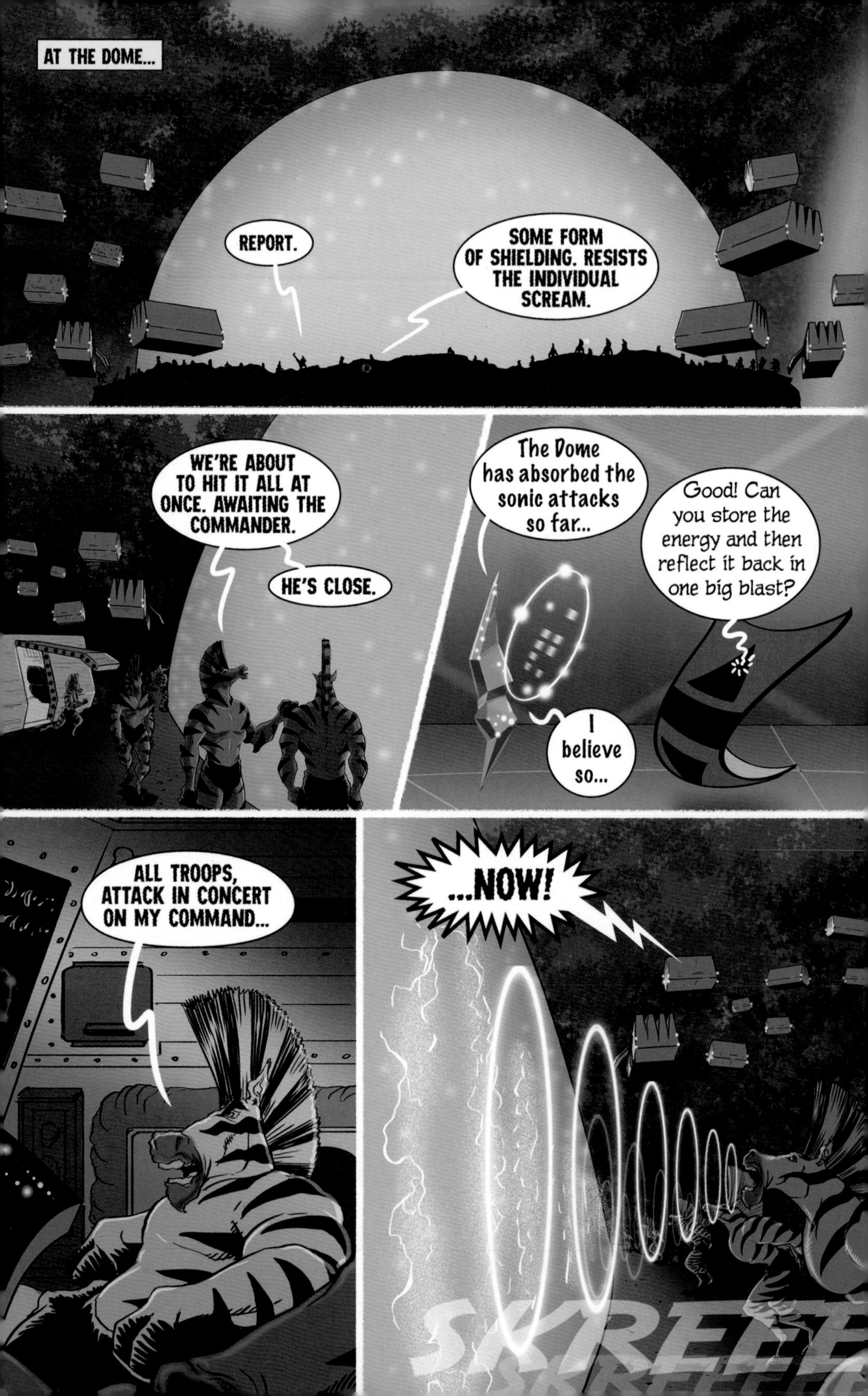
AT THE DOME...
REPORT.
SOME FORM OF SHIELDING. RESISTS THE INDIVIDUAL SCREAM.
WE'RE ABOUT TO HIT IT ALL AT ONCE. AWAITING THE COMMANDER.
HE'S CLOSE.
The Dome has absorbed the sonic attacks so far...
Good! Can you store the energy and then reflect it back in one big blast?
I believe so...
ALL TROOPS, ATTACK IN CONCERT ON MY COMMAND...
...NOW!
SKREEE

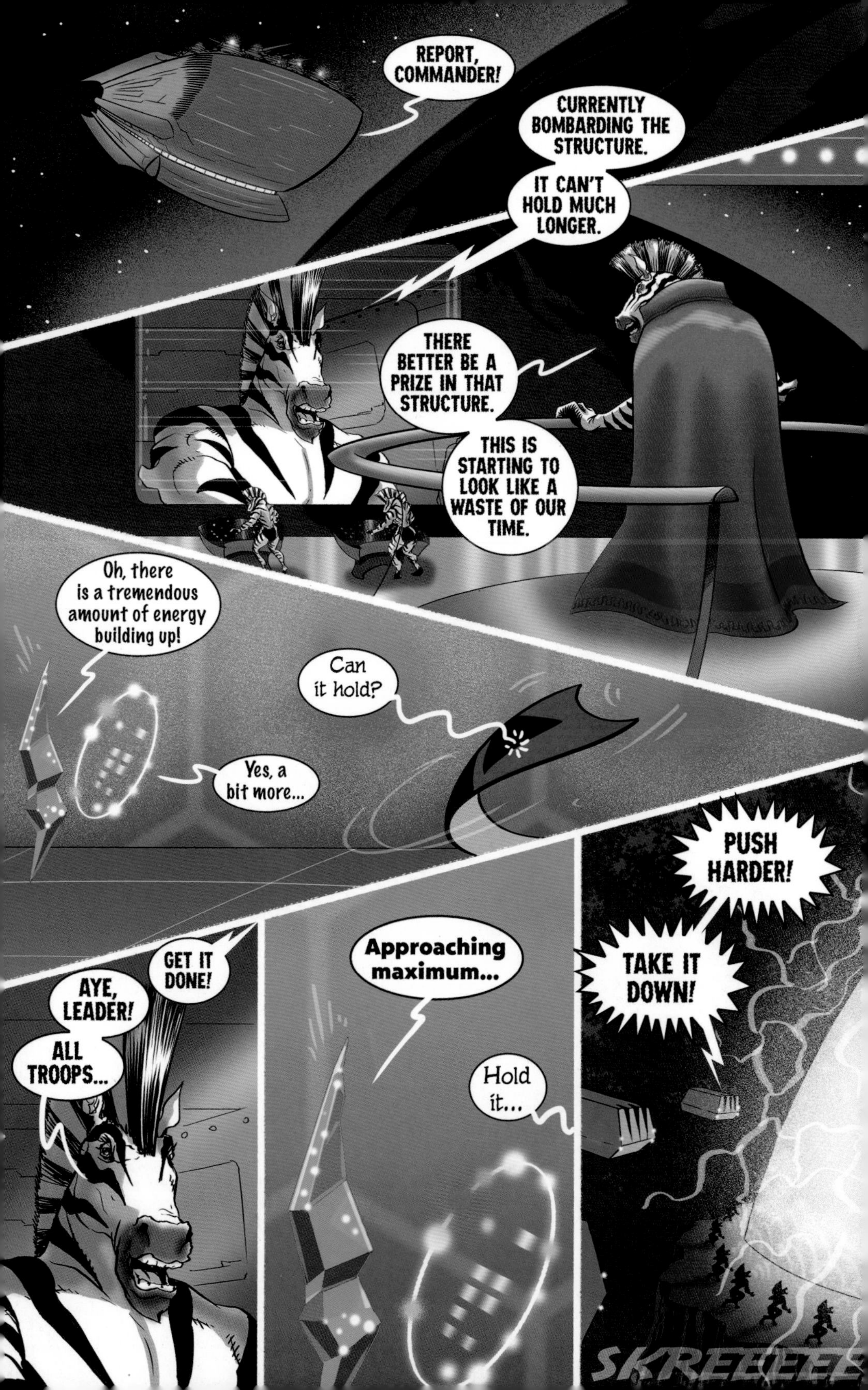
REPORT, COMMANDER!
CURRENTLY BOMBARDING THE STRUCTURE.
IT CAN'T HOLD MUCH LONGER.
THERE BETTER BE A PRIZE IN THAT STRUCTURE.
THIS IS STARTING TO LOOK LIKE A WASTE OF OUR TIME.
Oh, there is a tremendous amount of energy building up!
Can it hold?
Yes, a bit more...
GET IT DONE!
AYE, LEADER!
ALL TROOPS...
Approaching maximum...
Hold it...
PUSH HARDER!
TAKE IT DOWN!
SKREEEEE

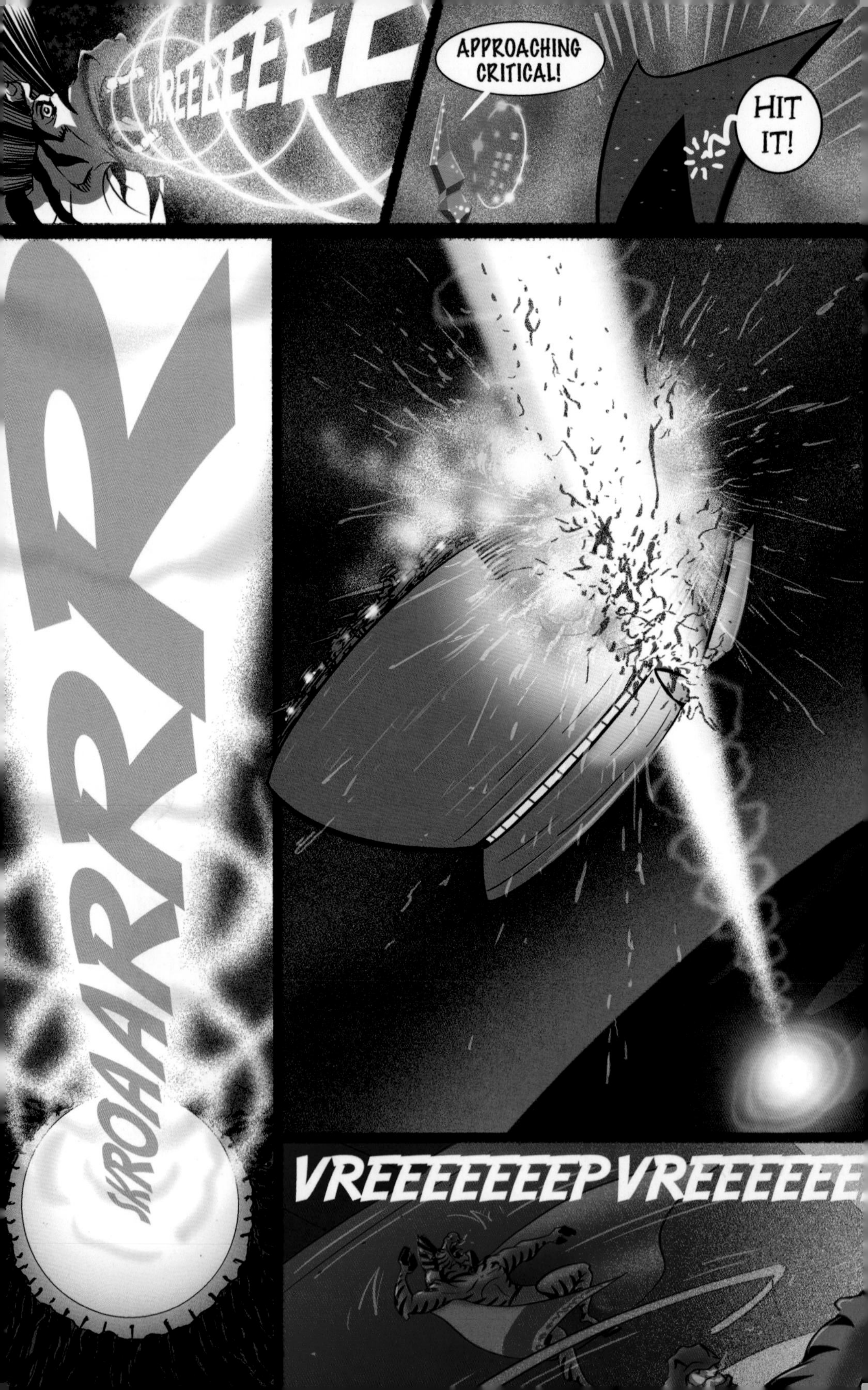
SKREEBEEEEE
APPROACHING CRITICAL!
HIT IT!
SKROAHARRR
VREEEEEEEEP VREEEEEE

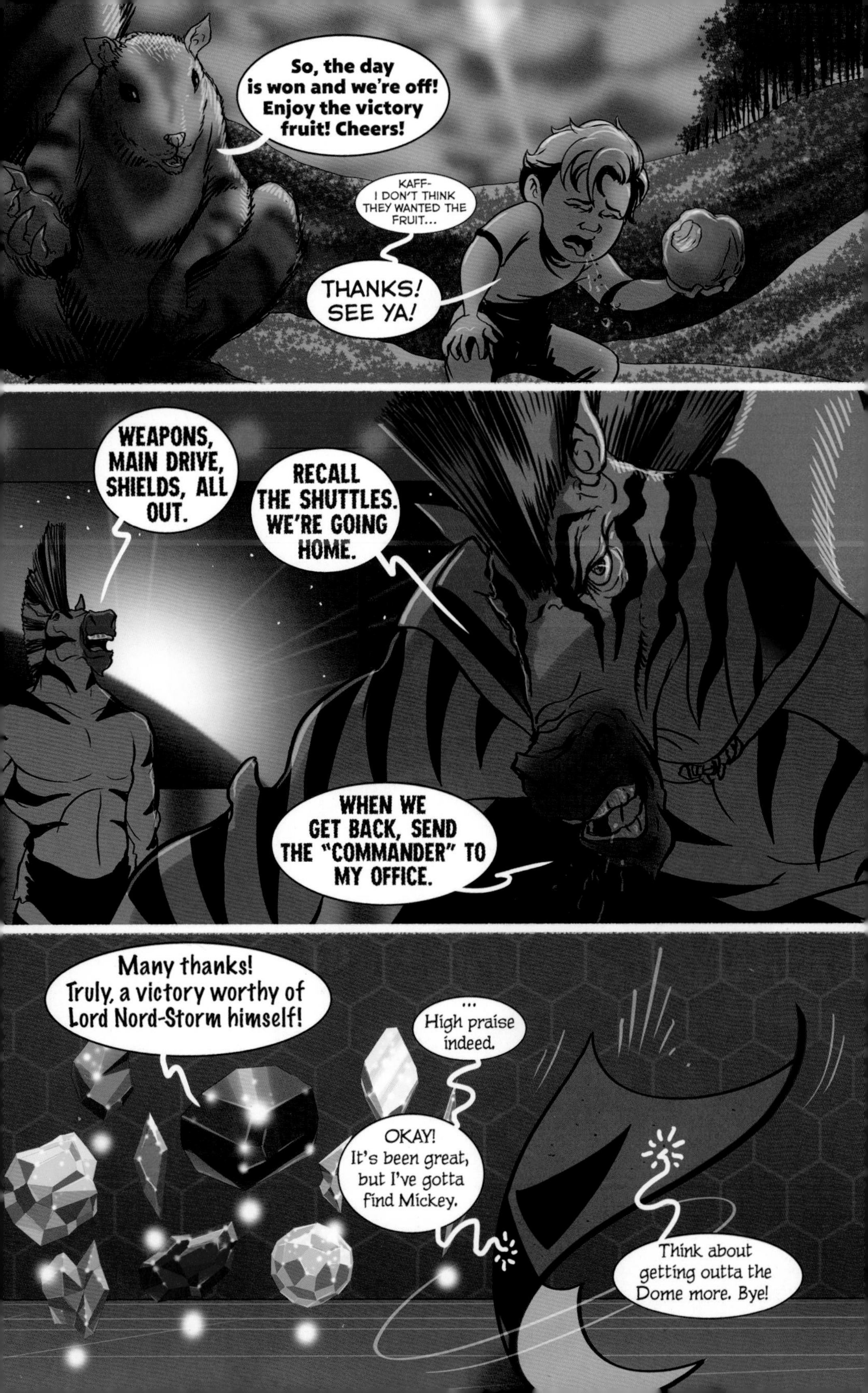
So, the day is won and we're off! Enjoy the victory fruit! Cheers!
KAFF- I DON'T THINK THEY WANTED THE FRUIT...
THANKS! SEE YA!
WEAPONS, MAIN DRIVE, SHIELDS, ALL OUT.
RECALL THE SHUTTLES. WE'RE GOING HOME.
WHEN WE GET BACK, SEND THE "COMMANDER" TO MY OFFICE.
Many thanks! Truly, a victory worthy of Lord Nord-Storm himself!
... High praise indeed.
OKAY! It's been great, but I've gotta find Mickey.
Think about getting outta the Dome more. Bye!

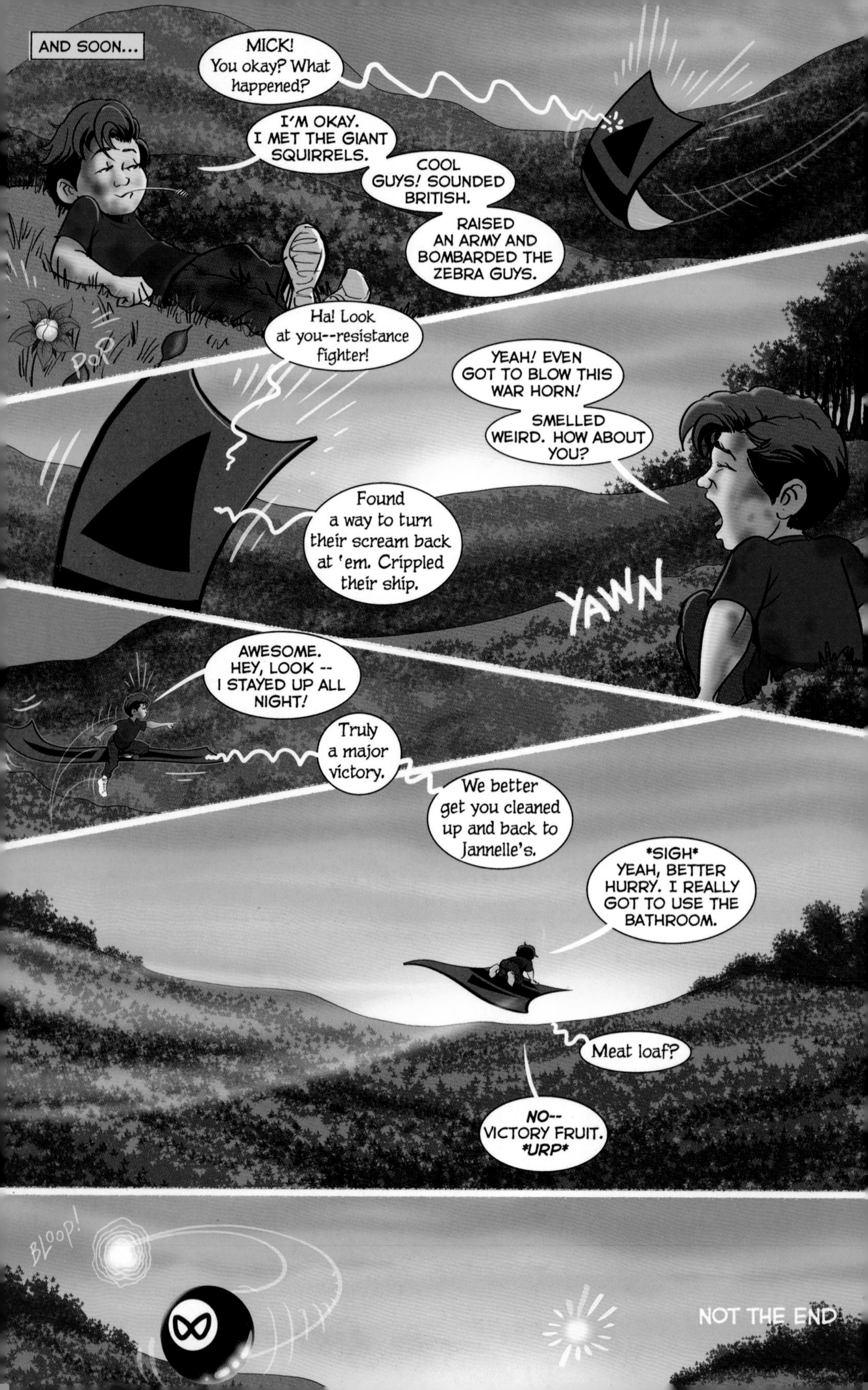
AND SOON...
MICK! You okay? What happened?
I'M OKAY. I MET THE GIANT SQUIRRELS.
COOL GUYS! SOUNDED BRITISH.
RAISED AN ARMY AND BOMBARDED THE ZEBRA GUYS.
POP
Ha! Look at you--resistance fighter!
YEAH! EVEN GOT TO BLOW THIS WAR HORN!
SMELLED WEIRD. HOW ABOUT YOU?
Found a way to turn their scream back at 'em. Crippled their ship.
YAWN
AWESOME. HEY, LOOK -- I STAYED UP ALL NIGHT!
Truly a major victory.
We better get you cleaned up and back to Jannelle's.
SIGH YEAH, BETTER HURRY. I REALLY GOT TO USE THE BATHROOM.
Meat loaf?
NO-- VICTORY FRUIT. *URP*
BLOOP!
NOT THE END

The Azure King

A traveler sought an audience with the great Kublai Khan
It was granted and on this day, The Khan met The Weaver
Who rolled out a magnificent carpet to the Khan's throne
The Khan of Khan's eyes widened as he took in its beauty

In shades of blue, it spoke boldly of the sky he cherished
The East, The West, The Sun, The Moon, noted in white
The Khan's keen mind recognized what this represented
The breadth and width of his mighty empire, here, at his feet

The Khan decreed that it shall always stay before the throne
A reminder to all of what was his and shall some day be
The traveler took his leave, while the Khan stared on happily
Later, outside the fortress, the Weaver looked back and smiled

Once night fell, the Great Throne room was abandoned, silent
The Khan's gift stirred... floated up, swept around the room
The Azure King was a Flying Carpet, and it had work to do
Wrongs to right and precious cargo that needed delivering

When the sunrise came, alarms did sound and men did shake
For all the Khan's prisoners were gone, his weapons destroyed!
When Kublai stormed to his throne room to plot his revenge
A massive cry rang out! "AND SOMEONE STOLE MY CARPET!"

MEMBERS OF THE TAPESTRY.

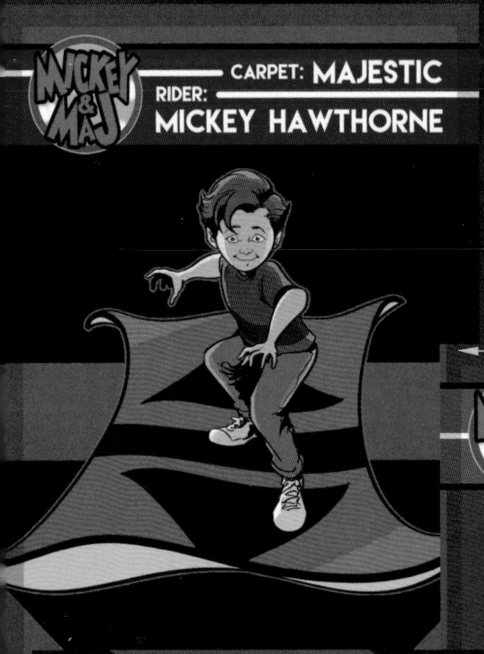
CARPET: MAJESTIC
RIDER: MICKEY HAWTHORNE

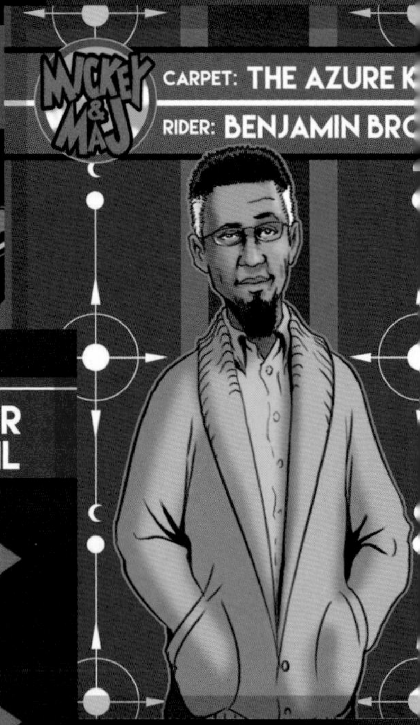
CARPET: THE AZURE
RIDER: BENJAMIN

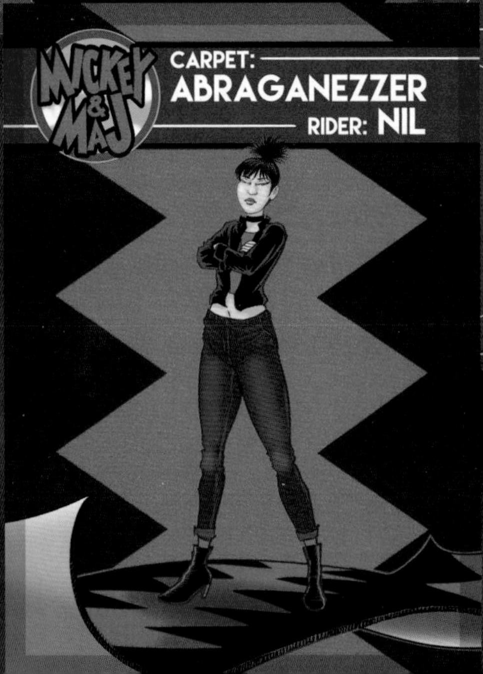
CARPET: ABRAGANEZZER
RIDER: NIL

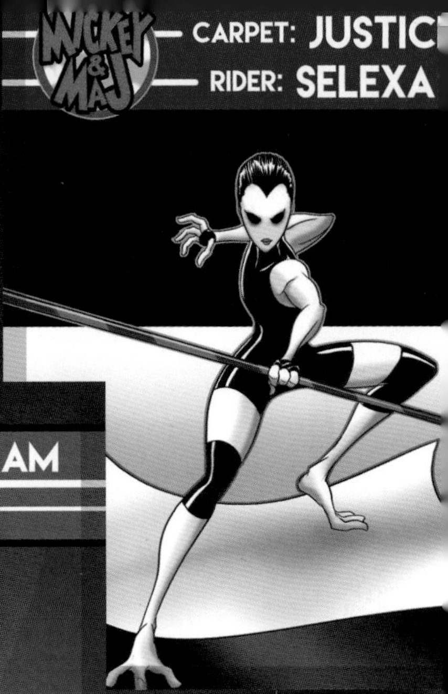
MICKEY & MAJ
CARPET: JUSTIC
RIDER: SELEXA

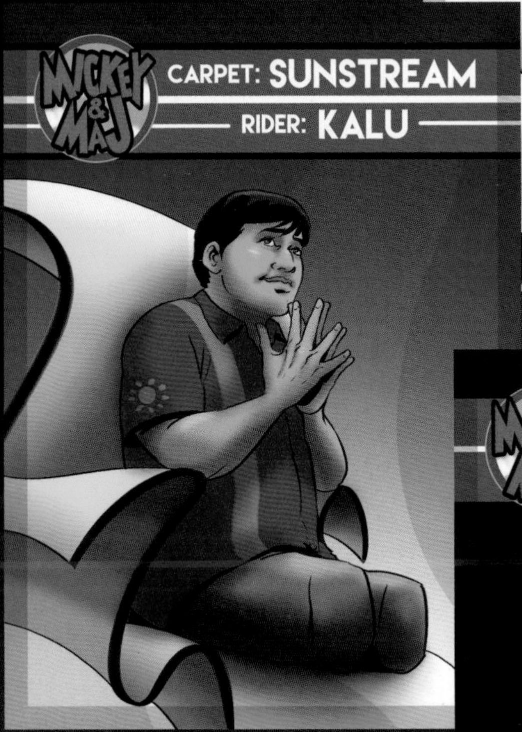
MICKEY & MAJ
CARPET: SUNSTREAM
RIDER: KALU

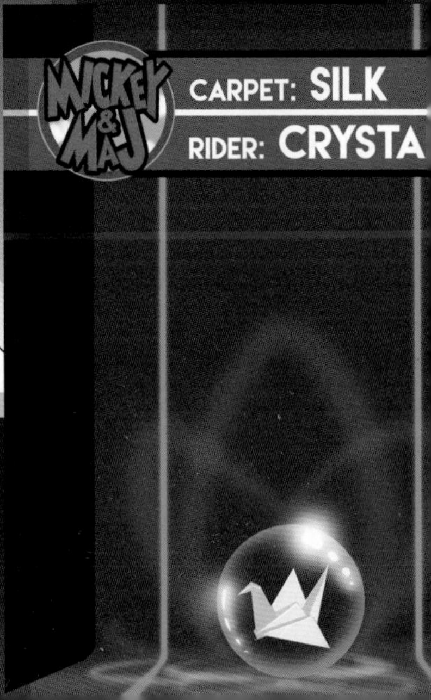
MICKEY & MAJ
CARPET: SILK
RIDER: CRYSTA

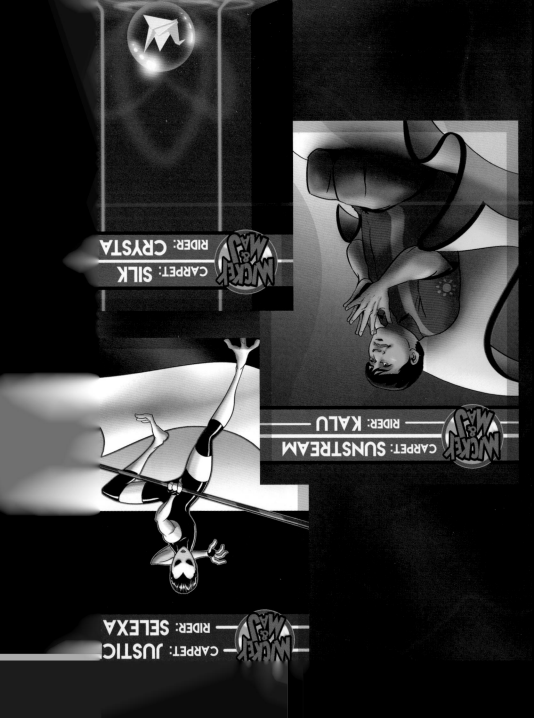

LET'S RIDE

THANKS TO PIP, NEIL AND ESPECIALLY LIN!

MICKEY AND MAJ.COM
RICKJLUNDEEN@GMAIL.COM